Praise for Hair of the Dog

"An enjoyable and well-paced mystery with a surprise kicker. O'Neil's third Cypress Cove Mystery is a delightful addition to the series."

— *Kirkus Reviews*

"Carlene O'Neil brings us the next chapter in her delightful Cypress Cove series. With its charming wine-country setting and a smart, savvy protagonist who won't quit until the truth is revealed, HAIR OF THE DOG has enough intriguing characters and compelling twists and turns to keep readers guessing to the very last page. I thoroughly enjoyed this book!"

—Kate Carlisle, *New York Times* best-selling author

"HAIR OF THE DOG offers up a rare blend of great plot, appealing characters, and gorgeous setting. Carlene O'Neil has crafted a suspenseful page-turner with the skill of a master mystery sommelier. This latest addition to the Cypress Cove series is a gold medal read."

—Ellen Byron, author of the award-winning Cajun Country Mystery series

Praise for Carlene O'Neil
and the Cypress Cove Mystery Series

"[A] good series with just the right amount of mystery to keep the reader coming back for more."

—*Suspense Magazine*

"[A] barrelful of textured plot twists, robust characters, and sparkling suspense . . . [A] mystery of the highest reserve."

—Jenn McKinlay, *New York Times* best-selling author

"Piquant, heady, and satisfyingly surprising."

—Carolyn Hart, *New York Times* best-selling author

"O'Neil has penned a witty and welcome entry into the field of the traditional mystery, with a smart and level-headed sleuth and a plot with as many twists as a grapevine. Welcome to Joyeux Winery—but do watch your step."

—G.M. Malliet, Agatha Award-winning author of the St. Just and Max Tudor mysteries

"The author's experience as a wine specialist shines…Equally delightful is the truly likable heroine, whose intelligence is matched by her wry humor and dedication to upholding her particular ethics and sense of justice."

—*Kings River Life Magazine*

"A well-rounded mystery that is a welcome addition to the cozy genre. This was a good read and I can't wait to see what happens next in Cypress Cove."

—Dru's Book Musings

"The breathtaking setting and stellar cast of characters—from protagonists Penny and Antonia to their various employees and family members to Penny's pets, gray tabby Petite Syrah and malamute Nanook—made this a sparkling debut."

—Melissa's Mochas, Mysteries & Meows

Books in the *Cypress Cove Mystery Series*
by Carlene O'Neil

One Foot in the Grape

Ripe for Murder

Hair of the Dog

Carlene O'Neil

Hair of the Dog

Hair of the Dog

Cover Design by Victor Aello (aello4design@earthlink.net)

Edited by Kristen Weber

Copy Edited by Cara Quinlan

Interior Formatting by Polgarus Studio

ISBN-13 978-0-9992703-0-1
ISBN-10 0-9992703-0-3

First Edition

Printed in U.S.A

Chapter 1

My cousin Annie is a terrific veterinarian, so two deaths at her clinic was both tragic and unusual. Of course, that wasn't the worst of it. The real problem was that both casualties were human. The day the trouble started, I knew something was wrong the minute I opened the clinic door.

"What do you mean I'm fired? You can't fire me."

"On the contrary, I can and I have."

The second voice belonged to Brian, Annie's partner in the clinic. I had two choices: I could give them some privacy, or I could move closer to hear better. Naturally, I scurried across the empty lobby and poked my head around the corner of the clinic's dispensary, where Brian stood in front of a technician I recognized. She looked pale, and her lower lip trembled as she gazed up at him with enormous blue eyes. She hiccupped and dropped a prescription bottle. Little yellow tablets bounced across the floor. Several landed at my feet, and I stooped to pick them up.

"I wasn't doing anything." I could see her name tag: Nicole. "Honest, Dr. Grasser, it's time for Missy to get her medication."

"That may be," Brian said, "but that doesn't explain the pills you have in your pocket."

"I didn't take any pills." Nicole wailed.

"Then prove it. Empty your pockets."

Annie walked through the doors from the surgery room. Dot, Annie's office manager, came out of her office and stood in the hallway.

"What's up?" Annie asked. "I can hear you all the way in the back."

"I've just asked Nicole to empty out her pockets," Brian said.

"But I didn't take any of Missy's pills. I wouldn't do that!"

"Then there shouldn't be any problem if we take a look," Annie said. "I'm sure Dr. Grasser is hoping you prove him wrong."

"Right, that's fine," Brian said. "Show us your pockets are empty, and we'll put this behind us."

Nicole was tiny with short blonde hair. She could be perky when she wanted to be. I'd seen her with the male clients. They just loved to drop off Spot when she was at the front counter. Her big baby blues glittering with unshed tears might have worked with them, but in this room they weren't cutting it. Nicole seemed to realize that, because she narrowed her eyes and threw up her hands. "Fine. A couple of pills. No big deal. It isn't like I took pain medication."

Annie pointed toward the clinic door. "You can stop back tonight to pick up your last check, but you need to leave the clinic."

"I'll be here late," Dot added. "Come back after eight, or I can mail it to you. Also, leave your keys for the door."

Nicole took the keys from her pocket and slapped them onto the counter. "I'm busy tonight. I'll come back tomorrow for my check." Nicole started walking toward the door and then stopped to look at Brian. "I don't understand. You were on the other side of the clinic. You couldn't have seen me."

"I didn't see you. I knew someone was taking pills, and you were the only one with access during the hours they disappeared. I guessed."

Nicole looked at Annie, her eyes full of appeal. "Dr. Moore, can't we talk about this?" She tilted her head and wrung her hands.

"There isn't anything to discuss," Annie said.

"But this will go on my record," Nicole pleaded.

"Maybe you should talk to a lawyer."

"I'll lose my license as a vet tech."

Annie nodded. "I'm hoping."

The smile disappeared, and Nicole's jaw tensed as she clenched her teeth. She walked to the rear door and turned back to us, her eyes on Annie.

"Bitch."

She threw open the door, shoulders rigid as she walked to her car, a cute little white Audi.

"That's a nice car for a vet tech, especially one who just lost her job," I said. "Are you going to call the police?"

"Damn skippy," Annie said.

"Good," I said. "Do you need to cancel lunch?"

"If you have time, I'd still like to go. Just let me call Lucas first."

Lucas was our police chief. He was young, still in his twenties, and was dating my niece Hayley. We'd spent some time together recently, when I'd managed to find a body on my neighbor's property.

Annie came out of the office a few moments later and threw up her hands.

"We didn't actually see her take the pills, so Lucas isn't confident the courts will pursue it."

Dot shook her head. "But she admitted to it."

"Just to us. Lucas is convinced a lawyer would come up with a different conclusion to our conversation." Annie grabbed my arm. "Come on, Penny. Food will help, or it certainly won't hurt."

At least once a week we made a point of having lunch together, just to catch up. We always ate at Sterling, the best restaurant in Cypress Cove and possibly along the entire Central California coast. With white stucco walls and fresh flowers on every table, the restaurant felt warm and inviting. Ross, the owner, was a close friend, and he waved from the bar when we walked through the doors. We grabbed a table near the large stone fireplace, the warmth a welcome balance to a dreary, wet spring day. It had been raining for two weeks. The sky was gunmetal gray, and all the local winery owners, me included, were beginning to worry. As much as California needed the water, too much rain and the entire grape harvest could rot on the vine. Joyeux Winery, the small winery I'd inherited from my aunt, wouldn't survive if I lost

4

an entire year's worth of work. Between the weather and the confrontation with Nicole, our normal banter was stilted, and I decided to address it head-on. "Back at the clinic. Does that happen a lot?"

"More than people realize," Annie said. "We're more careful than most. Accessing the painkillers takes two keys. One is kept with the tech on duty and the other with either Brian or myself. I read of one case where the doctor was taking the pain medicine. She'd record the pills as going to the animals she'd operated on and then take them herself. Lost her license. Went to jail for a while."

"I should hope so," I said. "What did Nicole take?"

"Phenylpropanolamine."

"In English."

"PPA. Keeps you alert. Cuts your appetite. Now that I think about it, I'm not sure the PPA was all she's been taking. She may have been helping herself to some of the profits. Most people pay by charge card, but you'd be surprised how much cash we bring in. Lately there are too many days when the register is off."

"Well, now she's lost her job and her reputation. I just hope it doesn't ruin your evening tonight."

"It won't. She only has herself to blame." Annie waved her hand through the air, as though pushing away thoughts of Nicole. "Now, tell me about the festivities."

Years ago, wineries were for one thing: making wine. Now, hosting functions was one of the more reliable ways wineries made money. This week, the town of Cypress Cove was sponsoring several benefits for the local animal shelter, and Joyeux Winery had been selected to host two of them.

"Tonight, we have the California Society of Veterinarians."

Annie nodded. "And tomorrow?"

"Tomorrow is the Fabulously Ugly Dog Contest. For dogs that are 'beauty-challenged.' First time at our winery. It's a pretty big deal, actually. Lots of news coverage."

"Now that's going to be fun," Annie said.

"And tonight won't be?" I asked.

"I need to be there for Eric, but it feels more like work. An evening with my colleagues. Plus, I have to dress up. Ugh."

"I get it," I said. Dr. Eric Sloan leased space from Annie and Brian at the clinic, where he focused on rabies research. Tonight he was going to receive the Silver Paw award, the highest honor veterinarians can give to one of their own. "How is his research coming?"

"Outstanding. One pill instead of a series of painful injections? The market can't wait to get their hands on it. The clinical trials are nearly done. Testing on humans should start soon, and the results look highly promising."

"I never see him when I come into the clinic," I said.

"That's not surprising. We hardly see them."

"Them?"

"Denise. His lab assistant. She's the only one allowed in. He needs a controlled environment for the clinical trials. Door kept locked, no visitors, that kind of thing." Annie took a bite of her chocolate mousse. "It's a fascinating disease, but vicious. After it gets in your system, there isn't anything anyone can do to help you. Nothing. Kaput. You're finished."

I put down my heavy silver fork and glanced at the other tables. Annie has a voice that carries. "I wasn't aware of that, no." I took a bite of my fruit tart. "Eat your dessert."

Annie went on, "It's sometimes called 'hydrophobia disease' because, even though the person is dying of thirst, they can't swallow water. It's supposed to be pretty gruesome."

"Seriously, Annie, too much information."

She looked at me, shaking her head. "I still can't believe you worked as an investigative photojournalist. You've got no stomach at all."

It was true. Being behind a camera lens was different. I'd always felt invincible. In real life, I'm not particularly courageous.

"No stomach whatsoever," I agreed. "Let's talk about something else. How about tonight. You okay with Eric being the one to make this breakthrough?"

Annie and Eric had gone to Davis School of Veterinary Medicine together. "Sure, why not?"

"Because you've always said more could be done to prevent this disease. I thought you might be the one to look for a solution."

"The important thing is finding an easier way to administer a rabies vaccination that works," she said. "I've been studying some of his results. He's going to change the world."

"When his tests are complete, will he stay on at the clinic with you and Brian?"

"I doubt he'll need the space, although I wouldn't mind.

Even with him there, we still have more than enough room. He's the perfect person to lease to, since he doesn't have patients and never uses the reception and exam rooms. The hurdle is that he's always had a high opinion of himself, and all this press he's getting over the vaccine hasn't helped."

"Does he act overbearing in the clinic?"

"Not at all. In fact, he's always a perfect gentleman. Polite. Opens doors. You can still tell, though, that he really does think he's the smartest one in the room. Of course, he probably is."

"But still," I said, "isn't it strange that he's perfected a rabies vaccination when it's something that you've been fascinated with for as long as I can remember?"

Annie considered. "He did the work and developed the science, so he deserves the recognition. I must say I could have used the contract with Amerigen."

"That's the company backing the drug?" I asked, and Annie nodded. "How much does Eric stand to make?"

"He hasn't confirmed anything, but the contract could be worth millions. That hurts a little. But it's a tremendous breakthrough."

"Well," I said, "you're taking it a lot better than I expected."

"Uh-huh," Annie said. "I'm taking it so well I might need to order more dessert." She eyed the rest of my tart. "You going to finish that?"

"Damn skippy."

Chapter 2

After lunch I dropped Annie back at the clinic and headed down the coast toward home. Even in the fog and mist, this part of California, just south of Monterey and Pebble Beach, is striking. Swirls of damp ocean air curled around the car and the cypress trees that lined the twisting road. I glanced down at the beach. Despite the chilly air, a few brave souls walked along the shore, heads down, braced against the breeze.

I drove through the entrance to my vineyards, the grape canes silver-gray in the subdued light. I skirted around the house and parked outside the barrel and fermentation building. It was designed after a French chateau my aunt had lived in years ago in France. Like the house and other buildings, the exterior was slate, with a copper roof aged to a green patina. Large double doors in French oak opened to the main room. French and American oak barrels stood in rows and reached almost twenty feet high to the ceiling. The wall sconces cast a warm glow off the wood-paneled walls, the air heavy with a fragrance only found on a winery—a

9

mixture of grapes, oak, and fruit. I'd recently redesigned the building to include an open area in the center for tables and dancing, and the results were better than I'd hoped. On the other hand, I'd spent the last of my reserves to finance it. If the weather didn't break soon, by this time next year someone else could own this building, along with everything else. Resolutely pushing the thought aside, I walked to the rear storage room and pulled out a selection of tablecloths. My winery manager, Connor, walked by, and I waved the cloths in his direction.

"What colors?"

He looked at my choices. "Assume I'm like a dog and can't distinguish colors. You're on your own."

"Right. It's for the Silver Paw Gala. Silver, black, and white it is."

"Good choice."

Connor stacked cases of chardonnay behind the tasting counter. He moved with fluid grace, comfortable in his jeans, work boots, and an ivory fisherman knit sweater. His dark blond hair held just a touch of wave and stopped at his sweater collar. I was aware of everything about him without needing to look. We'd flirted and danced on the edge of a relationship since I'd been back, but every time we moved forward something had gotten in the way. He was in his late thirties, about my age, and had worked for my aunt before me. When I lost her last year and she left me the winery, I'd asked Connor to stay on as manager, and he'd agreed, at least for the time being. He'd grown up on his own family vineyards not far from here and had lost the land in a family dispute. It was only a matter of time before he would want a greater challenge than what I could offer him. I pushed the thought from my mind.

"How many bottles do you think we'll need tonight?" I asked.

"Two to three glasses per person, a hundred guests. About sixty bottles. I'm prepping a little more than that just in case. As for the food, Ross will be here shortly." Ross had recently branched out with Sterling-to-Go, his company catering high-end events throughout the area.

"You've taken care of the wine. I'll finish the tables, and we should be set. Where's Hayley?" In addition to being my niece, she was the assistant manager at the winery.

"Still out. She should be back soon."

"It's going to be a late night. Are you staying?" Connor had recently purchased a home out at the beach but still kept an apartment above the winery office.

He nodded. "Frost warning." In the evenings, a blanket of fog comes in from the shore, and frost isn't a concern. If the sky is clear, though, frost is always a threat on cold nights, and we might need to fire up the frost protection system and spray the entire vineyard with water.

Hayley came in through the rear door. "I just checked all the sprinklers. On the outside chance the sky clears and we get frost, we're ready for it." She looked around the room. "Want some help?"

"I'm fine," I said. "All I need to do is finish with the tablecloths. Ross will have his servers set the tables, so that's it for me."

Hayley stretched. Now in her mid-twenties, she looks more like me than her mother. She is tall like me, with streaky blonde hair and hazel eyes. We're close, and always have been. My sister is ten years older than me, and lives in Boston, so Hayley relied on me as her favorite aunt. Without children of my own, I was glad she was in my life.

"I have an idea," I said. "Before it gets too crazy, you should grab a bite."

"I'm just in time." Ross walked up behind us. A big, lumberjack type of man in Tommy Bahamas, he moved behind the counter with ease. We'd been friends for ages, and nothing more. I'd figured out early on I wasn't his type. Thomas, the man I'd introduced him to several years ago, was. Ross steered us to the back, where his assistant was stirring a large kettle.

"That smells delicious," I said. "What is it?"

"Cream of mushroom soup. Here, let me get you a couple of bowls."

"Excellent suggestion, but can you put it in something for us to carry back to the house?"

"No problem." Ross ladled the soup into a small pot. "So, I heard Nicole got fired from the clinic."

"You didn't tell me," Hayley said to me.

Small towns. Nobody misses a thing.

"It happened right before I went to lunch with Annie. I haven't had a chance."

"Why was she fired?" Hayley asked.

"There might be some legal reason why Annie wants to keep it quiet, but you can ask her yourself tonight."

Ross stirred the soup. "Nicole had her hand in the pharmaceutical cookie jar. One of my waiters saw Nicole in town. She was on her phone, and said she was going to get Brian. Annie too."

"I don't know what she can do. I saw for myself that she had the pills."

"Just let Annie know she didn't make a friend today. Neither did Brian." Ross handed me the soup.

"Thanks for dinner. And the warning."

We reached the house, and Hayley took a seat at the kitchen table while I grabbed two bowls. I stepped over my malamute, Nanook, and pushed Syrah off the table. I'm not proud of the fact that my cat sits on the kitchen table whenever she can, but I've learned to pick the battles I can win with her. There aren't many.

"How was today?" I asked.

"We aren't able to do much with all this rain. The poor vines are all waterlogged."

"Annie said we're supposed to get more rain."

"Speaking of Annie, what happens next to Nicole?" Hayley asked.

"Not much, unfortunately. She's fired, but Lucas doesn't think there's enough to press charges. Brian didn't actually see her take the pills."

"At least she lost her job, and there won't be patients going without their medication," Hayley said.

"That's how I feel," I said. "Annie too."

Connor walked in. "Is there enough for me?"

13

I pushed the container toward him. "Grab a bowl. We need to make it quick, though. People will be arriving soon."

We ate quickly and left to change into our event clothes. Nothing fancy, just black turtlenecks with black blazers and black dress pants. We returned to the barrel room just as the first of the guests started to arrive. With Ross supervising the food and the serving, this event was an easy one for us. I stood near the entrance, pointing guests to the various wine and food stations. Joyeux Winery is known for our sparkling wine, the California version of champagne, and the waiters were busy pouring.

Shortly after six, Annie showed up, looking beautiful in a floor-length black fitted dress.

"Fabulous dress," I said. "I couldn't pull it off. I can't keep those off-the-shoulder dresses in place."

"I bet you get lots of sympathy for that one. Too busty. Boo-hoo. I'm just trying to look taller than five-two. Another problem you don't have. How come you ended up with the boobs and the height in the family?"

"Because you got the perfect hair and the great ass."

"Oh. Yeah." She smiled.

"You look gorgeous," I said.

"Thanks. As uncomfortable as this thing is, I better."

"Is Brian coming?"

Annie nodded. "He had to pick up his wife. I just saw him parking the car."

"Did he say anything else about firing Nicole?"

"He was sorry for the scene. I told him not to be. I'm just glad he suspected something was going on, and that he caught her. He knew what to look for from Claire."

"That's right," I said. "I forgot his wife was a doctor."

Annie nodded. "General practice. She said it's far more common in hospitals than people realize, especially with pain medicine."

"That's terrible."

"What's terrible? I thought we were here to have fun." The voice came from my left and belonged to Brian. He wore a tux and stood alongside his wife.

"Penny," Claire said, "the winery looks lovely, absolutely lovely." So did she. Claire's British, with a perfect complexion and jet-black hair cut in a sleek bob. Her accent, smooth and serene, floated above the crowd. "The new renovations turned out beautifully."

I looked around the room, warm and candlelit. Classical music drifted across the space, accompanied by popping corks and laughter.

"It's great to see you, Claire," I said. "How have you been?"

"Smashing," she said, but it came out softly, and she seemed unusually reserved, even for a Brit. "I mean, today was difficult for Brian, of course. Normally I have to listen to how much he enjoys working with you, Annie, which naturally I love to hear."

Brian shrugged. "Today wasn't fun, but for the most part, I get to practice sound medicine, with Annie as a partner."

"Tonight, though, we're here to have a good time, and I think I'd like some wine," Claire said.

"I'll go with you." Brian placed his hand on Claire's back. As they walked away, I turned to Annie.

"Brian seems fine. What happened today doesn't seem to have bothered him."

"I know," Annie said. "Claire seems more upset than Brian."

"Hopefully they have a good time tonight." When Annie didn't answer, I tried again. "I said—"

"Oh, I heard you," Annie said. "It might be difficult, though, with Amerigen here."

"The pharmaceutical company buying Eric's vaccine? Why would that make it more difficult?"

Annie was looking past my shoulder. "The president of the company just walked in, and look who he has on his arm."

Chapter 3

I turned to see a man about fifty just inside the doors. He had dark hair with a touch of silver at the temples. With a wide smile and quiet confidence, packaged in a beautifully cut tux, he looked like George Clooney pre-marriage, right down to the young, whippet-thin girl on his arm. She had pale blonde hair, short and teased high around her face, and was sporting a tube of a dress in cobalt blue. It took a double-take to realize it was Nicole.

"I wondered if she'd come with Jason tonight," Annie said next to me.

"What is she doing with him?"

"They're dating."

"Back up a second. How did they meet?"

"At the clinic. She told everyone they were seeing a lot of each other, but I think they've only been out a couple of times."

"Does Jason live here?"

"In the city. Apparently he has a penthouse overlooking the Golden Gate. He's a nice guy, the whole package. I hope with time he sees through her."

"Have her turn sideways, and he will. We all will. There's nothing to her. With that puffy, bleached hair, she looks like a Q-tip."

Annie nodded. "Those pills she took. The phenylpropanolamine. In animals it has other uses, but in humans it suppresses appetite. It was sold for years as a diet pill, until it was banned. My guess is that she was taking them to be skinny."

I remembered her behavior at the clinic. "Is the bad attitude a bonus?"

"Usually is, with most drugs used incorrectly."

We watched the couple cut through the crowd, Nicole anchored securely on Jason's arm. Annie rolled her eyes. "You've got to be kidding me."

I shrugged. "I don't get it. You said he's a decent guy. What could he possibly see in her?"

"What every man staring down fifty sees in a hottie in her mid-twenties. His own fleeting youth, slipping through his fingers like grains of sand in the hourglass of life." She sighed and took a big slug of wine.

I looked at my normally cheerful cousin. "The hourglass of life? What's *wrong* with you?"

She shrugged. "Got the blues. I'm turning forty next year. Beats me where the time went. I was going to be married. I was going to have kids. No husband. No kids. I was going to make a medical breakthrough. Instead, it's Eric. They say you can have it all. I'm not so sure anymore."

I put my arm around her. "Don't worry, you still have me."

"True. And a killer ass." She took another sip of wine. "So, what about you?"

"What about me?"

"No new men?"

"No new men, no old men, no hint of men in the future, and only dim memories of any men in the past. No men at all. Just Nanook."

Annie nodded toward the bar. "And, of course, Connor." We watched him direct the staff behind the counter.

"He's very handsome in that sweater," Annie said. "Anything going on there?"

"Under the sweater? Sure. A lot, from what I can tell."

"So?"

I didn't want to talk about it. "So nothing. It's work as usual. We get along great. That's enough."

"Sure it is."

Moments later, Eric entered the room with a woman I didn't recognize. I'd only seen him a few times, either in town or at the entrance to his office at the clinic. He had on a tux as well, the crisp white shirt looking spectacular against his naturally dark skin. He had a silver-gray beard, cut short, with hair long enough to be gathered into a short ponytail.

"I've never liked that hairstyle," I said. "A little too Hollywood for me."

"Well you might not like it, but there's been a steady stream of women coming in and out of the clinic to meet Eric who apparently disagree with you, including Denise."

"His lab assistant?"

Annie nodded. "The one who just came in with him, as

usual a few steps behind. She'd like to be more than his assistant, from what I've seen. Just the way she looks at him." Annie shook her head. "She's always so meek around him, even though she's as smart as can be. I don't get it."

I took a better look. With short-cropped medium brown hair and no makeup, she would be completely overlooked if it wasn't for her sleeveless dress, which drew attention to her strong, sleek arms.

"She looks in shape, but not at all flashy. Not the sort I'd expect him with," I said.

"Oh, he'll never date her, as much as she would like it."

I studied Eric as he made his way across the room, Denise still trailing behind. "He's so tan. Does he spend a lot of time in the sun?"

"He's always been that dark, even when we were in college and spent most of our time in classes," Annie said. "His background is South American. I forget where. Maybe Chile."

Denise lifted two glasses of wine from the nearest tray, handing one to Eric. She raised her glass as though to share a toast, but he turned away from her, weaving his way through the crowd, stopping every few feet to accept congratulations. Denise paled but recovered, stepping to the bar and taking a seat. I scanned the crowd for Eric but managed to snag Nicole's attention instead. She studied me for a moment, then, reaching for another glass of wine and Jason's arm, moved through the crowd.

"Get ready," I whispered to Annie as Nicole swivel-hipped to a stop in front of us.

"I bet you're surprised to see me. Jason had to be here, though, and lately we've been spending every minute together, haven't we?" She dragged a hand down his arm.

"Yup. So far it's been a swell third date." He kept his gaze on Annie, and I could see that his cheeks were flushed. He squirmed and seemed to be embarrassed by Nicole's overt display of affection. I studied Annie to see if she'd caught his look, but her face was blank. She'd missed it, of course. She spends too much time with the four-legged, hairy type of males, and never notices when a good-looking man is interested in her. That's what I was there for.

Nicole squeezed Jason's arm. "Since his company is going to make a fortune on Eric's vaccine, we needed to make an appearance tonight, didn't we?"

Jason smiled at her, but the warmth didn't quite reach his eyes. "The money isn't the important part of this venture. Rabies is nearly unheard of in America, yet it impacts thousands in other countries every year, all because the vaccine is hard to get. Until now."

Nicole nodded, her attention on flagging down another server. "Of course. That too. But still, the money will be nice."

"I'm not doing it for that." Jason stopped. "Some things are more important than—"

"You don't need to explain yourself, honey." Nicole spotted Brian and Claire in the crowd. "I suppose I should go say hello to Brian. Show there aren't any hard feelings over today."

She had to be joking. Annie didn't say anything, though.

Trying to take the high road, and all that. Over the years, I've learned you can't take the high road with people like Nicole. Too much climbing.

"You might not have any hard feelings, but I wouldn't speak for Brian," I said.

"Why? What happened?" Jason asked.

Annie shot me a look. I think she was trying to tell me this wasn't the place. I happened to disagree. "Brian caught your girlfriend here pocketing some medicine meant for a patient at the clinic." Jason's face paled. "Didn't she tell you?"

"Just a misunderstanding," Nicole said. "One that I won't forget you fired me over, Annie."

Jason looked over at Annie. "You had to fire her?"

Nicole stomped her foot. "You aren't hearing me. She didn't have to do anything." She looked at Annie. "Haven't you talked to Lucas? The police aren't going to pursue it, because nobody saw me take any pills." Nicole shot a quick look at Jason. "Not that I did, of course."

"Of course. Still," I said, "you do own a drug company, Jason. No wonder Nicole didn't tell you about it." I shrugged. "I'd watch her if I were you."

Nicole sputtered as Jason sat his wine glass down on a nearby table. "Excuse us." He glanced at Annie and turned to go, pulling Nicole behind him. When they were at the rear of the building, they stopped, and he crossed his arms. I could see her shaking her head as she pointed toward Brian, but I couldn't hear a thing.

"I think that went well," I said.

"You definitely ruined her evening," Annie said. "And the truth is, I'm not at all sorry you did. Come on, let's go socialize." We walked to where Brian and Claire stood. They weren't even trying to pretend they weren't straining to hear the conversation between Jason and Nicole, and I was happy to join in. After plenty of hand-wringing and foot-stomping on Nicole's part, Jason shook his head and turned toward the bar. Nicole tried to follow him, but Jason shook his head, firmer this time, and walked away.

"So, let me get this straight," Brian said. "I fire her today for drug theft, and she has the nerve to come here tonight, knowing we would all be here."

Claire nodded. "It's denial. With addicts, all their problems are someone else's fault."

"What did you say to Jason?" Brian asked me. "He looked pretty upset when he walked away."

"Why do you assume it was me who said something? It could have been Annie." Nobody responded. "I mean, it wasn't, but it could have been."

I stopped talking at the sound of breaking glass. When the second glass hit the deck, everyone started looking around, myself included. I shot a glance at Connor, still behind the tasting bar, but he shook his head and raised his palms. It wasn't him. The tap of high heels carried across the room, and I turned in time to see Nicole raise another empty glass from a nearby table and toss it over her shoulder. The glass shattered as people scurried to move away from her. I looked behind Nicole, but Jason was nowhere to be found.

"She's crazy," I said.

"She's obviously on something," Claire said.

"I'm going with crazy, and if she breaks any more of my wine glasses it's going to get really interesting." I spotted Jason just as he walked back in. Before the door closed, I saw his car, up front and running. He took Nicole by the arm and steered her toward the front door. Nicole turned and saw us.

"Bitches. You're both bitches." She shrugged off Jason's grasp and moved toward us.

I shrugged. "So you've said. If you know any other clever, pithy insults, now's the time to use them."

Nicole was short, about Annie's height, so nothing about her was intimidating. Then I got a look at her eyes. Wide, unfocused pupils ringed by red. Crazy is never pretty.

"Take responsibility, Nicole," Annie said.

Nicole moved closer to Annie, and I stepped between them. "Get out, Nicole. Now."

She pointed at Annie. "This isn't over."

"That's enough." Jason took Nicole by the arm and turned to us as he propelled her to the door. "I'm sorry, I didn't know." He kept his eyes on Annie. "I didn't know."

Chapter 4

"That's going to be a long ride home, for one of them anyway." I looked around the room. Servers and guests alike were talking about Nicole. I squeezed Annie's arm. "Go, circulate, and have some fun. I'll catch up with you later."

Annie nodded while I darted back to the bar, signaling Connor. "We need to do something," I said. "The mood in here is less than festive."

"I just spoke to the organizer," Connor said. "They're starting now." I heard the introduction for Eric begin. Connor handed me two bottles. "What this crowd needs is more wine."

I spent the next two hours circulating the room and filling glasses. Eric wisely kept his speech short, and guests appeared to enjoy the evening, but Nicole's meltdown continued to dominate the conversations, and the evening ended early. Once the first invitees departed, the rest were quick to follow. Shortly after the last of them left, Ross came around the corner, apron in hand.

"I hear Nicole really livened up the evening. I didn't get

to see it, unfortunately, but my staff gave me regular updates. Told you she was someone you needed to watch."

Ross and his warning dogged me late into the night, and it took a long time to fall asleep. In the morning, when I finally managed to stumble out of bed, it was to the

welcome sight of bright, clear skies. Grabbing that crucial first cup of coffee, I took a quick shower, donned jeans and an oversized purple sweater, and headed out the back door. Connor was hanging the banner for the Fabulously Ugly Dog Contest, and he smiled at me over his shoulder. He had a great smile. My heart did a little happy dance, and it took all my energy to focus. Focus on anything but him, in jeans, from behind, up on a ladder…

"Do you mind holding on?"

No, I wouldn't mind at all. I pulled my eyes up to his face. "I'm sorry. What?"

"The ladder. Since you're here, would you mind giving me a hand and steady it?"

"Of course, sure." Smooth.

The contestants were starting to arrive, and if the rest of them were in the same class as the early arrivals, the competition was going to be stiff. Though adorable in their own way, so far I'd seen some truly hideous dogs.

Connor folded up the ladder. "How many are we expecting?"

"There were maybe thirty dogs last year."

"I meant the kind who might want to buy wine."

"Right. I was told there were a couple hundred attendees

last year, and since we finally have a little sunshine, there will be at least that many."

The event featured a fashion show with four-legged models strutting the red carpet, and a variety of pet care booths. All of the models came from the local shelter and were available for adoption. For the main event, there was an outdoor stage and bleacher seating. There was also a chili cook-off, and even though it couldn't be considered standard breakfast fare, I couldn't take the aroma anymore.

"I'm starving. I'm going to hit up the Sterling booth." I took one last look at Connor, wearing another one of those great sweaters, burgundy this time, and those form-fitting jeans. He turned to me, and I jerked my eyes up off his backside. Subtle. Yup, that's me.

Connor climbed off the ladder. "Let me put this away, and I'll go with you."

"No need to run off just yet."

The voice came from just over my shoulder, and I didn't need to look to know it belonged to Chantal, without a doubt the most annoying person I've ever met. She stood upwind, which meant I caught a good whiff of the Obsession perfume she always wore. In a tight-fitting red cashmere sweater and molded-on black yoga-type pants, she slunk over to Connor and rested a hand on his shoulder, her perfect red nails squeezing ever so slightly.

"I haven't seen nearly enough of you lately. Penny, you should let him get into town more. It doesn't do the rest of us any good for you to keep him to yourself."

"He's free to do whatever he wants." I could hear the

strain in my voice but couldn't help it. Chantal had been under my skin since junior high. "I thought your mother would be here by now."

Chantal pointed one of the fingers still resting on Connor's shoulder. "There she is."

I turned to see Antonia Martinelli, the owner of one of the largest wineries in California. Antonia's winery ran adjacent to mine. Connor helped her on occasion, since she was well into her eighties, not that she'd ever admit it. Ramrod straight, with silver hair piled high and her standard black dress, she looked to be from a different century. Tough as nails, but loyal.

"I really hate to pull Connor away." Sure I did. "But we do have some work to do."

Chantal raised her brow. "I'm certain I hate to let him go." She turned to Connor. "Promise me we'll get together later?"

"Penny's right. It's going to be a busy day."

Chantal did a flouncy thing that emphasized her cleavage, something she certainly didn't need. Every guy in the adjacent area stopped and instinctively looked her way. With her signature phony finger wave, she strolled off in the opposite direction of where her mother stood with the mayor of Cypress Cove. The mayor seemed to be doing a lot of head shaking, which didn't surprise me. The larger wineries drive tourism to the area, and Antonia Martinelli didn't let the local politicians forget it. She also owned half the real estate in Cypress Cove, so when she had something on her mind, everyone in town quickly knew what it was.

"I don't encourage Chantal, you know." Connor closed the ladder, holding it with one hand.

"Everyone knows it doesn't take much to get Chantal going." The fact that he was by far the best-looking guy there didn't help, but I managed to keep that to myself. We walked to the rear of the fermentation building. It was a bit of an incline, and I was huffing a bit while I watched Connor hang the ladder. I really needed to work out more.

"So, who's judging this contest," Connor asked.

"There are three judges. Antonia, a local newscaster, and Brian."

"They have their work cut out. Honestly, how do they decide? Did you see the guy trying out the stage with his dog? What was that? I've never seen anything like it."

I nodded. "Nothing like the Chinese Cresteds. I mean, come on. Hairless except for bangs, and those long, hanging tongues. It doesn't get any uglier, in a cute sort of way."

We left the fermentation building, walking past the Sterling booth. Ross saw us and nodded his head toward the pot, at least two feet across. He stirred it with a spoon that could double as a boat oar.

"Care to help with the stirring?"

"If it will get me a taste. It smells delicious."

"Good," he said. "You two can be the first to try it. It's tequila and cactus chili. The bowls are under the counter."

I grabbed bowls and spoons, and Ross ladled out the piping-hot chili.

"Complex. You have several layers of flavor," Connor said.

I looked up. "You sounded like Ross just then."

"What? Straight men can talk food too. I'll have you know I'm a very good cook."

"I guess you'll just have to make dinner for me sometime. I mean, if you want." Sometimes I just needed to stop talking, but he smiled.

"Just tell me when."

The happy dance in my chest started up again, and I couldn't stop smiling as the remaining competitors arrived and filed past, getting ready for their big moment. The dog to beat was Bubbles, out of Boca Raton. Bubbles was down in front with her human, who was passing out pink T-shirts with a photo of Bubbles on the front, trying to rally the crowd. Bubbles didn't need the extra help. Bubbles was ugly. She knew it. Her mom knew it. We all knew it.

Connor shook his head. "Look at her, soaking it up. I can't believe they traveled all the way from Florida for this."

"Hey, it's a big deal. The winner gets five thousand in cash, a modeling contract with *Dogue* magazine in San Francisco, and a segment on the show *Dog Planet*. This has become one of the biggest ugly dog contests in the country."

"There's more than one?"

"Are you kidding? This is just a qualifier for the Ugliest Dog on the Planet. A bulldog with a tremendous underbite won last year, and he's back again fighting to keep the title." I jerked my thumb toward the main parking lot, where several news crews were parked. "All those news vans are from different stations. One of them is covering this for French Television."

Reporters scurried around to get set up before the competition. An attractive woman stepped out from behind one of the vans, and it took me a moment to recognize that sleek bobbed hairdo. Claire worked her way around the cameras and sound equipment, and she wasn't alone. Eric stepped into view and pulled at her arm. She turned and pushed him off. Eric said something and waved her away, kicking at the dirt before he disappeared behind the vehicles. Claire hurried down the path, and I waved her over.

"Hey, so what's up with Eric?" Subtlety was never my strength.

"You saw that," Claire said.

"Hard to miss. What's going on?"

"Oh, nothing really. I just think he's a pompous ass."

I'd seen the way Eric had pulled on her arm. Whatever they were fighting about was more than just Eric's lack of modesty. I took a long look at Claire. She was pale, but she's always pale. This was different. There was a faint sheen to her face, and she stood with her arms securely folded in front of her, shoulders stiff.

"What's he doing with the TV crews?" I asked.

"Several want interviews to cover his vaccination. They can have him." She grimaced. "As a doctor, I can appreciate what he's done, but that doesn't mean I have to like him."

"I didn't know you felt so strongly about him."

"He just isn't one of my favorite people." She shook her head. "We go back a long way. We met at UC Davis."

"Annie went there."

"So did Brian."

31

"Is that where you two met?"

"Yes, we all met there." Eric stepped out from behind the vans, and reporters surrounded him. Behind them, a thin woman with short hair jostled to watch the interview. I recognized her.

"That's Denise, isn't it?"

Claire followed my gaze, then nodded. "Always nearby."

I watched Denise work her way to Eric's side. There was a flash as someone took a photo. Eric turned to the cameras, his smile wide. Claire tsked next to me. "As I say, I've known him a long time. Let's just leave it at that."

"Sure, no problem." I checked the time. "Is Brian looking forward to being a judge in the contest?"

"He seems to be. Chatted about it all the way here." With finality, Claire turned from Eric. Her brows were drawn, her shoulders tight, but she took a deep breath. "Look, he's just over there." She pointed through the crowd. "Let's join him."

By the time we reached him, Claire had relaxed, her face calm. The improvement lasted until Brian spoke. "What was the problem with Eric?"

Claire stiffened. "Nothing. It was nothing."

"I saw him grab your arm."

I wasn't leaving. Not until I had to, which occurred seconds later.

"Penny, might I have a few moments with Brian, alone?"

"Oh. Sure. Of course." I moved away, far enough to comply with Claire's request but close enough to catch bits of their conversation.

Annie walked up to me. "What are you staring at, Miss Nosy?"

I silenced her with my palm, but it was too late. Claire pulled Brian off in the other direction.

I told Annie about Eric grabbing Claire by the arm. "Brian saw it. Claire said it wasn't anything, but I don't believe it, and I don't think Brian does either."

Annie shrugged. "I've never noticed any tension between Brian and Eric at the clinic. Of course, Eric's usually in the back and we don't see him all that much. Claire's never been very fond of Eric, though."

"I got that. I didn't know you all met in college. I wonder if something happened back then."

"Maybe. I've never heard of anything."

"How is it when Claire comes into the clinic and Eric's there?"

"I'm always stuck in back. Ask Dot. She never misses anything. That's why she's such a good office manager. She's around here somewhere."

The crowd was starting to grab seats for the contest, with several entrants having entire sections of fans, most in matching attire. The pink shirts were for Bubbles, of course, but there was Tiny, another Chinese Crested, with a big throng of fans in yellow, and Scootch, the bulldog with the tremendous underbite and one lazy eye. His fans were numerous, and all wore red.

"I need to run. When the contest is over, this mob is going to be thirsty, I hope. I need to make sure Connor is good behind the bar."

"Behind the bar, on top of the bar…"

"Go watch the contest, and we can talk about that some other time."

"That's always your answer: some other time." She arched a brow. "And you accuse me of missing what's right in front of me."

With a wave, I turned and made my way to the tasting room, which already had a crowd. Connor and Hayley were both behind the counter, and I joined in, spending the next hour pouring tastes and discussing our varietals. We don't make a lot on the tastings, but this was for a good cause, and hopefully when visitors return home they'll seek out our wines in the future.

During a lull, I heard a roar from the crowd. On stage, Bubbles from Boca Raton was being lifted high above her mom's head, relishing her victory. The finale created a flurry of sales as the onlookers disbursed, and I kept my head down until I felt a shadow fall over me.

"I guess ugly is the new cute." It was Jason from the pharmaceutical company.

"It certainly is for Bubbles," I said. Not overly tall, but with broad shoulders and silver-streaked hair, he really was attractive. And, after all, Annie was only five-two. "So, in the future, I don't expect we will be seeing as much of you. Unless, of course, you will be around because of Nicole…"

"No, that won't be happening."

"I'm sorry, I didn't mean to pry." Jason didn't know me well enough to realize that's exactly what I intended, and he answered easily.

"I don't mind you asking. Last night, Nicole and I came to an agreement."

"An agreement?"

He nodded. "We agreed we wouldn't be seeing each other again."

"That's probably a good move. For one thing, she was a little young for you." Mentally, I slapped myself. Nice and tactful. Fortunately, he started laughing.

"I'd come to the same conclusion. Besides, I run a pharmaceutical company. When I heard yesterday that Nicole was taking medicine from Annie's clinic, well, that put everything in a different light."

I bet it did. "What about Annie? I think you two might be a good fit. Besides, I've seen how you look at her."

He laughed again. "You know how to get right to the point, don't you?" He rubbed a palm along his chin, thoughtful. "She is pretty terrific, isn't she? You think she'd be interested?"

Gee, I don't know. Does she have a pulse? "Maybe, if you can get her out of the clinic long enough. She's pretty busy. So, it's definitely over with Nicole?"

"We're through all right, but she wasn't happy about it. I don't mean to sound arrogant. It was just my decision to end it. I don't know what I'd been thinking, to be honest."

"I'm not sure clear thinking occurs when a twenty-five-year-old with a twenty-five-inch waist is involved."

"Not my finest hour, I'll admit. And sadly, I think you're overstating her waistline. She's ridiculously skinny. It's more like twenty-two inches."

35

"That's pretty specific," I said. "Not sure your memory can be trusted."

"I'm not relying on memory. She's coming up behind you."

Jason stepped around me and stopped Nicole in her tracks. She looked like she had a bad night. She winced in the morning light, her hair was flat on one side, and I think her sweatshirt was on inside-out.

"Your problem isn't with Penny, Nicole. It's with me."

"I wouldn't have a problem with you if it wasn't for Penny and her stupid cousin. Annie could have let the whole thing drop, and then I wouldn't be in this mess." As if on cue, Nicole teared up. "Jason, we need to talk." Her voice broke. "I really want to talk to you. Alone."

"There's nothing more to say. And if there was, I certainly wouldn't discuss it here."

"I can meet you at the Marquis later."

"Please don't show up at my hotel. I promise you, nothing will come of it."

Like magic, the tears dried on Nicole's face. "Fine. I don't have time for this." She turned to look at me. "Tell your cousin I'll be by the clinic later to pick up my check." She turned to Jason. "You'll regret this. You and that bitch who fired me are both going to be sorry."

She disappeared into the crowd before either of us had a chance to respond.

"So, you were dating that, huh?"

He pressed his thumb and forefinger to his eyes and shook his head, as though trying to erase the memory. "It was only a few dates. Not long enough for me to see this side of her. I think she's dangerous."

"I'm not worried. She's ninety pounds."

"Just because someone is small in stature doesn't mean they can't find ways to be vindictive. Your cousin's the one I would warn. Annie should know Nicole is holding a grudge."

"Point taken. I'll let Annie know."

A couple of hours later, the crowd began to disburse. Annie walked in as I was stacking wine crates in the back room.

"Where have you been?" I asked.

"Just chatting. A lot of my clients are here. Can I get a ride to the clinic?"

"No problem, but wasn't Brian going back tonight also?"

"He came with Claire, and they've left. I thought I would catch a ride with Dot, but she's gone too."

"Dot needed to prepare Nicole's last check. She told me she was coming into the clinic later to pick it up."

"When did you see Nicole?"

"A little while ago. I think she's stalking Jason. She interrupted as he was telling me he wanted to ask you out."

"Yeah, right." She waved away the comment.

"Okay, would you rather insist that it didn't happen or discuss the nice, successful pharmaceutical entrepreneur who could be George Clooney's twin and wants to go out with you?"

"All right, I'll listen, but if Nicole is the type he normally goes for, why would he want to date me?"

"Because you're a smart, successful veterinarian who's age appropriate for him. Not to mention, the crazy toothpick he was dating is now stalking him."

"Okay, that's a pretty good argument. Tell me all the details on the drive."

By the time we reached the clinic, the sun had dipped below the horizon.

"While I'm here, can I get some more of those vitamins you recommended for Nanook? I'm almost out."

"Sure, let me grab them for you." Annie closed the door and disappeared into the clinic. I pulled into a spot and turned off the engine. The fog was creeping in from the sea, an almost nightly occurrence this close to the ocean. It danced along the ground and curled around the car. There's a silence that accompanies this ritual. It feels like a blanket settling over the town of Cypress Cove and the Central California coast. It makes every noise stand out, and the car that pulled into the lot a few minutes later sounded jarringly loud. No wonder. It was Nicole's snazzy little sports car. I know a little about cars and drive a restored Jaguar X360 I'd found abandoned in a neighbor's yard twenty years ago. The Audi Nicole parked next to me was expensive. She didn't buy it on a vet tech salary. Somebody had helped with that neat little gift. She turned off the engine, and I got a sneer when she stepped from the car. I looked around the lot. Brian and Dot's cars were there. With an audience, I didn't think Nicole would have a chance to cause much trouble. Still, I didn't trust her, and by the time she reached the front door I was right behind her. Nicole didn't look at me as she pushed through the entrance, not bothering to hold it open. Classy to the end. We both entered the waiting area. The offices were on the left, and Nicole headed to the right, toward the exam rooms. The drug dispensary was also there, and I followed her around the corner.

Nicole guessed my thoughts. "Don't worry, I'm not making a drug run. I just have a few more things to say to your cousin."

We continued to walk through the clinic. "I think you should just get your check and leave. You got off easy last time. Keep it up, and next time you might find yourself short on luck."

We both came around the corner to the main operating room and stopped. Brian was face-down on the ground, a dark red stain spreading across the back of his white lab coat. Annie was above him, holding a knife. Her face was an odd gray, and her hand shook as she held the knife out.

"I just found him like this." She dropped the knife, and it clattered on the floor. "This was in his back."

"Sure it was." Nicole found her voice. "Look who's short on luck now?"

Chapter 5

I needed to think. The rapidly spreading stain across Brian's back wasn't helping. I'm not good with blood, and my breath shortened to pants that didn't go beyond my throat. Averting my eyes, I pushed some air into my chest. "Who else is here, Annie?"

"Just Dot. She's up front in the offices."

I raised my voice. "Dot, can you come in here?" My voice was shaky, but I heard the office door click open. I knew Dot was standing behind me when I heard the clatter of loose bracelets she always wore, followed by a sharp intake of breath.

"Nobody move. Annie, is he dead?" I asked.

Annie reached for his wrist.

Nicole tsked. "She just stabbed him. She shouldn't be allowed anywhere near the body."

Annie held Brian's wrist. "He's gone, and I didn't stab him, I found him like this." Annie looked at the knife. "It's from the operating room. It's mine."

"Annie, stop talking. Dot, don't come further into the

room so we can tell the police nothing was moved from this point." I reached for my cell. "I need to call the police."

"You can't in this room," Dot said. "Too much equipment. No signal. You need to use the hard line."

I gestured behind me with my hand. "Nicole, come with me while I call the police."

Nicole shook her head. "Forget it. I'm not leaving Annie here alone."

I didn't like where this was headed but could only take care of one thing at a time. "Fine, let's all go into the other room." Annie slowly got to her feet. She reached me, and I put my arm around her shoulder.

"Let Dot take you to splash some water on your face, then everyone wait in reception while I call the police."

A few moments later, I reached the station and asked for Lucas.

"I need someone else if he isn't in." I almost hoped he wasn't available. Since I moved back to Cypress Cove, I'd managed to find my share of bodies.

"No, he's right here."

"Great." I steeled myself. The deputy called out, "Penny Lively, line one," in the background. Moments later, Lucas was on the phone.

"Penny, what's up?"

I took a deep breath. "Somebody stabbed Dr. Brian at the vet clinic. Annie found the body. I was just dropping her off. I *swear* that's how it happened."

There was a muffled response.

"Lucas, you there?"

"Did anyone call 911?"

"We just found him, and Annie took his pulse." I remembered Brian's open eyes and shuddered. "He's dead."

"I'll be right there. Don't touch anything."

"Of course I won't."

"Listen, do you have your camera on you?"

"Always." I keep one in my trunk, a habit from my old job.

There was a pause. "I might regret this, but I don't like to wait for photos. Things get moved, and it will be hours before I can get someone down from San Francisco. I could use one of my staff, but they don't have your experience, and two of my deputies are out with the flu."

"Okay, sure," I said. "I won't touch a thing, and this way you'll have a second set of prints and a different perspective."

"And keep Annie as far away from the body as you can."

"Lucas, you can't—"

"I don't know what we have yet, but believe me, in the long run it's for her own good."

I returned to the lobby and its three occupants. Nicole was sprawled on one end of a bench, seemingly oblivious that someone she knew was dead just steps from her, while Dot sat next to her, hunched and weeping. Annie moved back and forth in front of the main windows, hugging her arms around her body.

"I'm going to my car," I said. "I need to get my camera."

"I want some air." Annie moved toward the front door.

Nicole wasn't as unaware as she seemed. "No, you don't.

42

No talking and deciding how you're going to make this look better for you."

I turned to Annie. "Maybe you should stay here."

I grabbed my camera from the trunk and returned to the lobby. "Lucas wants me to get some shots while we wait," I announced to nobody in particular. I started in the back of the clinic but couldn't open the offices to the rear of the building. I returned to the lobby.

"The doors are locked in the back."

"That's Eric's space," Dot said. "It locks from both sides. You can't get through."

"I think the police will probably want to get in there. You might want to call him."

She wiped her cheeks. "Guess I'll have to."

Dot moved to the reception desk as I worked my way quickly through the clinic, taking photos. I snapped shots of the offices, exam rooms, and, finally, the operating room. I shot the room wide-angle, staying away from Brian's body until I couldn't avoid it any longer. The knife remained where Annie had dropped it earlier, the stain on Brian's back now the width of his shoulders. I swallowed hard and wiped my clammy hands on my jeans before snapping a few final shots of Brian. I returned to the lobby and emailed the photo files to Lucas. As a backup, I emailed copies to myself, and then took a seat.

We waited in silence for the police to arrive. Nicole was now perched on the arm of a couch, while Dot stood by the window, looking out for the red and blue lights. I sat with Annie on the opposite couch. Over her shoulder, I could see into the operating room. Only Brian's face was visible. He could have been sleeping. I shuddered and turned my face.

We only had a short wait before we heard sirens. Moments later, two patrol cars pulled into the lot. Lucas stepped from the first car. I pushed open the glass doors and walked toward him. When he spotted me, he narrowed his eyes and drew his brows together.

"I was just dropping Annie off. I *swear* it."

"So you told me on the phone." He held up his palm to silence me. "Photos?"

"I shot everything." I looked behind him. Two deputies stepped from the second car. "Where are the rest of you?"

"This is it. As I said, we're short-staffed tonight. Email me the photos."

"Already done."

"How long ago did you find him?"

I looked at my watch. "Twenty minutes, twenty-five at the most. Brian was at the dog contest until just over an hour ago, so that will help us narrow the time of his death."

Lucas stopped in his tracks. "There isn't any 'us.' I'm going in there, and you're not going to say a word."

"But I might be able to help. At least with where everyone has been for the last hour."

Lucas sighed. "I will ask the group that one question, then I take it from there. Don't make me regret this."

I nodded, and we pushed through the glass doors. Lucas swept his hand again, this time to indicate all of us. "I'm going to talk to each of you. First, I need to find out where everyone has been for the last hour."

"I was in my office working," Dot said, her voice breaking. "I didn't know anyone was here until Penny called out to me."

"I was with Penny," Annie said. "We drove up, and I came in and found Brian."

Lucas took out a notepad. "Dot heard Penny call out after the murder, but she didn't hear you shout or yell when you found Brian?"

"Well, no." Annie stopped. "I did yell." She shook her head. "I think I did. I don't know." She pressed her hands together. "Why can't I remember?"

"Shock," I said. "Lucas, everyone reacts differently in these situations. You know that."

Lucas slowly turned his face to me. Oops. "Thanks, Penny. Yes, I do know that."

"Well then, why didn't Dot hear her?" Nicole sat back, satisfied.

Dot shook her head, a long braid of silver hair swaying behind her. "I didn't hear anything because I wear headphones while I'm working. Grateful Dead. I'd taken them off right before I heard Penny call out to me."

"Whatever." Nicole turned to Annie. "It doesn't matter if you did scream. You could have stabbed him and then screamed as though you'd just found him."

Annie was ashen, and her lips trembled when she spoke. "I *did* just find him."

Lucas held up his hand. "Stop. I'll be talking to each of you alone. You first." He pointed at Annie. "The rest of you wait."

"Oh, this is great," Nicole said as she took a seat.

Lucas led Annie out of the lobby and toward her office. She looked over her shoulder as they passed the door to the operating room. I tried to catch her attention and reassure her, but she didn't seem to realize I was even there.

We sat in silence for a moment. "I need to call Hayley." I left the lobby and stood outside the front entrance as a deputy strung police tape around Annie's clinic. Hayley answered on the first ring.

"Where are you?"

"At Annie's clinic."

"What's going on? You sound funny."

I stalled, as though saying it out loud would somehow make it worse. "Brian's dead, and Annie was found with his body, holding the knife that killed him. It looks bad, even to me, and I know she's innocent."

"Brian's dead." Hayley paused as she absorbed the news. "They can't think Annie's responsible. Just tell everything you know to the police."

"I will. The problem is that when I found her, I wasn't alone. Nicole was with me, and you can guess what she's saying."

There was a pause on the line. "Oh jeez, why her?"

"I know. I need to stick around. I'm waiting for my turn to talk to Lucas."

"He's there now?" Despite the situation, I could hear the warmth in her voice.

"Yes, and he wasn't necessarily thrilled at finding me at the scene of another murder."

"It isn't on purpose."

"I'll be sure to remind him of that. I'll call you when I know more."

I'd just closed the phone when a black SUV pulled into the lot. Eric stopped in front of the police tape. He jumped from the driver's seat and ducked under the tape. One of the deputies caught him right before he entered the clinic.

"You don't understand." Eric struggled to free his arm from the deputy's grasp. "I've got to make sure nobody's been in my offices. It could invalidate all of my work."

"Eric, the doors to your offices are locked," I said. "I tried to open them myself." The deputy looked at me. "The chief asked me to take pictures. I was there at his direction."

Eric relaxed, and the deputy let go of his arm. "Dot called me and told me what happened to Brian. I can't believe it."

"Why don't we sit here on the steps," I said. "I'm sure the police will want to talk with you. If nothing else, you have access to the clinic."

"Not really. We don't use the connecting doors," Eric said, pulling at the short ponytail skimming his collar. "We use the outside door." He abruptly stood. "I should check and see if that's been disturbed."

The second deputy moved closer at his words, and I shook my head. "You'll know soon enough. In the meantime, you might want to call Denise. See if she was in your offices tonight."

Eric shook his head. "She's in the city."

"She drove to San Francisco tonight? What for?"

He shrugged. "What she does with her personal time isn't my business."

He was dismissive and on the edge of surly, and I decided to dig a little. "That isn't what I've heard. It's my understanding she'd like very much to be part of your business."

He interrupted me with a wave of his hand. "Rumors. She's my assistant. Nothing more."

"Either way I'm sure the police will want to talk to her at some point."

Eric nodded. "I'm sure she will be happy to talk to them, as am I, although I don't know how much help either one of us will be."

"They'll want to know the basics. Where you've been for the last couple of hours. That type of thing."

"That's easy. I was down at the beach, Cliff Point, taking photographs."

"At night?"

"Sure. It's the only time bats come out to fly."

"Okay, then. Bats."

Eric studied me. "Considering the field I'm in, it isn't that surprising."

I held up my hand. "No, I get it. It's just not something you hear every day, going out at night to photograph bats."

I thought back to the tension between Eric and Claire earlier. "It looked like there was an argument between you and Claire this afternoon at the dog contest."

Eric hesitated. "This afternoon?"

I nodded. "Near the TV crews. I saw you grab her arm. Brian did too. He didn't look very happy about it."

His face cleared. "Oh, right. Before I gave my interview. It was nothing."

"It looked like more than—"

He stood, pulling out a packet of cigarettes. "I need a smoke." He walked the length of the front porch, stopping at the far end, just as Dot pushed open the front doors.

"I didn't know he smoked," I said.

"I see him smoke out back during the day," Dot said. "Smelly things rolled in brown paper. He brings them back from South America." She pointed over her shoulder. "Someone is getting real antsy, and both deputies are busy out here. Maybe you can help?"

Nicole. I nodded and pushed up off the step. I could see right away what Dot meant. Nicole was seated, but she was jiggling her foot and rubbing both arms as if chilled.

She spotted us. "So when it's okay to leave, is my check done? I want to get out of here as soon as possible. This whole thing is giving me the creeps."

Dot turned to Nicole. "I didn't have time to get it ready, but how can you think of something so unimportant right now? Brian's dead. Someone you worked with. Someone you knew."

"Yeah, I knew him. He was the guy who got me fired."

"Such a fluke," I said, "us getting here at exactly the same time."

"So?" She recrossed her legs, opposite foot now shaking.

"Nothing, really, I just think it's quite a coincidence." I decided to dive right in. "When did you leave the winery?" I said. "Did you leave right after you spoke with me and Jason?"

Nicole narrowed her eyes. "Why?"

"Just trying to work out the timing." She kept her gaze on me, and I got a good look at her eyes. They were glassy, her pupils dilated. She was certainly on something.

"If you think I had anything to do with this, forget it. I got here after you and Annie, remember?"

I didn't answer, but if she'd left the winery right after we spoke, she had plenty of time to kill Brian, leave, and return, calm and collected, for her check.

The second deputy dusted the locks on the front windows. "What are they doing out there?" Dot asked.

"Looking for fingerprints," I said.

She waited until he was finished and reached to close the blinds, but he raised his hand to stop her.

"You can't touch anything," I said.

She turned and shook her head, beaded earrings swinging. "I can't believe this is happening."

"Is there anything you remember that seemed off tonight?" I asked.

"Nothing. Dr. B was working, and I was in my office as usual. I can't hear anything from back there, and, besides, I had my headphones on." She gestured at the cord around her neck. "Classic rock. I didn't hear a thing." She pressed her palms against her eyes. "I just can't believe it." She sat down hard on the couch. "We were alone here. At least I thought we were." Her face grew pale. "I was alone with whoever did this. I could have, I could have…"

I grabbed her by the arm. "But you weren't." She nodded and took a jagged breath. "That's it," I said. "Keep breathing."

Chief Lucas was with Annie a long time. When they finished, she looked paler than when she'd found Brian, but the deputy joined us in the lobby and I couldn't ask her any questions. The time Lucas spent with Dot and Nicole was short in comparison, which added to my concern as I studied Annie's tear-streaked face. When Dot returned, she stopped to say something to Annie, but the deputy shook his head and pointed to the door. Dot gave Annie a soft smile and left. Nicole was in with Lucas for the least amount of time, but the smirk she gave us when she returned was hardly encouraging. I'm sure she'd had plenty to say to Lucas.

"Night, you two. Still didn't get my check, but the floor show was worth it. Want to know who Lucas thinks is the leading lady?" The deputy signaled for her to leave, but she ignored him. "Things are going to get real interesting for you now, Annie."

Lucas stuck his head around the corner. "That's enough, Nicole." He nodded in my direction. "Penny, you're up."

I gave Annie's hand a little squeeze and went into her office, where Lucas gestured to a seat.

"Before you say anything, all I did was drive Annie back here, and let me tell you, it's a good thing I did."

"What do you mean?"

"My presence keeps Nicole from embellishing the story. She might have said she saw Annie actually stabbing Brian."

"How do you know she didn't? Stab him, I mean."

My throat went dry. "You can't honestly believe Annie is a murderer." He frowned at me. "You can scowl, but we both know she didn't do this."

Lucas swiveled in his chair. "I don't know anything yet." He raised his voice as I started to interrupt. "I have a job here, Penny, and I intend to do it. You must see how it looks. Annie was found by both you and Nicole, bent over Brian's body holding the murder weapon, a knife that belongs to her, a knife thrust to the hilt into Brian's back."

The room took a little spin, and I swallowed before I answered. "She found him and took the knife out because she was trying to help him."

"Penny, we're dusting for fingerprints, but there aren't any signs of forced entry."

"That doesn't mean anything. Dot was here. All the staff have keys. I've even got a key for emergencies."

"Okay, we'll let it go for now. Annie has a couple things going for her. For one thing, she's well-known in town as a decent, stand-up individual."

I nodded. "Damn skippy."

"For another, she and Brian had a good relationship."

"The best. Friends and coworkers."

"But in the eyes of the law, that doesn't get you very far. What helps Annie is that she doesn't have a motive."

"Of course she doesn't," I said. "The clinic is doing fantastic, and they've always gotten along beautifully. Business has never been better. Annie loves…" I stopped. "Annie loved working with Brian."

Lucas made some notes. "How did Annie get along with Brian's wife?"

I had to shift gears. "Claire? They're friends. They've known each other since college."

Lucas stopped writing. "I didn't know they've known each other that long."

"They all did. Brian, Eric, Claire, and Annie all went to UC Davis at the same time." I stopped. "Claire. Someone needs to tell Claire."

"I've got a deputy at her house now," Lucas said. "Nicole had some strong opinions she was more than happy to share. She wasn't broken up about Brian's death, but she was downright happy that she was the one to find Annie in, well, in the position she found her in."

"You know Brian found Nicole stealing drugs and that Annie fired her over it. Annie called your office right after it happened. She spoke to you, didn't she?"

Lucas nodded. "Annie decided not to pursue it."

"After you told her there wasn't enough evidence. How much more evidence do you need beyond seeing the way Nicole just left here? Surely you could tell she's high as a kite right now, and you let her leave to drive home!"

Lucas hardened his look and folded his arms. Oops. "This isn't my first interview, Penny. Look, I don't know why I'm telling you this, but I had Nicole followed. They'll give her just enough time to clear the parking lot before they pull her over. Then she'll have to explain why she's driving under the influence, and this way we'll be able to get a drug test."

"Thanks, Lucas. Nice move."

"Glad you approve. I don't want Annie driving. Take her home, and let me do my job."

Annie was blue as she shivered and turned my car heater to the highest setting. We'd just left the parking lot when we spotted a patrol car, red lights blazing. I slowed down as they loaded Nicole into the back seat.

Annie kneaded her hands in front of the vent. "Other than seeing Nicole carted away, this will pretty much go down as the worst night of my life." She covered her face with her hands. "I can't believe I said that. Brian's dead, and here I am saying it's the worst night of *my* life."

"It's the shock, and this is me you're talking to. If it makes a difference, it could have been even worse. You might have arrived earlier, and don't forget Dot was there alone with the killer…"

Annie nodded. "You're right. The same thing could have happened to either one of us, although something about Dot being there is bothering me."

"What?"

"All she had to do was finish the check for Nicole. How long would that take? She said she was wearing her headphones, and it sounds like she was there a while, but she still didn't have the check ready?"

I thought for a moment. "What do you think she was doing?"

"I don't know. I've been blaming Nicole for the cash shortages, but in reality she didn't have access to the funds the way Dot does. I hate to think it, but what was Dot doing there, alone and at night?"

"Be sure to ask her the next time you see her. Also, you need to get the locks changed. Lucas felt that not having any forced entry looks bad."

"Bad for me, you mean."

Unwilling to add to her burden, I shook my head. "Not necessarily. It does narrow the suspect list to either someone Brian knew and let in, or someone with a key. A lot of people have access to the clinic. As far as Lucas, well, he needs to review all the angles." I sighed. "It's the way we found you. It wouldn't be so bad if I'd been alone, but of all people, why did Nicole have to be there?"

"I'll never forget how it felt to come around that corner and see Brian like that." Her voice broke, and she shuddered. "I don't blame Lucas for what he needs to do. Of course I look guilty, the way it sits."

I had to ask. "Why did you pull out the knife?"

"I don't know! I panicked. Somehow I thought it would help." She closed her eyes. "This is so bad."

I held up my hand. "It isn't as bad as it could be. Lucas told me the best thing you have going for you is not having a motive. People don't kill unless they have a reason, and you didn't have any reason for wanting Brian dead. The clinic is more profitable with two of you, you get along great…"

"I can't imagine the clinic without him. What am I going to tell his patients? Oh, damn!"

"What?"

"Claire. Who's going to tell Claire?"

"Lucas already has a deputy with her."

We drove in silence for a few minutes. I saw Annie wipe the side of her cheek and reach in the back for a box of Kleenex.

"No," she said.

"No what?"

"It isn't right that Claire is with someone she doesn't know."

I nodded. "Let's go."

"I suppose Lucas won't approve, since I'm his best suspect."

"That's easy to solve. We won't mention it to him."

A short time later, I pulled into the circular drive of the ranch-style house just outside of town. The lights were on, the curtains open.

"The deputy must be gone. Do you see Claire?"

Annie nodded. "She's on the couch. She's just sitting there."

We walked to the door and knocked. After a bit, Claire opened the door, her eyes red and glazed. It took her a moment to recognize us, then, without a word, Annie folded Claire into her arms.

"Oh, Annie. It can't be." She pushed back the door and gestured for us to follow. "Help me understand what happened." Claire took a deep breath. "The police told me how he was killed. They said he was found by someone he works with. Was it you, Annie?"

Annie nodded. "I'm so sorry."

Claire didn't respond and swayed slightly.

"Let's sit down." I took Claire to the couch, where she collapsed. Annie sat down beside her, and I remained standing. "Did Brian tell you why he was going back to the clinic?" I wasn't thrilled to be pushing Claire for answers.

She'd just found out Brian was murdered, but the police would be asking the same questions, if they hadn't already.

"He said he didn't like something that came back on a test result."

"Was that common?" I asked.

Annie nodded as Claire answered. "Sometimes the lab sends test results out late. He preferred to check them as soon as he could." Claire covered her face. "I dropped him off. He said he'd be home soon."

"Wait," I said. "You dropped him off at the clinic?"

She dipped her head. "He went in early today. I picked him up around noon. We had lunch and then drove together to your winery for the dog contest." Claire slid back on the couch. "I can't believe this has happened. I need to make some calls." She closed her eyes. "I need to tell his family."

"Do you want us to stay?"

She shook her head. "I'd really prefer just being alone for a bit." She let out a jagged breath. "Brian really loved working with you, Annie. I'm just so glad he was prepared in case something happened to him. It helps, knowing you'll be okay."

Annie paused. "I'm sorry, Claire, but I don't know what you mean."

"Brian didn't tell you?"

"Tell me what?"

"He took out a key man policy."

I shook my head at Annie, and she shrugged. "I don't know what that is."

"It's insurance a key person in a business takes out, in

case something happens to him. Brian said you'd discussed it."

"When Eric started renting from us we talked about extra insurance in general, but I didn't know he'd increased his coverage. It must have been fairly recent."

Claire nodded. "He got it just a couple of weeks ago. I feel so much better knowing you won't have to worry about that, at least."

I tried to keep my voice from betraying the panic I was starting to feel. "I'm sorry, Claire, but just one more question. Do you know how much the policy was for?"

Claire nodded. "It was really reasonably priced, probably because of his good health. They didn't think he was at risk." Claire's voice broke. "So he decided on a million."

"A million dollars?"

Claire nodded. "Brian said the equipment alone is worth that."

Annie nodded. "He's right."

"I'm going to lie down now." Claire raised her hand against any protests we might have made. "Honestly, I just want a little time alone."

Reluctantly we left and watched through the window as she walked back to the couch, tears streaming down her face. As we pulled from the driveway, I turned to Annie. "You know what this means, right, Annie?"

She nodded. "That Brian was more organized than me. It was his idea to get the additional insurance. Said that we'd both feel more secure if we didn't need to worry about the business. It was just like Brian."

I shook my head. "It was a smart move, but I wouldn't exactly say you should feel secure right now. Brian just gave you a motive. Make that one million of them."

Chapter 6

"I can't breathe. I can't breathe. *I can't breathe.*" Annie wiped her face on her sleeve. "I think I'm going to pass out."

I pulled the car to the side of the road. Annie pushed open the door, jumped out onto the grassy slope, and started pacing back and forth.

"How bad does it look that he took out insurance just a couple of weeks before he's killed?"

"Well, it isn't good."

"Even worse, he got the extra insurance and I didn't."

"Lucas is certainly going to ask you about that."

"I do one thing, and that's be a vet. Everything else gets filled in when I can."

"Wait a minute," I said. "Isn't that why you have Dot?"

"Yes." She stopped pacing and turned to me. "That's exactly why I have Dot. She must have known about the policy. She would have filled out the paperwork for Brian."

"Why wouldn't she have mentioned it to you too?"

"The paperwork's probably buried on my desk. There wasn't any hurry. We had plenty of time."

It was the middle of the night. I could see Annie's breath as she walked in circles.

"It's cold, and you're in shock. Let me get you home, or better yet come back to my place."

"I can't sleep. I can't even stop moving." Annie reached me and grabbed me by the arm. "You need to help me. You can find out who did this." In the moonlight, Annie's face looked ashen. "I mean it, Penny. Lucas's job is to find the most logical person, and right now I look like a pretty good fit, even to me. Please help. What is it they look for in a murder?"

I stalled, not wanting to answer. "Motive, means, and opportunity."

Annie nodded. "I have all three, Penny." She shivered. "All three."

"That's it, I'm taking you home."

"But you'll help me, right?"

I looked at my cousin, the person who'd always been there for me. "You don't even need to ask."

I got her back in the car, and we drove in silence until we neared her street. Annie pushed her fingers through her hair.

"It's so dark. I know this might be paranoid, but I'm glad you're here."

I pulled into the drive and left my lights on. We sat and looked over the yard.

"I don't think you're paranoid at all. You found your business partner and friend murdered. Whoever killed him had likely just left. You didn't see them, but they don't know that. You should definitely be more careful, at least until this is resolved."

"Great. I'm officially petrified. Now you're going to help me for sure."

I looked around. It's always dark in Cypress Cove at night. The town vetoed standardized street lights years ago, and the only light was from Annie's front porch.

"Let's go." The crunch of her crushed-shell drive underfoot echoed in the stillness, and we both breathed a sigh of relief when we'd made it through the front door and William, her lab mix, greeted us.

"Want something to drink?" Annie asked.

"No. What I want is for you to take a hot shower. Now go."

While I waited, I made her some chamomile tea. She returned a few minutes later in flannel pajamas that dragged on the floor, completely hiding her feet. She looked like a teenager. With her cup in hand, she curled up on the couch and turned to me.

"Where do you think we should start looking?"

"Well, I agree with you about Dot," I said. "I think it's strange. She didn't even have Nicole's check ready, so what was she doing?" I slapped my head. "I just thought of something. We can see what she was working on when Brian was killed."

"How?"

"The photographs I took for Lucas. I shot the whole place, including Dot's office. I have them on my phone. Let's look at them on your desktop."

Within moments she had the photos up on her monitor. She scrolled through the first few shots and then stopped.

"What?" I said.

"It looks like someone went through Brian's office." She enlarged the photo. "His desk is a mess. He always kept everything in order." She paused. "His laptop is still there, but I don't see his book."

"What book?"

"A notebook where he kept patient notes, clinic items, that kind of thing."

"He didn't use his computer?"

"Yes, all of us used the same system for patient records. This was more a habit of his."

"I'll tell Lucas it's missing," I said as Annie flipped through a few more shots. "The other pictures, the ones you shouldn't see, are at the end," I added. "The photos of Dot's office are coming up."

We clicked through and found the photographs showing Dot's desk. "What are we looking for?" I asked. "I see patient folders, maybe invoices. Does anything look out of place to you?"

"Not really, but there's no reason to come in after hours to do any of this." Annie shook her head. "I don't know what Dot was doing at the office, but there's no way she could have killed Brian. She isn't a murderer."

"Still, her being there is something out of place, something that doesn't fit." I thought back to Brian, and the way we found him. "Can we narrow it down to who was strong enough to use a knife like that? How much strength do you need?"

"More than you think, unless…"

"What?"

Annie bit her lip. "Anger. Anger will give someone the strength needed."

"If that's the case, then Nicole could have stabbed him. Just because she pulled in behind us doesn't mean she hadn't been there earlier," I said. "She could have circled the block and returned."

"But would she really come back to where she had just murdered someone?"

"Sure, otherwise everyone would be wondering why she didn't pick up her last check. If she doesn't show up, then she really looks guilty."

Annie shivered, tucking her feet under her.

"We don't have to do this now if you don't want to."

Annie shook her head. "I'll be okay. I asked you to help, but that doesn't mean it's going to be easy for me."

"It's going to be a lot harder if you're accused of murder."

Annie took a deep breath and squared her shoulders. "I get it. Find out everything you can about Dot, if that's where you think we should start. If there's something I need to know, it's better to find out now."

"Annie, it would have been better to find out yesterday."

I left her curled up and sipping tea, with promises to call her later. On the drive home, I cut through Pebble Beach. The night had given up the stars for the soft purple sky that heralds daybreak. I pulled to the side and parked along a stretch of empty beach. Otters bobbed along hunting for shellfish, their slick heads diving just before each wave broke on the rocky shore.

With a sigh, I pulled out my cell phone. I punched in Connor's number and promptly hung up. When he knew the details, Connor would certainly voice his opinion that I should leave the police work to, well, the police. It was a conversation we'd had before, but we both knew I wouldn't stay out of it. I couldn't. I just wasn't capable of walking away, once I was involved. That didn't mean I wanted to face it alone, though. What I needed was a friend, someone rational and completely in my corner, which led me back to Connor. I tried calling three more times before finally letting the call go through. He answered before I even heard it ring.

"Where are you?"

"At the beach," I said.

"Is that what I hear in the background? I thought you might be calling from the police station."

"Hayley told you."

"Right after she hung up with you." I tried to read his mood from the tone of his voice. Surprisingly, he sounded pretty calm. "I can only imagine how happy Lucas was to find you on the scene."

"I just happened to be there when Annie found the body, and it's a good thing I was." Connor remained silent, and I lifted my chin. "Well it was. Otherwise, Nicole would have been the only one to find her, and Annie would have really been in trouble."

"You mean she isn't in trouble now?"

"Well, yes, but it would be worse if she had to face it alone. Good thing I was there."

"Uh-huh. Good thing. I spent the night at the winery, so

I'm here. Why don't you come home and tell me what happened?"

"Because I don't want to hear why I shouldn't get involved."

"So you were planning on never telling me about it?"

"The thought crossed my mind."

"Well, then." His voice dropped. "Why did you call me?"

The waves rolled in while I thought about my answer. "I really wanted to talk to you."

There was a pause. "You want me to put on some coffee? There's some French roast down at the office. Whole bean."

"I'm not sure even coffee will help."

"It'll be a perfect cup of coffee."

I started the car. "I'll be there in ten minutes."

Hayley was pacing in front of the window as I drove up, and when I reached the porch she opened the front door and hugged me tight.

"I'm fine," I said. Hayley bit her lip, her eyes troubled. "I mean it." I lifted my arms and shifted from one foot to the other. "See? Everything's working." Hayley didn't look convinced, and so I tried again, keeping my voice light. "Look at you, standing here waiting for me. Doesn't anybody work around here?"

Hayley gave me a small smile and nudged me in the ribs. "Sure, and now we can get to it. It's your own fault for making us worry."

I nodded. "I get it. Believe me, I'd give anything not to be in this situation. Same with Annie."

"I know, and I know you'll help her."

"Lucas isn't thrilled with the situation."

Hayley shrugged. "Can you blame him? Your ability to turn up bodies complicates things for him."

"Yeah, it complicates things for me too. On your next date, can you put in a good word for me?"

"You want me to influence a cop?"

"Sure, if you can. Let's get some coffee."

We walked into the kitchen as Connor flipped an omelet onto a plate. I plopped into a chair, and he handed it to me.

"Eat this, then tell us what's going on."

I filled them in between bites, skimming over the way I'd last seen Brian. I finished with the insurance policy that Brian had taken out on himself.

"So Annie has a motive," Hayley said.

I nodded. "I'm sure that's the conclusion the police will come to." I pushed away my empty plate. "You'd think with everything that's happened I wouldn't have an appetite."

"I knew you'd be hungry." Connor poured himself another cup of coffee. I wasn't sure how to respond. I caught a reflection of myself in the sliding door and decided reflections operated like cameras—they add ten pounds.

Connor pulled out the chair opposite mine. He turned his coffee cup in slow circles, a sign he had something on his mind.

"So, what happens now?" he asked.

The words rushed out, fueled by exhaustion. "Now I help Annie figure out what really happened. She didn't do it, so logically, someone else did. It happened at the clinic and there wasn't any sign of a break-in, so it's either someone Brian knew and let in or someone who had a key. Either way, it's likely someone we all know." I was talking too fast, but I couldn't seem to slow down. The reality was setting in. Annie was likely to be arrested for murder.

Connor studied me. "You okay?"

"Better. The coffee's helping." It wasn't bad to be sitting in the morning sun with him, either.

"So, exactly how do you help Annie, and how do you propose finding who killed Brian?" He focused steel-blue eyes on me, eyes fringed with lashes any woman would kill for. I had to look away to concentrate.

"Annie thinks it's strange Dot was there last night, supposedly working, yet Nicole's check wasn't ready, and there wasn't any other reason for her to be in the office."

Hayley sat down beside me. "I can't see Dot killing anyone. She's one of the original flower children, right?" I nodded, and Hayley continued, "That's what I thought. I've never seen her without her peace sign earrings on."

"I find it hard to believe myself," I said. "Annie agrees. We have to start somewhere, though, and Dot's unusual behavior is the only thing we've got."

"So, you're going to find out why Dot was there at that time of night and see if it could have anything to do with Brian's death?" Connor asked.

"Yup, that's the general idea."

"That's not very well thought-out," he said.

"You sound surprised. You know I'm not big on planning things."

"At least you're admitting it."

"Tough to deny it." I rolled the tension out of my neck and took a swig of coffee. "More coffee, a shower, then I'm going to have that talk with Dot."

"Why don't you try to sleep for a couple of hours first?" Hayley asked. "You've been up all night."

I took a good look at both of them. Hayley's eyes were red, and she couldn't seem to sit still. Connor's hair was tousled, and he stifled a yawn. "I think we were all up the entire night. Sorry I worried you."

"Yes, well." Connor stood. "Hayley, we'll have a short day, but we do need to get that irrigation line replaced today. Can you get started, and I'll meet you out there?"

"Sure," Hayley said. As she left the room, she turned and caught my glance, a question in her eyes. I shrugged. Connor clearly wanted to talk to me alone, and I didn't need to guess at the topic. He rinsed out his cup, left it in the sink, and, with two strides, was at my side. He bent down until his face was inches from mine. I needed to regroup. It was a lot easier to brace myself when he was across the room.

"Would it make a difference if I said you've been in similar positions before, and it's almost gotten you killed? That the police are better equipped to handle this, and if Lucas wants you to stay out of it, you should?"

I'd never really noticed the cleft in his chin before. "Lucas can't possibly think I'd stay completely out of it. He knows me better than that, and so should you." He smelled like fresh air. "I'm not standing by to watch a murderer pin the blame on Annie."

Connor nodded. "That's about what I thought." He pushed himself up and walked away, and my pulse slowed. I think he may have muttered "Here we go again" under his breath, but I couldn't be sure.

When he'd gone, I sat in the sun for a few extra moments. Syrah sprawled on the floor next to me, content to keep an eye on the birds from a comfortable position, while Nanook rested up against the glass. I took my time and finished up the coffee, then took a quick shower and changed into my go-to outfit: an oversized sweater, this one in coral, jeans, and boots. After a quick pin-up of my curly hair, I hit the door and called Annie from the car. When she answered, it sounded like she dropped the phone. Twice. Finally she spoke, her voice sounding like she had a mouth full of gravel.

"What time is it?"

"A little after nine. Did you get any rest at all?"

"Between finding…" She paused. "Between finding Brian, and knowing that certain people think I might be a murderer, I barely closed my eyes."

"Other than being exhausted, how are you?"

"I'm terrified, absolutely terrified, of what happens next."

"What happens next is that I go talk to Dot and see what she was doing at the clinic last night. The police are going to work it their way, but that doesn't mean we can't try to push them in the right direction." I frowned. "I'm just trying to think of a reason to stop by Dot's house. I don't know her that well."

"You could say I asked you to check on her, that I wasn't

70

up for it. Or you could tell her I sent you to see the fosters."

"And what is that exactly?"

"She fosters dogs for the shelter. Just one more reason I can't see her being a killer."

"Well, she was doing something at the clinic last night. Let's find out what it was. Text me her address, and would you call her and tell her I'm coming?"

"The address is on its way."

Chapter 7

After days of rain, the air was fresh, and my spirits lifted. The possibility of Annie being charged with murder seemed remote as I lowered the top of the car for the first time in weeks. I plugged Dot's address into my phone and took side streets, pulling into her drive a short time later. The house, a one-story brick tudor-style, sat back from the street. The fence on both sides of the drive enclosed an oversized yard— a good thing, considering the level of noise coming from the house. If she had one dog, she had fifty. I walked up the gravel path, and before I had a chance to knock the door swung open.

"Kinda figured you were here. No need to ring the bell. I wouldn't have heard it anyway over the ruckus." She pushed at the cattle dog blocking the door. "Move, Cody."

I opened the screen. "How many do you have?"

Dot flipped her braid over one shoulder. "Only two of my own. The rest are fosters. The numbers fluctuate, but right now there are three."

"I didn't know five dogs could make so much noise."

"This isn't anything. Wait until you're trying to take a nap and the mailman comes. Now that's barking."

She shooed everyone outside and turned to me. "Of course, I was glad for the company last night, I can tell you."

I didn't picture her as someone who frightened easily, an impression she confirmed with her next words. "Not that I was scared, just angry with myself. I could have helped Brian. I could have saved him."

She must have been in her mid-sixties, but she looked fit. Her white peasant blouse framed broad shoulders, and she moved with purpose. If the killer had known she was there, it might have been enough to scare them away. She was right. She could have stopped the killer. On the other hand, she could *be* the killer. I shook that unpleasant thought off and concentrated on what Dot was saying.

"I didn't hear the phone earlier and just listened to Annie's message that you were coming. No surprise I missed the call with the dogs barking, but I could have saved you the trip. All three fosters are spoken for. They're siblings, so it's wonderful we get to keep them together. A family not far from here with some acreage is taking them. Sadly, there are always more at the shelter."

She was right. The dogs scampered around my feet. Perhaps it was time for another dog. Company for Nanook. I considered it as Dot gestured toward the stove. "You've probably been up all night. I know I was. Coffee?"

"Sure. Just black." I took a seat at the table, and she joined me with two mugs.

"So, how is Annie holding up?" Dot said. "She has a lot

73

to handle right now. I just wonder how long the clinic will be shut down."

"Annie said the chief would call her today. Lucas knows she needs to get the clinic reopened as soon as possible."

"We needed to call all of Brian's patients this morning that had appointments." With one hand she twisted an earring, the peace symbol Hayley mentioned. It was difficult to picture this woman hurting anyone, but I thought of Annie and pressed on.

"How did the owners take the news?"

"Shock and disbelief. You know what people think of both Annie and Dr. B." Dot paled, and she cradled the hot cup as though chilled. "It wasn't easy, last night, seeing Brian. Do you think Annie will be okay working there?"

"I think so," I said. "Annie's always been better at bodies and death than most. Certainly better than I am. Even when we were young she seemed to understand death is a part of life."

Dot nodded. "They worked well together, and were friends, so maybe Annie will draw strength from that."

"Tell me about their partnership," I said.

"Well, like most good business partners, at their cores they were different people. They had different strengths. Annie was better with the owners. Brian wasn't such a people person and was more reserved, but he was terrific with the animals. Take last night. He liked coming in after hours to check on all the patients."

"There weren't patients at the clinic last night. Claire said he went in to check on some test results. Do you know what tests those could be?"

Dot shrugged. "We get test results around the clock, and Brian liked to know the results as soon as he could."

I rested my hand over the cup, the steam rising between my fingers. "Did you frequently see Brian in the evenings?"

She nodded. "That's right."

"But why? I mean, why do you go in after hours? I could see last night, with you needing to get Nicole her check, but it wasn't necessary for you to be there on most nights, was it?"

She didn't answer, and I waited. Sort of.

"Dot? Why were you spending so much time at the clinic after hours? And last night, Nicole's check wasn't ready, so what were you doing there?"

Dot pushed back from the table and stood, hands on hips. "Why are you asking? Does Annie have an issue with me?"

"She's just relieved you weren't hurt, but yes, she wants to know why you were there so late. It's a reasonable question."

Dot toyed with her bracelets, her head down. "I'd been talking to Brian a short time before he was killed. I was there just steps away when it happened." She turned to me, her face flushed.

"Don't think you could have prevented Brian's death. It's just as likely you both would have been killed." Dot didn't answer, and I decided to press. "Sooner or later, it's going to come up why you were there. I'm surprised the police haven't asked you already."

Dot took a deep breath and let it out slowly, dropping

back into the kitchen chair. "They did. I told Lucas I was just catching up on paperwork." She looked down. "I knew that wouldn't float with Annie, but the chief didn't question it."

"What's going on?"

Her hands trembled, and she pressed them into her lap. "The truth is that I'm slipping. Not physically. Physically, I'm as strong as an ox. Mentally, I can't remember figures and my memory is shot. I've worked with other peoples' money my entire life, and now I find myself losing my place when I'm adding up basic sums. Lately it's been getting worse. When I caught my mistakes before I made the deposits, I've made up the difference myself, but I know the books were off a couple of times."

"You need to talk with Annie."

Dot nodded. "I know. Last week I forgot to put the deposit for the entire weekend in the bank. I had it in the back of my car. Thousands of dollars in cash and checks, and I leave it on the back seat in my unlocked car! How could I have done such a thing?"

I rested my hand on hers. "Have you gone to the doctor?"

"No. I'm afraid of what he might tell me."

"You need to do that, and you need to talk to Annie. She said she'd noticed something off with the books, but you've been with her so long I'm sure there's a solution. I don't want to speak for her, but you are so good with the clients and staff. I can't imagine the clinic without you there."

Dot smiled, and her shoulders relaxed. "Now that it's out there, I feel a lot better. I'll make an appointment."

"Do you want me to tell Annie what's going on?"

Dot shook her head. "I'm going to call her right now. It's something I should have done before this."

"Before I go, is there anything that you remember about last night? Something that stands out?"

"I told Lucas everything I could think of, Penny, honest."

"Then let's change our focus. Perhaps Brian wasn't killed because of something that happened last night at the clinic." I shook my head. "Maybe it wasn't a random act of violence. As far as the police can tell, it wasn't a break-in. No forced entry, and the computers and expensive equipment were left untouched."

She straightened. "I see what you mean. Someone was after Brian specifically."

"That's what I believe," I said. "Has anything changed lately with Brian?"

Dot pressed her palms to her cheeks. "I thought about it all night. Only two things stand out. The first, of course, is Brian firing Nicole. The police shouldn't dismiss her so fast for Brian's murder just because she arrived at the clinic after you and Annie did. She could have driven around the neighborhood and doubled back."

"Believe me, I've had that same thought."

"I thought you might." Dot hesitated. "The other thing is harder for me to discuss, because I don't have any proof and I'm very fond of the person involved…"

My voice rose an octave as my throat tightened. "Annie is in trouble, and I don't care who's involved. If you know something, you need to tell me."

Dot nodded. "Of course, you're right. It's Claire."

"Claire?" I shook my head. "We saw her last night, and she's devastated. She and Brian seemed very much in love."

"They are. That is, they were, or maybe they still are."

"I'm not following you," I said.

"I know I'm not explaining very well." Her concern showed in her drawn brows. "I'm sure they're still in love, but something's changed. They've been acting different lately. Claire usually works nights at the hospital, and most days she would pick up Brian to have lunch with him. That stopped a couple of weeks ago. Another thing—Brian has ordered flowers to be delivered to her at the hospital every Monday for ages, and he hasn't done it in weeks."

"Any idea what's going on?"

Dot raised her brows. "I don't know any specifics, but I can tell you it began just about the time Eric started using the clinic for his research."

"What are you saying? That Claire was involved with Eric?"

"Now, I didn't say that." Dot shook her head. "I'm going to let you decide for yourself. I'm not one to gossip."

"Really? Cypress Cove would shut down if people shut their mouths."

"Nonetheless, I really don't know any more than that. It just seems a bit of a coincidence that Brian and Claire's relationship changed when Eric came into the picture."

"I saw Claire with Eric right before the dog contest," I said. "Claire was upset, but when I asked her about it, I didn't really get an answer. Can you think of anything else?"

When Dot remained silent, I pressed, "Annie needs every bit of help we can give her."

Dot didn't say anything, lost in thought, and I waited. Finally, she nodded decisively. "All right, I know one other thing." She scooted the chair closer to me. "I handle the deposits that go from the clinic to both Annie and Brian's personal accounts. As the two owners, they take set salaries weekly from the business."

"And?"

"Three weeks ago, Brian took Claire off his bank account. Why would he do something like that?"

Chapter 8

Why, indeed. Unable to learn anything more from Dot, I left a short time later and followed the coastal route, taking the turn-off for downtown. Ocean Boulevard is the main street through Cypress Cove, and the specialty boutiques lining the boulevard buzzed with activity. Flowers bloomed year-round in the mild climate, and lavender scented the air. Tourists, with their cameras and carefully selected treasures, strolled the shaded walks, snapping photos of gardens tucked between cottages with thatched roofs and uneven edges.

My stomach growled, and I pulled into the lot for Sterling Restaurant, determined to have a salad. I even managed to reach the door before my resolve crumbled. The smell of baking drifted through the open windows, and I fell apart like one of Ross's chocolate croissants. I pulled open the front door and headed to the bakery case. This is why I carry around ten extra pounds. Ross came to stand beside me as I contemplated my options.

"Have the strawberry delight. Very little added sugar, and it has fruit and fiber."

"Done." I paused. "I'm going to need a little of your clotted cream with it."

"Of course you are." He raised a brow. "Especially after what you've been through." When I didn't answer right away, Ross leaned in. "You are going to tell me what you've been through, right? Or do I have to beg?"

Thanks to Ross, Sterling is also the best place in town for gossip. Still, he's very fond of Annie, and I could see concern in his eyes as well as curiosity. "Sit and have coffee with me."

"Excellent idea." He pulled up a chair. "I was going to call you. How's Annie holding up?"

"When did you hear about the murder?"

"This morning. All morning. Everyone was talking about it. You know how news travels in this town."

I did, actually. "She's worried. She found Brian dead, and that might not be the worst of it. She could very well be arrested for his murder." I filled Ross in as he rested on his elbows and latched onto every word.

"Poor dear."

I nodded. "She's pretty shaken up, and it didn't help that Nicole was with me when I found her."

Ross rolled his eyes. "Nothing but trouble there. I'm going to go see Annie. Bake her something."

"If anything will cheer her up, that'll do it."

I got a box of pastries and left a short time later. Driving to Claire's, I weighed my options. She lost her husband just a few hours ago, but Annie might be arrested for it. Any hesitation I felt dissolved, and I pulled into the circular drive. Claire stood at the window looking out, arms hugging her chest. She opened the door as I walked up the front steps.

"I hope I'm not bothering you," I said as she opened the door. "I just wanted to check on you, see if there was anything I could do or if you'd heard any updates."

She shook her head, the sleek black bob swinging around her pale face. "I haven't talked to anyone this morning. I just keep staring out the window. I can't help it; I'm expecting to see Brian walking up the front steps, like it's some sort of crazy mistake."

"I'm sure you didn't sleep and must be exhausted. Do you want anything to eat?" I held out the box. "I brought fruit tarts from Sterling."

"Maybe later," she said. "I'm just not capable of eating anything right now."

"Would you like some coffee?"

She paused. "I wouldn't mind some tea. The British woman's cure for everything." She gave me a weak smile. "Let's have strong black tea."

We walked into the kitchen, and I reached for the refrigerator door. "Let me put the tarts in here for later." There was a list on the door, and I took a closer look.

"You won't be able to make anything of that," Claire said.

"I didn't mean to pry," I lied, "but now that you mention it, that's what I call doctor's handwriting. I can't understand a single word."

She perched on the corner of the breakfast bar. "Brian and I had our own shorthand. We came up with it in college." She glanced at the paper. "It's a shopping list. Buy eggs. The last thing Brian wrote to me." She turned to wipe her eyes with the back of her hand as I busied myself filling the pot with boiling water and loose black tea. Morning light filtered in through yellow sheers. Pictures lined the window ledge, mostly of Brian and Claire. I picked up the closest. It was taken out at the coast, Cliff Point in the background, just as Brian brushed the hair from Claire's face. They looked happy. I replaced the photo, poured the steaming tea into two cups, and handed one to Claire.

"I have to be honest, Claire. I need your help. The police might charge Annie for Brian's murder. Lucas won't accuse her lightly, but if all the evidence points that way, I'm not sure how much choice he'll have."

Claire brought down her cup. "What rubbish. They can't possibly believe Annie would have done such a thing."

"They're trained to focus on the facts, and, as much as I hate to say it, Annie was found"—I looked at Claire—"well, she was found in a damning situation."

"But why would she kill Brian? She had no reason."

"You brought up a very good reason last night. People have killed for much less than a million-dollar insurance policy."

Claire pressed her fingers against her forehead. "I'm so sorry. I wouldn't have mentioned it if I'd thought for an instant it would point the finger at Annie."

"Don't even think that. The police would have found out. That's exactly the type of thing they look for."

Claire nodded. "I suppose you're right. I'd assumed it was a robbery. A theft of some kind that went terribly wrong."

"No, nothing was taken, although Annie thought Brian's notebook might be missing. You haven't seen it, have you?"

"No. He usually has it with him. I would think it's at the clinic." The silence settled around us as I decided how to best proceed.

"Is there something else, Penny?"

"Actually, there is. I know this isn't easy for you, but what really happened between you and Eric at the festival?"

"You don't think it was Eric, do you?"

"He has offices at the clinic, so he has access."

She sighed. "It's stupid, really. He had a crush on me, years ago when we were all in school together. I never took a second look."

"So, what happened at the festival?"

Claire shrugged. "I think his success has gone to his head, as if that would make a difference to me. He just wanted to remind me once again that he was available if I was interested. I reminded him, again, that I was neither available or interested."

"Brian saw what happened and asked you about it."

"Yes. He was tired of Eric flirting with me. I always thought one day Brian would find Eric's schoolboy advances as silly as I do." Her eyes fell. "Of course, now that day will never come."

I took a sip of tea. "Do you think there's any possibility that Brian confronted Eric at the clinic later?"

"If you're suggesting that Eric killed Brian in a jealous rage, that's just not possible. Eric only flirts out of habit. He doesn't take it seriously, and I certainly don't."

I didn't respond. Passion can simmer for years and flare up again from the smallest of sparks. I knew all too well it was a common cause for murder. Claire had finished her tea and the color in her cheeks had improved, but I wasn't finished yet.

"I need to ask you about something else."

She looked at me expectantly, and I hesitated just long enough to remember Annie and what was at stake.

"Why did Brian take you off his checking account? Were you two having trouble?"

I'd been hoping to surprise her, and succeeded. Claire turned white, with two bright spots flaming her cheeks. "Whatever you think, my financial problems have nothing to do with Brian's death."

"But why would you be having financial problems? Help me understand. I know you're still on staff at the hospital. You're one of the best doctors in town. What's going on?"

Claire stood and moved to the window, her back to me. Without turning, she said something too low for me to hear.

"I'm sorry, I didn't hear what you said."

With a sigh, she turned to face me. "Have you been to Shiloh Gaming Resort?"

I shook my head, confused. "The new place down by the county line?"

Claire nodded. "It's got something for everyone. A beautiful hotel, conference center, gaming and sports facilities, and, of course, the casino. I've never seen anything like it."

"Then I take it you haven't been to Las Vegas."

Claire shook her head. "Never. It wasn't a trip at the top of my list, and now I wouldn't risk it."

"What do you mean, risk it?"

Claire sighed. "I grew up in a small town north of London, and the only gambling was the occasional card game, or perhaps a friendly wager on the local football match. I didn't like it much, really." She pressed her fingertips together. "It's different in a casino, isn't it? I knew the first time I stepped through the doors. The lights, the chips. Dice rolling across the table make my palms itch to play. I can watch a roulette wheel for hours."

"You have a gambling problem."

Claire nodded. "I can't stop once I start. I'd never leave if I could help it."

"Brian found out."

"Of course he did. I think he saw the change in me the first time we walked into the place. I didn't even go to gamble. I tagged along while Brian played racquetball in the sports center. The second I walked into the casino, I felt my face flush. I managed to resist that first night with Brian there, and even got through the next few visits without anything going horribly wrong. Unfortunately, that was just enough time for me to learn the games, taste the thrill of watching your number come up, or the wonderful feeling when you see cherries along the top of that alluring, hateful little window."

"What happened?"

Claire walked to the sofa and settled on one arm. "One day while Brian was at the clinic, my shift ended early. I decided to drive to the casino and take a peek, see what it was like during the day." Claire turned to me. "You know what? It was exactly the same. It could have been midnight. The lights, the sounds. There aren't any windows in that place. No clocks."

"Vegas casinos are like that. They're designed so people lose track of time. What did you do?"

"I took a seat and lost four thousand dollars."

"And Brian noticed."

"Not then. I shifted some money around and swore to myself I'd never go back. I lasted a week. I really thought I could control it. It's not like I'm stupid or don't know anything about gambling addictions. I just somehow missed the signs in my own behavior."

"How did Brian found out?"

"We got a call." Claire gripped the back of the sofa. "I got a call, that is, and Brian happened to answer it. I took advances against our credit cards. I thought I'd get a chance to pay it back before Brian found out, but I couldn't break even, forget getting ahead. The more I tried, the worse the problem got."

"What did Brian do?"

"He was so confused." Her voice faltered. "And hurt that I hadn't told him."

"That's when he took you off his accounts?"

"It was the only thing he could do, really. He took me off all the credit cards and accounts we had together."

"I'm sure that was a difficult thing for him to do. I'm sure it was difficult for you, too."

"I didn't blame him. I told him to do it. It was better that way. Brian comes from a very wealthy family, you know."

"Actually, I didn't."

Claire shrugged. "He never acted like it, which is one of the many reasons I loved him. I didn't even know he was rich until after we were married. With this problem I have, I was glad he took me off all the accounts. I didn't want access to any of it."

"And what about now?"

Her shoulders stiffened. "Yes, I see what you're asking. I get it all. No children, no other heirs. Only me."

She reached for the table, picking up her cup of tea. She took a sip and set the cup down with a grimace. "We Brits hate tea that's anything less than scalding hot. I wonder why." She squared her shoulders and turned toward me. "I go to Gamblers Anonymous meetings twice a week, I avoid roads leading anywhere near the casino, and I resolve not to gamble today. I plan on doing the same thing tomorrow, and every day thereafter, but for now I only have to worry about today." She gave a soft smile. "Since I found out you can gamble on-line, I've stopped carrying my phone and I'm staying off the computer. I won't even buy a lottery ticket now, something I used to do once a week."

Claire seemed to tire. Her shoulders sagged as she twisted the bottom edge of her sweater in her hands. She appeared sincere, and if things were different I wouldn't have questioned her devotion to Brian for an instant. But Annie was on the line. All I had was Claire's version of events, and now she was a wealthy woman. What if Brian had removed her from his finances because of something else entirely? As though she could sense my doubts, she grabbed my gaze and held it.

"I realize that Brian's wealth gives me a motive, but you need to find other suspects who benefit from his death. It wasn't me. I loved him. I want him here with me now."

If she was lying, she'd missed her calling. "If what you say is true, who else had reason to kill Brian? Eric? You said that his crush on you was ancient history. Who else?"

Claire buried her face in her hands, and when she looked up her eyes were red and swollen. "Honestly, I can only think of Nicole. She was furious with Brian after Annie fired her. You saw her behavior at the party."

I nodded. "It's possible. She arrives early to get her check. Brian's there. Things escalate, and she stabs him."

Claire paled, and I bit my lip. "I'm so sorry."

Claire shook her head and placed a trembling hand on my arm. "Your hands are like ice," I said. "You're freezing."

"No, I'm fine." She took a broken breath. "Let's finish this. Did Nicole have a key to the front door?"

"Perhaps. She left her set at the clinic when she was fired, but she could have made a copy earlier without Annie's knowledge."

"Then she might have gotten in without Brian realizing it."

I nodded. "It's possible. Getting fired and having Jason break up with her really seems to have pushed her over the edge. Jason avoided a lot of trouble there, especially since he owns a pharmaceutical company."

"Jason hasn't broken up with Nicole," Claire said. "Whatever gave you that idea?"

"Nicole told me herself, yesterday at the ugly dog contest."

"Well, that's quite impossible. I saw them myself after the contest. I went out for a quick bite after dropping Brian off at the clinic. They were in a back booth, and believe me, nothing about them said they'd broken up. She was all over him, and he wasn't putting up a fight." Claire paused and bit her lip. "I remember thinking I'd call Brian and tell him."

I stood. "I'm making you some more tea and then I'll leave you alone."

Claire studied me. "You're following up on this."

"I need to find Jason," I said. "He's got some explaining to do."

Chapter 9

I left soon after. My disappointment in Jason settled in my throat, and I was determined to find him. I tried Annie at home, but thankfully she didn't pick up. I needed to tell her Jason wasn't the person we thought he was, but I was glad for the delay. As I left a message for her to call me, the phone rang. I looked at the caller ID and picked up.

"Should I even ask how you're spending your day?" Connor launched in without preamble.

"It would be better if you didn't."

He sighed. "That's what I thought. I hate to interrupt your busy schedule, but with the fields this muddy, we're behind on the pruning."

He didn't need to say anything more. "I'm on my way."

In the spring, it's a race to get the vines pruned before the buds appear, and that's when everything goes to plan, including the weather. So far this spring, nothing was on schedule. I spent the rest of the day in the fields with Connor and Hayley until it was too dark to see. We finished, showered, and met in the kitchen.

I love good food, especially when it just shows up on my plate. That's my favorite dish, actually. Tonight it was Sterling leftovers from the Silver Paw Gala. I piled my plate with mini quiches and asparagus wrapped in prosciutto. I eyed Connor's plate. "I'll trade you two quiches for three of the crab fritters."

"How is that fair?"

"The fritters are small."

- With a sigh, he held out his plate. Hayley had the rest of the soup, and we joined her at the table.

"So, how's Lucas?" I asked.

She put down her spoon. "That didn't take long."

"What?"

"You know he isn't going to talk to me about the case," Hayley said. "Even if you weren't involved, he wouldn't talk to me."

"I just asked how he was." My voice rose. It might have squeaked. "Does he seem worried, or confident maybe? Does he have something on his mind, or just the normal things?"

"I'm not sure how normal any of this is, especially in Cypress Cove. He's investigating the murder of a friend." She shook her head. "I've got nothing. If I did, I'd tell you, only because I know you'd get it out of me anyway."

"So," Connor said, "how about you?"

I carefully avoided his piercing gaze. "How about me what?"

"Fair play. If you can ask questions, so can the rest of us."

I twirled a fritter. "Fine, what do you want to know?"

Connor leaned in. "Where were you all morning?"

Hayley nodded. "And what did you learn?"

I pushed my plate away and faced Connor. "If I tell you, you have to promise me you'll just listen."

"Oh, I'll listen fine. I might have a few things to say afterwards."

I lifted my chin. "Then I won't tell you."

"Yes, you will. For one thing, you can't keep anything to yourself. For another, you're going to get yourself into a corner and come to me to get you out." He leaned across the table and I could smell the eucalyptus that grew along the winery border. I focused on what he was saying. "And don't pretend you don't know what I'm talking about."

Hayley shifted her head from side to side, weighing it out, and came down on Connor's side. "He's right. You can't keep things to yourself, and you've asked for his help on more than one occasion…"

"Fine. This is what I know so far." I told them of my conversations with both Dot and Claire. Connor listened without comment until I'd finished, and then I waited. I waited some more. The silence stretched, and I glanced at Hayley. She averted her eyes and hid a small smile behind her palm.

"Well?" I asked. He rubbed his eyes, something he does a lot around me.

"How do you do it? I mean, really, how do you get people to tell you the things they do?"

"It isn't easy."

"I'm not kidding," he said. "Dot tells you she's losing her memory, and Claire admits to a gambling addiction?"

"I had a couple of things going for me," I said. "They're smart enough to realize they could be considered suspects. This way they've offered explanations for behavior that could be questioned. Dot explained why she was at the clinic when Brian was killed, while Claire explained Brian removing her from their finances. For all I know, they were just practicing on me before the police ask them the same questions."

"But you believed them." He said it like a statement.

"I'm inclined to. This doesn't mean they're innocent. It just clears up some unusual behavior. Either way, it gives me something to work with. Now, if I find out they were lying, then the question becomes, why?"

"What was the second thing?" Hayley chimed in. "You said you had a couple things going for you."

"That one is easier." My chest tightened, and I gripped the edge of the table. "I don't care who I embarrass, harass, or annoy. I don't care what it looked like, or what motives the police think Annie had. She isn't a murderer. She didn't do this, and I'm not stopping until I find out who did."

Despite my lack of sleep since Brian's death, I tossed most of the night, finally giving up toward dawn. With a sigh, I rolled to the phone and tried Annie's number. She didn't answer. Hopefully she was sleeping. If I didn't hear from her this morning, I was going to stop by. I yawned and fell back on the pillows, but my exhaustion didn't prevent Syrah from assuming her regular morning stance. She climbed onto my chest and stared at me with jewel-green eyes. The persistent whipping of her tail was telling: I'd kept her waiting long enough. With a moan, I managed to make it out of bed and into my robe. Stepping over Nanook, I opened the sliders to a sky patterned with white clouds. Although the vines growing up along the house were silver and thick with morning dew, the rain was gone, at least for now.

After I fed Syrah and let Nanook out the back, I poured coffee from the pot. There wasn't much left. Hayley and Connor had started the day early, taking full advantage of the break in the weather. I finished off the coffee, took a quick shower, and dressed in jeans and a lemon-yellow sweater, all without focusing on what had kept me awake. The worry over Annie had been replaced with anger at Jason, and, for a while at least, that was easier. I'd suggested Annie might be interested in him. Why would someone who owned a successful pharmaceutical company date anyone like Nicole? Even more astounding, why would he keep dating her once he found out the truth? I wasn't going to wait any longer to ask him that very question, and so I left a short time later. Fortunately, I knew where to look for him. Nicole and her big mouth had finally come in handy.

I pulled into the curved drive of the Marquis Hotel and handed the valet my keys. He eyed my car with appreciation. I pulled out my wallet, handed him a bill, and pointed to an empty spot. "Let's put it right there."

Dramatically overlooking Monterey Bay, the Marquis Hotel looks like an elegant European villa. Thick, white-washed walls, containers of lavender and rosemary, and intricately designed tile floors led into the lobby and ended with sweeping coastal views. Just a block from Cannery Row, it's where the rich and beautiful stay when they come to town. I've never spent the night, but even having a glass of wine in the polished mahogany bar was an experience.

I walked up sweeping stairs to the hotel lobby. A grand piano sat opposite the reception counter, and straight ahead was a large patio with panoramic views of Monterey Peninsula. The tuxedo-clad pianist played something jazzy, and the scent of white jasmine drifted in from the patio.

I was hoping Jason was here, and started toward the house phone. As I crossed the lobby floor, I glanced toward the patio, where a few people sat having breakfast. Jason was there, with his back to the ocean, reading a newspaper.

I turned, made my way out the French doors, and stopped at his table, waving off the waiter approaching with a menu.

"Mind if I join you?"

Jason glanced up. His eyes shifted between me and the paper, but it wasn't clear if he was avoiding me or just wanted to keep reading.

"I'm surprised," I said. "I would have thought you were an online news kind of guy."

"Who isn't?" he said. "This hotel still delivers a paper to the room, though, so I grabbed it."

"Good article?"

He shook his head. "No, not especially." He ran his hand through his thick dark hair and absently gestured toward an empty chair.

"Join me, please." He glanced at his watch.

Not exactly an offer I couldn't refuse, but I took a seat nonetheless. "I don't want to keep you from your reading." My pitch rose at the end in an effort to sound sincere.

"No problem. It's the financial section. Probably better if I put it down."

I turned to look out over the water. "Especially with this view."

He glanced over his shoulder. "Ironic, isn't it? I moved to the west coast because this entire stretch of the Pacific is just so damn beautiful, and I'm too busy to enjoy it anymore."

"You're staying here. You certainly know how to pick nice hotels."

He surveyed the patio. "I didn't pick it." His face tightened, the tension knotting his brow.

"Ah." He'd given me my opening. "Nicole likes staying here."

"Liked," he corrected me. "I won't be spending any more time with her."

My eyes grew wide, and I threw up my hands. Miss Innocent. "See, that's what I thought. That's why I was so surprised to hear that you and Nicole were tucked into a back booth recently." I leaned on my elbows and moved in closer. "I heard it was pretty cozy too."

Jason examined his palms for a moment, and I took the opportunity to study him. He was a big guy, solid, with dark brown eyes and a slightly crooked smile. Dimples. Beige Dockers and a tweed blazer with leather elbows. An expensive but understated watch on his left wrist. Loafers, again expensive-looking, but simple. He was a man who liked nice things, but of the understated variety.

"Honestly, Jason, Nicole is the last person on earth…"

He held up his hand. "I get it. I told her we were finished, then I get to the restaurant and realize she's followed me there."

"What, you mean she's actually stalking you?"

"All I can tell you is that I'd just ordered, looked up, and there she was."

"So why didn't you tell her to leave? How come she was wrapped around you like a skinny python?"

"I was trying to avoid a scene."

"How'd that work out for you?"

He caught the irony in my voice and smiled. "I get it. Everything with Nicole is a scene, but that's the last one I'll be having with her. I pulled her off and left. She followed me back here, but I wouldn't let her in. I told hotel security I wanted her kept away, and I didn't hear from her again."

"She definitely didn't come back?"

"No," he said. "I didn't leave, and I didn't hear anything else from her."

"So you don't know where she went after she left here."

"Not a clue." His eyes narrowed. "Is it important? Where she went?"

"She went to the clinic to get her last check. She arrived the same time as I did. We walked into the clinic together."

"You mean she was there when you found Brian?"

I answered the question with one of my own. "When did you find out about the murder?"

"Eric told me."

"When did he tell you?"

"Yesterday morning."

"He said he was out photographing bats when Brian was killed," I said.

"That sounds about right. He's fascinated with the things. Their movements, their habits." He drew his brows together. "When did you see him?"

"The night of the murder, the police spoke to everyone with keys. Dot called Eric, and he came to the clinic. He was concerned someone could have broken into his lab."

"It's not impossible someone would try. This treatment is worth millions. Someone could have been trying to steal it and Brian surprised them. Aside from that, all the clinical trials need to be carefully controlled or the medical board won't approve the results. Eric said nobody had entered his lab, which is good news." Jason shook his head. "Of course, what happened to Brian is terrible. How's Annie taking it?"

"As well as can be expected. Her friend and business partner has been murdered, her clinic's closed, she isn't making any money, and she's currently considered the main suspect."

"Brian must have surprised someone." Jason shook his head. "He forgot to lock the door, or it was someone with a key, which would explain why there wasn't any sign of forced entry." He stilled, thoughtful. "Maybe someone looking for drugs."

"Someone like Nicole."

He raised his palm flat to me, as though pushing the thought away. "I didn't say that. She may have her troubles, but that's a long way from being a murderer."

"Is there anything else you can tell me?"

He shrugged. "Nothing. Brian was in fine shape the last time I saw him."

"When was that?"

"We met for a coffee the day before he died."

"I didn't know you two knew each other."

"We had some business to discuss."

"What business did you and Brian have together?" He gave me a quizzical look, his brow raised. "I mean, I thought Eric was the only veterinarian involved in the vaccine."

"He is. Brian was interested in the investment opportunity. Apparently he came from money, and he mentioned several months ago he might be interested in investing."

"Did he? Invest, I mean."

Jason glanced at the paper yet again. "Yes." He studied his hands, tapping the pads of his fingers together, lost in thought. With a sigh, he looked up. "You may as well hear it from me. We met because he wanted to tell me he'd changed his mind. He wanted out."

"Any particular reason?"

"He didn't say, but I got the feeling he needed the money for something."

I wondered if Brian needed the money for Claire and her gambling, but I kept that thought to myself. "Did you let him out of the investment?"

Jason smiled, but it didn't quite reach his eyes. "It isn't that easy. I would have helped him if I could, but once shares are bought it's out of my hands."

A server walked up, and we fell silent. When he'd left, Jason turned to me.

"What else can I help you with?"

A polite way to dismiss me. I chose to ignore it.

"Back to Nicole. What time did she leave here?"

"It was around nine, give or take." He pointed over my shoulder. "Last I saw her she was being led down those steps right over there, kicking and screaming the entire way. She made sure the security guard escorting her was miserable."

"I'll bet." I calculated. She had plenty of time to get to the clinic and murder Brian before we arrived.

"I wonder where she is now," he said.

"Are you worried about her?" I knew I sounded testy but didn't care. "I would have thought she'd be the last person you'd be asking after." My fingers drummed away on the table. "You seemed interested in Annie. I almost believed the Nicole episode was just a foolish moment on your part."

He raised a hand. "I didn't see the crazy side of Nicole until just the other night, and, in spite of the impression Nicole was trying to convey, we were never serious. I'm only asking where she is because I'm relieved she hasn't been back here."

I paused and took a breath. "All right, that makes sense. It's just that Annie deserves the best. I don't want her to get mixed up with someone...um, someone who dates women like Nicole."

"You don't hold back, do you?"

"Sorry, but Annie's my cousin and best friend."

He grinned. "I try not to make a habit of stupid behavior, or of dating women who behave stupidly. I promise you, Nicole fills that quota for a lifetime."

His eyes met mine and held there. The silence lengthened. "Okay," I finally said. "Let's say I believe you." I wasn't sure I did, but he didn't need to know that. "The last time I saw Nicole, she was attempting to leave the clinic after the murder. She tried to drive away high on something, even with police everywhere. They arrested her. I don't know where she is now, but if she's still in jail, it's nothing more than she deserves. She made Annie look as guilty as she could to the police." I stopped. "Now that I think about it, I'm surprised you didn't hear from her."

"I made it clear I wasn't interested in keeping in touch," he said.

"Still, if she was in jail, who did she call?"

"It wasn't me."

"Well, I for one hope to never see her again," I said.

"That makes two of us." He glanced at his watch. "I don't mean to be rude, but I've got a conference call I need to jump on. Investors like to be taken care of."

I smiled and gave a small wave as Jason made his way into the hotel. The newspaper he'd been reading was on the table, and I picked it up. Folded to the business section under a column entitled "Heard on the Street," I found what had been of such interest to Jason: "Amerigen struggles amid rumors of lost investor backing." I scanned the article, which cited higher than anticipated expenses as the cause.

Tucking the paper under my arm, I made my way through the lobby and to my car. I didn't know how much Brian had invested, but if Amerigen was having a hard time holding onto investors, and Brian was one of them, Jason had a motive. How much would he lose if Brian pulled out? Why had Brian reversed his interest in the first place? Jason said he'd stayed at the hotel after having Nicole removed. He had time to get to the clinic, confront Brian, and kill him before Annie and I arrived. Jason had looked worried when I'd first seen him. When he'd said that Brian was no longer interested in investing, he'd glanced down at the paper. Brian had wanted out, but was that enough to get him killed?

Chapter 10

After I left the hotel, I called Annie. She answered on the first ring.

"Where have you been?" I asked. "I was getting worried."

"I'm sorry. I didn't count on the press and fair-weather friends calling, pretending to offer sympathy but really just looking for tidbits. I unplugged the phone and have been trying to rest."

"That's the best way to handle it. Don't talk to the press, or anyone really. In the meantime, let me tell you what I've found out." When I finished she blew into the phone, like she'd been holding her breath.

"This is good news, Annie. There are motives for other people, other suspects. Jason might have needed Brian's investment, Claire has a gambling problem, and Dot could be a thief. These are all good arguments for the police to take a harder look elsewhere, anywhere, other than you."

She took another deep breath, and when she spoke there was a bit of Annie in her response. "Only you would consider finding motives to commit murder good news. What are you doing now?"

"Timing the drive to the clinic from Jason's hotel."

"Bye for now. Call me if you learn anything."

It took less than ten minutes to reach the clinic. At night, without traffic, the trip would be even faster.

I pulled into the lot, the building still surrounded by police tape. Parking up front, I turned off the engine and stepped from the car. The clinic is located just outside of town, with hills on one side and a nature preserve on the other. I'd never really noticed how isolated the location was—of course, I'd never been here alone, and just a few short steps from where a body was found. I leaned against the car as the pines whispered in the soft afternoon breeze coming in from the ocean. Seeing the clinic, empty and without clients, clarified how much this was going to impact Annie.

Turning to leave, I spotted a white sports car in the back of the lot. Nicole's car. It was parked on private property, so it hadn't been automatically towed when she'd been arrested. I looked around, but the place was still empty. The police had likely gone through the car already, although perhaps not, since they seemed to be focused on Annie as the main suspect. Either way, I knew Lucas wouldn't appreciate my next move.

I scurried across the lot. I wasn't entirely sure what I had planned, but I was glad I didn't have an audience. I stopped at the driver's door and was rewarded for snooping—the window was halfway down. Nicole would have lowered it when trying to talk her way out of trouble, and the police officers would have spotted her pupils. With a flashlight in her face, they must have been spectacular.

I tried the handle. The door eased open, and I slipped into the driver's seat. The car was low to the ground and not particularly comfortable, but it was easy to imagine a steep price tag. All leather and silver, with screens and plugins and a seat that somehow gripped my sides. I opened the glove box. Nothing but a small packet of car information. Less than three hundred miles on the odometer. I shuffled through the paperwork until I came to the purchase receipt, dated six weeks earlier. It was in Nicole's name, but the financing box wasn't checked. I flipped to the last page. Nicole had paid cash or, more likely, someone else had.

I put the paperwork back and shifted to look in the rear. In contrast to the car's front seats, which were empty, the back was in shambles. Shoes, makeup, several hangers, and assorted clothing covered every inch of space. I tried to reach through the narrow gap between the front seats to sort through it, but quickly gave up. I stepped out, pushed the driver's seat forward, shoved all the clutter to one side, and crawled into the back seat. By keeping the driver's seat tipped forward, I had just enough room to dig through the flotsam of Nicole's life. I searched the pile, moving items to the front seat to make room as I went along, but found nothing of interest.

As I walked back to my car, a truck pulled in and stopped just inside the entrance. I was standing in the middle of the parking lot, completely exposed. Relieved that it wasn't the police finding me at the crime scene, I took a closer look. A white baseball cap and sunglasses hid the driver's face. The truck, a big silver Ford, idled, and I got the feeling the driver was contemplating putting it in reverse to leave. I took several steps forward and was rewarded with a better angle as the sun revealed muscular but feminine bare arms. Denise. I waved, and she dropped her head slightly, as though upset at being recognized, but then she slowly pulled the truck forward. She parked and stepped from the cab.

"Denise, right? We haven't actually met. I'm Penny."

"I know. I've seen you here before. What are you doing?" She held up a hand. "Sorry, that didn't come out right. I'm just surprised to see anyone." She waved toward the clinic. "The police won't let us in, even to our offices in the back. Our work is being delayed."

Our work. Denise was implying some ownership of Eric's vaccine. I wondered how she would word it if Eric had been there.

"It must be exciting to be part of the team that came up with the vaccine," I said. "What is it you do exactly?"

"Oh," Denise said, "the science behind it is too complicated to explain, but my role is field work."

"Field work?"

"That's right. Collecting samples, tracking specific subject animals and studying their movements and patterns, that kind of thing."

"It sounds like hard work."

"It is, but physical labor suits me."

I believed her. She looked strong and healthy, and I didn't doubt for a minute she had the strength to kill Brian. Unfortunately, I couldn't think of any reason why she would. Still, showing up this way seemed off. The clinic was locked, so what was the point?

"You said you're just checking up on things?" I asked, and she paused, tension building across her jaw. She shifted from foot to foot as she held one wrist, cracking the joint in an unconscious manner. I wondered what she had to hide and decided to pursue it. "I heard you were in San Francisco the night Brian was killed."

The foot shifting halted, and her wrist stopped mid-twist. She stood immobilized by the question, then slowly resumed circling her hand. "That's right. San Francisco. Seeing friends."

Maybe she was in the city, and maybe she'd seen friends, but that wasn't the whole story, and we both knew it. The silence stretched until finally I shrugged. "Well, I guess I'll be going."

"Yeah, I need to get going too." The relief on her face was clear. "Good to finally meet you, Penny."

Denise was hiding her real reason for being at the clinic. She also wasn't sharing why she'd been to the city, if she'd even gone at all.

I returned to my car and drove out of the lot. Denise left right behind me, taking the right out of town, toward the beach. I wondered if she was going bat-watching at Cliff Point. Possibly Eric had sent her to check on things, or perhaps he was meeting her now. I made the left toward Cypress Cove, driving up Ocean Boulevard, and parked at Sterling.

"How's Annie?" Ross asked as soon as I got through the front door.

"She's been better. She needs to be working, and right now she doesn't even have that."

Ross pulled me to the bar. "Eat here and we can talk. I'm a bartender short today."

I collapsed on a stool as Ross poured me a glass of chardonnay. I briefly waved it away, a feeble gesture I didn't really commit to. Thankfully Ross didn't pay attention, and I sipped and talked in equal measures.

"What are you going to do?" Ross asked when I'd finished. "Wait, what am I thinking? You're going to find the killer yourself." He lowered his voice. "Who's your main suspect so far?" Now this was the Ross I knew, loved, and doled out information to...carefully. As much as he cared for Annie, he couldn't be trusted with anything you didn't want everyone in town to know. I mumbled a noncommittal answer.

Before he could press me further, I raised a hand. "I need comfort food, and lots of it." Ross disappeared and came back minutes later with a plate piled high with coq au vin. Half an hour later, my anxiety was buried under a big pile of chicken and mashed potatoes.

As much as I'd enjoyed my meal, the tightness in my neck told me food wasn't going to be enough. Ross was busy, so I waved and left a short time later. I needed to talk through everything with someone who would keep it to themselves. Annie's the one I rely on most when I need a sounding board, then Hayley and Antonia. I couldn't talk to Annie, not when she was the main suspect. I didn't want to upset her further. And Hayley was working, not to mention dating the investigating officer, so she was out.

I drove to Antonia's winery and pulled in through the massive front gates. I parked and, despite my anxiety, stopped to admire the view. Martinelli Winery is the largest winery on the Central Coast, and one of the most beautiful in the entire state. The two-story stone mansion, with circular turrets and a slate green roof, faces out across the valley toward the Pacific Ocean. The turrets are bare stone this time of year but will soon be covered in dark green ivy. In the fall, this same ivy covers the front in golden bronze.

I climbed the steps and knocked on the massive double doors. Chantal answered immediately, as though she'd been standing there waiting.

"Oh, it's you." She turned away.

"Nice to see you too, Chantal." She wore a red silk dress that floated over her voluptuous figure. Red lipstick complemented her cat-green eyes and her hair, a perfect cascade of dark waves, framed her oval face. She looked great, and she knew it. Of course, I immediately regretted my lack of makeup, frizzy hair, and the mashed potatoes for lunch. She managed to bring back all my adolescent insecurities. I wanted to kick her three-inch heels right out from under her. Very mature. Before I had a chance to embarrass myself, though, she stopped and turned back to me. Something in her manner suggested I wasn't going to like what she had to say next. "Actually, I thought you were my date."

"Nope." I'd been right: I didn't like it. "Just me."

She didn't move.

"Just going to squeeze on past you."

She reluctantly removed her hand from the knob.

"Here to see your mom."

She didn't budge.

"Yep, kind of tight." I pushed around her. "There we go. I'll just show myself in."

"Yes, well, Connor should be here any minute."

I stopped in my tracks and Chantal smirked, glad to get a reaction from me. Connor and I had a relationship in our future. We just needed a little more time, something the praying mantis in front of me would do anything to prevent. I forced a smile. "You two are going out, huh? Well, have a good time."

She tossed her mane. "We're going to Sterling."

I nodded.

"For dinner," she added, in case I'd managed to miss her meaning.

I nodded again.

"Honestly," she said with a shrug, "I don't know what took him so long to ask me. I've wanted to go out with him for simply ages."

"No kidding." This wasn't the first time we'd had this conversation. Moments like this made it clear Chantal wasn't giving up on Connor anytime soon.

I heard his car, a sleek black number, so different from the truck he drove around the winery. "Where's your mom?"

She pulled out a small vial of perfume. "In the library." She gave me another grin, showing perfect white teeth surrounded by Chanel-Rouge lips.

"You have lipstick all over your teeth."

The smile fell away as she finger-scrubbed non-existent lipstick stains. I took my revenge where I could.

A car door slammed as I turned to the door on my left. I wasn't going to stand there and watch Chantal leave with Connor. I turned the handle and let myself in.

"Didn't anyone ever teach you to knock?"

"Don't be testy," I said. "I had to get out of the hallway." The peal of Chantal's laughter mingled with the deeper sound of Connor's voice, and Antonia nodded. She was seated behind the desk wearing a black cashmere sweater that complemented her silver hair.

"I understand that seeing the two of them leaving together might not be your favorite thing, although I don't think there's anything for you to worry about. Chantal's representing me at a wine growers association dinner tonight. She wants to take a more active role here at the winery, and I've been trying to encourage her."

I tapped my forehead. "That's right. Connor said he was going. It's being held at Sterling." My face grew hot. "Chantal said Connor was taking her to Sterling for dinner."

"Naturally that's what she said." Antonia walked to the windows flanking the fireplace and craned her neck to see the front of the house. "Chantal's not going to miss a chance to needle you. Heaven knows, you give her plenty of opportunities."

"You know how much she gets on my nerves," I said.

"Of course I do. So does she."

I joined her at the window. Connor looked great in a

brushed lightweight blazer with fitted twill slacks in moss green. I could even imagine the smell of his hair, still slightly damp from a recent shower. Chantal laughed up at him as he opened the passenger door and let her in.

"It doesn't bother me in the least they're attending this thing together."

"Then why do you have your nose pressed against the glass?"

She was right. I forced myself to turn and take in the room. Peach silk walls glowed in the afternoon sun and complemented the cherry bookcases that ran floor to ceiling. Waterford vases held magnificent floral arrangements, and damask sofas flanked the fireplace, so inviting during the winter months. A wine bar occupied one corner, and Antonia walked there now. "Care for a glass? I have a bottle of our cabernet open."

I joined her, taking a seat. "Sure. So, I need to bounce something off you."

She handed me the glass. Her thin wrist was a clear reminder of Antonia's advanced age, but those vibrant Martinelli green eyes were as bright as ever, and she proved her mind was still keen with her next words. "Something to do with that terrible business at Annie's veterinary clinic, I presume?"

I nodded.

"From what I gather, it appears the police think Annie might be involved." She shook her head in disgust. "Nonsense. What is Lucas thinking?"

"That someone found bent over a body with a knife in

her hand might have some explaining to do."

"Can she? Explain, I mean."

I nodded. "She found Brian and pulled the knife out. She has medical training, of a sort. She was trying to help him."

"But it didn't help, did it."

"No. Brian was already dead." I closed my eyes.

Antonia circled the bar and sat down next to me. I smelled her lavender-scented hand cream. She patted me on the shoulder, and I jumped a bit, surprised. Antonia had been close to my aunt and I'd known her my entire life. She's smart and I trust her opinions, but she isn't known for being warm and fuzzy. She must be mellowing with age.

"How are you planning to help Annie?"

"I can ask questions with the best of them, as you know. Of course, the police want me to stay out of it. You should have seen Lucas when he realized I was at another crime scene. His reaction was tame compared to Connor's, although I'm not even sure he's entitled to an opinion."

"Aren't you? He manages your vineyards, your labels, and everything else associated with Joyeux Winery. He's even managed to make a darn good vintner out of you. He's certainly entitled to an opinion. Whatever happens to you impacts him."

"Okay, fair enough, but Annie is my cousin and best friend." I rolled my head back, staring at the ceiling. "I don't know what to do."

Antonia slammed her cane hard against the wooden floor, and my head snapped forward. She stood. "Yes, you do. Come here."

I followed her to the French doors leading directly out onto a large stone terrace. Beyond that, orderly rows of grapes undulated over the next ridge and out of sight. Nearer to us were the fermentation building and winery office.

"Remember the last time you were in that building?" She pointed to the office, a little red cottage where, not so long ago, Antonia and I had found the body of her own winery manager. I nodded. "You didn't give up then," she said. "You followed your instincts, and they proved correct. Annie needs you to do the same thing now. Trust yourself. Some might be upset with you, and the guilty party certainly won't appreciate you meddling, but Annie's future is at stake." Antonia raised her brow. "If Connor has anything to say about it, send him to me."

Antonia was right, and I felt calmer when I arrived home a short time later. That lasted until I found a note saying Hayley and Lucas were having dinner together. Lucas is a terrific guy, and he's good to Hayley. It was unthinkable he might be building a case against Annie, but in my heart I knew Lucas would follow the clues where they led him.

I poured a glass of iced tea and grabbed my camera. For as long as I can remember, the easiest place for me to find perspective has been behind a lens. The camera has a way of bringing into sharp focus how small my troubles were compared to so many people I'd photographed over the years. The images, though, could be haunting, and I'd been ready to leave that life behind. Now I concentrate on landscape photography, which rarely keeps me awake deep into the night. I specialize in abstract shots: real subjects shot to compel the viewer to take a second look. The shots sold well. Several galleries in town had standing orders, and last year I'd won national acclaim with a shot that matched the Santa Lucia mountain range in the background with the rough-edged outline of grape leaves in the foreground.

I set my tea on the step and spent the next hour wandering the vineyard with Nanook, taking random shots until dusk moved in. I tried not to wonder how Chantal and Connor were getting along. If he were with someone else, any other woman in town, I wouldn't mind nearly so much. I lied to myself a little longer and then went in to make dinner, a frozen entree with hardly any calories, fat, or taste. As I finished, I heard voices at the front door. Moments later, Hayley walked into the room. Lucas and Connor followed, their voices trailing off.

"Please, no need to stop talking on my account," I said, and they exchanged glances. "Seriously, why bother trying to keep anything from me when you know I'll find out one way or another." I focused on Lucas. "Do you have any updates?"

"You know I can't tell you that."

I tilted my head toward Connor. "You told him."

"No, I didn't. We weren't discussing any of the case particulars, just…"

"My getting involved, perhaps?"

Lucas sighed. "I'll tell you what's in the public records. Brian was killed shortly after nine from a single knife wound. There were no traces of drugs in his system, and no defensive wounds. The killer was someone he knew." He grunted. "You know enough to realize the first thing we look for is motive, and Annie's the only one so far who has one. Brian recently took out extra insurance—"

"How did you find out so quickly?" He shot me a look. "I mean, that was fast."

"Nowadays there are databases that do nothing but spit out that kind of information," Lucas said.

"I thought something like that would be private."

"Most people sign away their rights to privacy without even knowing it. The insurance companies love when the police suspect foul play. It doesn't cost them anything to have the police investigate, and if a crime is proven, sometimes they don't have to pay on a claim."

"What about the way he died? I've heard it takes a lot of strength to kill someone with a knife. That it isn't easy to do, especially since he was stabbed just once."

Lucas nodded. "Usually that's true." He paused. "The knife nicked his heart. He died almost instantly."

"Either the killer was lucky or knew what they were doing."

He caught my eye. "That's about it, but we're leaning toward someone with basic medical training, and that includes veterinary."

"Hold on," I said. "Nicole had basic training. Eric is a vet, Claire is a doctor, and even Jason must have some basic medical knowledge. He owns a pharmaceutical company. There's even Denise, Eric's lab assistant, although she says she was in the city that night. Whatever. None of these people are above suspicion."

"See, that's what worries me." Lucas put his hands on his hips. "You tracking suspects isn't exactly staying out of it and letting me do my job. I'll be the one to decide who's a suspect. Got it?" He stared at me until I bobbed my head once. It was a token agreement, and we all knew it, but he continued. "Now, why don't you level with me on what you've learned? Like you, I'll find out, one way or the other." He was drumming his fingers on the counter, and he wasn't smiling.

"All right then. Let's start with Dot. She said she was working at the clinic late the night of the murder. She just happened to be in the back office with headphones on when someone is killed yards from her?"

Lucas nodded. "When I questioned her, she said she's often there in the evening."

"Well I've met with her since then," I said. Lucas raised a brow, but I pressed on. "She says she's losing her memory and was there that night trying to catch up on her work." I was encouraged to continue when Lucas pulled out a notepad. "Annie said the receipts have been off lately at the clinic. What if Dot was embezzling money and Brian surprised her?"

Lucas looked at me over the pad. "What else?"

"Well, Denise, Eric's lab assistant, said she was in the city the night Brian was killed, but I know there is something she isn't telling me."

Lucas paused. "I don't know what you expect me to do with that."

"Just confirm she really was in the city. Something's there."

He bit at his lip. "What else?"

"Then there's Eric. He said he was out filming bats, but he was alone. Pretty weak as an alibi."

"Bats?"

"Research. He claims he was at Cliff Point."

"What motive would he have?" Lucas asked.

"He's been in love with Brian's wife, Claire, since they went to college together. Unrequited love, the classic motive."

I ticked off the remaining suspects on my fingers. "Speaking of Claire, she wasn't getting flowers from her husband on Fridays anymore." Lucas and Connor exchanged glances. "Trust me," I said, "when a man sends you flowers every week and then suddenly stops, it means something."

Lucas still looked skeptical. "How's this?" I said. "A few weeks back, Brian took her off all of their joint accounts. Why? Apparently she has a gambling problem."

That got his attention. "How did you find this out?"

"Well, if you must know, I went to her house and asked her."

Lucas threw his palms in the air. "And she just told you?"

"People just seem to tell me things."

Lucas took a deep breath and let it out slowly. "Anything else?"

"Well, yes, actually. Jason said he was at his hotel, but he was alone and I only have his word for it."

"And Jason said this to you…"

"Um, when I went to his hotel and asked him."

Connor stifled a groan.

Lucas held up his hand. "You can't be tracking down murder suspects and confronting them."

"It was fine. He was sitting on the patio having breakfast."

Connor spoke up. "Lucas, this is an old argument, one I've had with her many times. Good luck if you think she's going to stop now."

"We were in a public place. What could happen?"

Lucas momentarily closed his eyes. "Why would Jason be a suspect?"

"He wasn't, not until I spoke to him this morning. I saw an article in the paper that said Amerigen is losing investors. Then I found out Brian had tried to back out of investing. Who knows how Jason took it? Maybe he went to the clinic to try and change Brian's mind and things got out of hand."

I took a breath. "Finally, we come to Nicole. Sure, she conveniently shows up just in time to find Annie kneeling over Brian, but it's possible she arrived earlier, killed him herself, left, and then came back. She might have seen us arrive and changed course to be with us when we found Brian. Then we become her alibi."

Hayley took a seat at the counter as I waited for a response. Connor let out a sigh, and Lucas slapped the notebook shut, his jaw twitching with tension.

"What?" I said. "That's some useful information. It wasn't hard to get, if you want to know the truth. I just asked a few questions." I studied Lucas. "I can practically hear your teeth grinding."

He looked up and appeared to be searching for the

appropriate response. "Look," I said, when he'd returned his gaze to mine, "I know these people. They talk to me. It's easier than talking to the police. I consider them my friends, or at least my acquaintances. All of them except Nicole, that is." I thought of her car, still parked at the clinic. "Which reminds me. What happened after you arrested her?"

"A DUI is an expensive mistake," Lucas said. "It took her some time to post bail. She got out this morning."

"Who posted bail for her?"

"Nobody. She came up with the cash."

"See, I didn't know that. We can exchange information."

Connor spoke up. "You've got to admit, Lucas, she does have a knack for digging stuff up. Short of getting her to stop, which is unlikely, I've learned it's best to have her on your side."

"I'm willing to share everything I learn with you." I leaned in toward Lucas. "And what I've learned is that there are plenty of motives to go around, motives as strong as what you've settled on for Annie. None of these people should be discounted."

"I didn't say they were." Lucas massaged the back of his neck and looked over at Hayley, who gave a dismissive wave of her hand.

"Our dating shouldn't influence you one way or the other," she said, "but I would just like to go on record and say Aunt Penny will try to solve it, with or without your approval."

He turned to me, and I bobbed my head from side to side as though weighing it out. Finally, I spoke. "Yeah, she's right. I'll be trying to find the killer. If I denied it, I'd be lying."

Lucas shook his head. "All right. You be careful, keep your eyes open, and tell me everything you find out."

"Agreed," I said. "Have you learned anything else?"

"The only other thing of significance is that we've confirmed no forced entry."

I bit my lip. "With no defensive wounds, that makes sense. It certainly sounds like someone Brian knew." I felt the tightness in my chest. "Eric, Nicole, Claire, Jason, Denise. He would have let in any of them without a thought, and Dot was already inside."

Lucas held up both hands in surrender. "I promise you we're looking at all options." His face tightened. "Listen to me now. I will follow up on every lead that comes across my desk, but there's an order to investigations that we follow. That's just how it works, Penny. Nothing you've told me changes the fact that Annie was found over Brian holding the knife that killed him. It was her knife, from her surgery kit. She had motive, she had means, and she had opportunity."

"But you know Annie. You know she couldn't have done this."

He paused, staring over my shoulder, then nodded slightly, as though coming to a decision. "You need to know the DA wants to charge Annie. He's not doing anything for the time being, but I know where it's headed. I don't necessarily agree with him, but there's only so much I can do, and I promise you I'll go after whoever's guilty based on the evidence."

"Sure, I understand what you need to do." I certainly knew what I was going to do.

"It isn't much, but I've cleared Annie to reopen the clinic," Lucas said. "She's free to operate her business as of tomorrow morning."

I wondered for how long as Lucas said goodnight and Hayley walked him to the front door. I felt frustrated by the conversation. I wasn't convinced anything I'd shared with Lucas would help persuade the DA that Annie was innocent. The DA didn't know Annie. My frustration boiled over when Connor passed close to me. Instead of the hint of spice he normally carried with him, I caught a lingering wave of perfume.

"How was your evening?" I wrinkled my nose. "Did you fall onto Chantal's bottle of Obsession or just the particular parts of her body where she pours it?"

Connor raised his brow. "I spent the evening at a wine growers association meeting. Yes, I drove Chantal. Yes, we sat next to each other. Yes, she had perfume on. We even had dinner, and during dinner we discussed the business of selling wine. She's trying to take a bigger role in running Martinelli, and she wants to learn the inside workings of the association."

"The only thing she's working is you."

Connor smiled. "I really think I can take care of myself. Some guys might fall for her brand of seduction. I don't know why. It's a little obvious for my taste."

I couldn't help myself. "So, what's your taste?"

He walked up to me and leaned against the counter. I'm

tall, and he still has several inches on me. He wore a soft green chambray shirt. The sleeves were folded above strong and slightly tanned wrists. Steady blue eyes gazed down at me, and a soft smile played along his lips.

"My taste? I go for women who don't try too hard. Someone with a sense of humor who knows what she wants. Someone smart. Someone kind." He laughed. "Not Chantal. I caught her checking out her reflection in the butter knife."

"So, I guess it would be okay with you if a woman wanted to help someone wrongly accused of murder. You did say you wanted someone who knows what she wants."

Connor shook his head. "I also said I wanted someone smart."

"Annie didn't do it, and you just heard she's the main suspect."

"You're getting in over your head. Again."

"Didn't you just hear the DA wants to charge her with murder?"

"It's early. Lucas will get all the facts and figure it out."

"I'm not willing to take that chance. Not with Annie." I pushed away from the counter and walked out of the kitchen.

Chapter 11

I didn't see Connor for the rest of the evening and had another fitful night. When the clock read five I gave up on sleep, pulling on blue sweatpants and a matching sweatshirt. I caught my reflection in the mirror. I looked like a blueberry. I really needed to get more exercise, but at the moment it took less energy to just turn away from the mirror. I stepped to the sliders leading outside. Wind buffeted against the glass. The sky was gunmetal gray and littered with dark clouds. I hoped for the best and pushed open the doors. Nanook ran past me, excited to be out in the weather. He turned back to look at me, hoping I'd join him.

"Not a chance," I said over the rush of frigid air, thinking once again of adding another dog to the family. "Maybe it's time you had a friend."

I entered the kitchen for much needed coffee and could still smell Chantal's perfume. My annoyance from last night returned, and in spite of the icy wind I threw open the doors while the coffee brewed. When I had my first cup in hand I settled in at my desk and spent the remainder of the morning going over orders. It didn't matter how fabulous the wine was if it didn't sell. The good news was that we were still in black ink. When I finished up, I made peanut butter on toast and dialed Annie at the clinic.

"Lucas told me he was letting you reopen this morning, but I wasn't sure you'd be in."

"Are you kidding? I'm swamped. Hold on." I heard a door close. "There, now we can talk."

"How are you holding up?"

"Not great."

"Is it hard to be there, you know, after Brian?" I asked.

"Not as much as you'd think. My conscience is clear and Brian would want me to be all right, so that helps. Plus, I've always been better with death than you."

She's right. I have a real aversion to bodies, which in no way hampers my ability to find them.

"Maybe you can make it a short day."

"Nope. I had patients scheduled already, and I needed to field calls from Brian's clients."

"I forgot on top of everything else you'd have Brian's patients to manage. Didn't your staff help?"

"Sure, but almost every one of them still wants to talk to me."

"Speaking of talking," I said, "did you hear from Dot?"

"Yes, she called me yesterday and we talked again this morning. She told me her memory isn't what it was. It explains why she was working here late the night Brian was killed."

"What did you do?" I asked.

"I made her an appointment with a specialist, switched her to the front where she isn't dealing with finances, and started looking for a new bookkeeper. Dot's been with me a long time. I wasn't going to let her go."

"I'm so glad that's settled, but what are you going to do at the clinic? You've got to think about your business long term without…without Brian."

"I have a relief doctor coming in, one I've used before. Most of the clients know her, but it certainly isn't a long-term fix."

"Do you think Brian's patients will stay at the clinic?"

"Maybe most, but either way the business is going to take a hit. Not now, though." She lowered her voice. "I swear we're busier than normal here today. I think some of them just wanted to come by and see where it happened."

"In a small town, this is big news. How can I help?"

"Just find proof I didn't kill him. I get the feeling Lucas doesn't have a lot of leads. He isn't very encouraging." Her voice shook. "I'm afraid, and I don't know what to do."

"We'll get you out of this, Annie. I promise. Now let's talk about what I can do right now. Today."

"Well, I never did get Nicole her last check. We didn't give it to her the night…I mean, Brian's last night, and since then the clinic's been closed."

"Not to mention she just got out of jail this morning," I said. "I'm sure they took her license. Look out the window. Is her car still there?"

"I don't need to look. I saw it when I pulled in. She hasn't been back. We could mail it to her…"

"No, don't. Let me shower and change, and I'll come by and get the check," I said. "I'll bring it by her house."

"I'd love it if she never stepped foot in here again. You don't mind?"

"Mind? On the contrary, I'd welcome the chance to see her again. We have some unfinished business."

I didn't see Annie when I entered the clinic a short time later, but she hadn't been exaggerating. The waiting area was standing-room only, dogs and cats sharing the space in an uneasy truce. The noise level was low considering the number of patients, and the mood difficult to place— somber, but with an underlying buzz of excited tension. Annie was right. Some of the patients were there to see where it happened. Dot was behind the front counter with the receptionist. She saw me and walked over, envelope in hand.

"It's been a long morning without Brian." She looked around the room. "It's almost as if the animals can feel something is different. I told Annie it will take some time." Dot shook herself and handed me the envelope. "Here's Nicole's check. The last thing I'll do as a bookkeeper." She leaned in. "Annie let me move up here to focus on checking patients in and out. No money-handling at all."

"She told me." I studied Dot. "Even with everything going on here, you look more relaxed than the last time I saw you."

"I'm just so glad Annie still wants me to be here. I don't know what I'd do without this job, without this place."

"Do you think you'll miss being the bookkeeper?"

"Hardly," she said, the bangles jangling on her arm. "It's a relief." She signaled to a man with a terrier mix as a vet tech came up behind her.

"Wait." The tech skimmed the paperwork in her hand. "This isn't the right file."

Dot didn't miss a beat as she rattled off a ten-digit patient number, pausing only to reach down and scratch the dog between the ears. "Hi, Clyde. Haven't seen you in a while."

I heard little warning bells going off in my head. Dot claimed to be so forgetful that she was leaving money bags in her car, yet she rattled off that code without any trouble, and certainly faster than I would have remembered it.

"See you later." I scooted around the dog and out the front door, taking a seat in my car. I'd been willing to believe Dot, *wanting* to believe her. Now doubt tightened my shoulders, and I drummed my fingers against the steering wheel. If Dot had taken money for years, it would total a large amount, certainly more than she could replace. Brian might have found out and confronted her. She had just said she didn't know what she would do without this job. So what would she do to keep it?

I left the clinic with the check and directions to Nicole's house, which turned out to be a townhouse in a very exclusive area. When I arrived, I pulled to the side of the road. The complex was gated, and a security guard sat there watching me. I fingered the sealed envelope containing the check and decided that in this case honesty might actually work best, especially since I had a legitimate reason for being there. I pulled up next to the kiosk and turned on my brightest smile.

"Hi there," I said. "Could you let Nicole..." I didn't know her last name. It wasn't written on the envelope, and I didn't want to listen to Nicole yammer that I'd opened her mail. "Hmm, this is awkward. I'm here dropping off a check for one of your residents and I don't know her last name." I gave a little laugh, hoping the large gentleman with the slicked-back hair and steel gray eyes would join in. He didn't. "She's in her twenties and whippet-thin, drives a white Audi. Totally obnoxious." I said this last part under my breath, but apparently loud enough for him to hear, because one side of his mouth rose. Just a touch, but I was encouraged. "Honestly, I'm just here to give her this."

"You can leave it with me."

I thought fast. "Sorry, she has to sign for it."

He studied me. "I know who you mean. I'm going to have to call her to get her approval before you go in."

"No problem." It might be a problem, but I didn't have any choice. "Tell her it's Penny Lively."

I waited while he dialed a number, and was encouraged when he nodded and hung up a few moments later. Pushing a button, he leaned out the window while the gate slowly opened. "You don't look like her regular guests."

"What do her guests usually look like?"

"Rich. And male." He pointed up the hill. "Unit 208. Third building on your right."

The complex I drove through was woodsy and secluded. These townhomes came with every amenity, and Nicole's building was next to the tennis courts. I pulled right into her driveway, figuring she wouldn't be using it anytime soon. I parked, walked up the meandering path, and knocked. The door moved and I pushed against it with my fingertips.

"Nicole?"

"In here."

I stepped into a foyer that would have been attractive if it were clean. Instead, it was the residential version of Nicole's car, and featured an assortment of shoes, magazines, rollers, and several plants in desperate need of watering, and that was before I reached the living room. I stepped through the mess, rounded the corner, and spotted Nicole on the couch. She was watching television, but the sound was off. She didn't look up, and for a moment I questioned if it actually was Nicole. For one thing, she had the remnants of a dessert in her lap. I think it once had been a cake. Chocolate. I got a better look at her when she pushed herself upright and lobbed the cake pan onto the coffee table. The cute pixie hair was gone, replaced with a tangled mess. She had raccoon eyes from left-over makeup, and her outfit consisted of cut-off jean shorts and an oversized white tee dotted with chocolate frosting.

"Where's my check," she asked, without looking up.

"I have it, but I want to ask you something first."

"Why should I tell you anything?" Her voice rose as she turned to face me.

Good question. "Because if you give me some answers, I'll give you your check and leave."

She shrugged. I was going to need more. "How's this. If you *don't* answer my questions, I'm going to tell Annie she should have your car towed off the clinic's parking lot. There's no reason Annie should be doing you any favors." I had her attention now. "I hear it's pretty expensive when they impound your car. Not to mention what towing can do to a vehicle, especially one that's as close to the ground as yours. Be a shame to bang up such a nice little number."

"Fine," she said. "Let's just hurry up and get this over with."

I thought back. "Where were you the night Brian was killed?"

She snorted. "I was with you, remember? You know, when we found Annie." She smiled, a nasty little grin. "Right after she killed Brian."

I ignored the bait. "Before then, earlier in the evening."

Her head slumped back on the couch and she stared at the ceiling. "I was with Jason at his hotel."

"Jason said he had you removed from his hotel."

Her head snapped up. "That's a lie!" Her answer was sharp, but it seemed to exhaust the last of her energy. Her head dropped to the couch once again. "I left because I don't want to date him anymore."

"Really?" I said. "That doesn't sound like you."

She shrugged. "I've decided he's too old for me. Boring."

"Okay, let's say I believe you. Jason told me what time you left his hotel. You had a full hour before we found Brian's body. Where did you go between Jason's hotel and the clinic?"

For the first time since I'd arrived, she focused on me. "Why do you want to know that?"

I didn't have anything to lose. "Because you had time to go to the clinic early and kill Brian."

Her eyes narrowed. "Why would I do that?"

It was my turn to shrug. "He fired you, not to mention ruined your chances to date Jason. I guess it's a good thing Jason's too old and boring for you, since a man who owns a pharmaceutical company can't really afford to date someone caught stealing medications from her job."

I looked around for things she might be able to throw at me. "By the way, you owe me for three broken wine glasses."

As easily as it had come, Nicole's focus faded once again and she waved me away with her hand. This was a different Nicole. She was listless, and the chocolate cake…

"Now I get it. You're out of drugs, aren't you? What was it Brian caught you taking?" Nicole didn't answer. "Phenol something? Annie said it gave people energy and killed their appetites. That's what's going on with you. Now that you don't have access to the clinic, you're cut off."

"Just go," she said. "Even if you're right, so what? You can't do anything about it now."

"Maybe not, but I can stay on the police, and eventually you'll need to tell them where you were after you left Jason's hotel and before you showed up at the clinic."

She turned to me, not lifting her head from the sofa. "I wasn't at the clinic earlier. I can't prove it, though. I guess you'll just have to take my word for it."

Not likely. "Where were you?"

"It doesn't matter. I just said I can't prove anything."

"I'd still like to hear where you were."

She took a deep breath and pushed it through her teeth. "Fine. If you must know, I can't remember."

"That's a likely story. I'm sure the police will be just fine with you telling them you can't remember."

"It's the truth."

"Wait a minute," I said. "It's the drugs. You honestly can't remember. You drove that way. You know you have a problem, right?"

She tossed her head the same way the old Nicole would, but with the unwashed hair, raccoon eyes, and chocolate stains, the effect was lost. She seemed to realize it mid-hair flip and folded against the arm of the couch. "Whatever."

"If you really don't remember, you can't prove you weren't there when Brian was killed."

Under the mascara streaks her face paled. "And you can't prove I was, or that I had anything to do with Brian's death." Picking up the remote, she stood. "You'll do anything to get your cousin out of this, but you aren't going to pin it on me." With that, she hurled the remote at the wall. For someone with arms the size of chicken wings, she had a vicious swing. The remote shattered, sending pieces of plastic across the room.

"Now there's the Nicole I know." I picked up my bag. "Well, I'll be going now."

"Where's my check?"

"Really? That's all you have to say?" I pointed to what was left of her remote. "I hope you like this channel because you're going to be watching it for a while." I pulled out the check and dropped it onto the couch.

"Where do I sign?"

"What?"

"I need to sign. You told the security guard at the gate you couldn't leave this with him because I needed to sign for it."

Right. "Sure, I know that." I pulled a pad from my purse. "I'll just write up a receipt..."

"I didn't have to sign for anything." She placed one hand on her hip. "You just made that up so you could come in here and bother me."

"Oh please, I'm bothering you? I'm sure right when I knocked you were getting the vacuum out to clean this mess." The absurdity of the situation hit me all at once, and I moved quickly toward her. Her eyes grew wide but she didn't back up, trying to hold her ground. It didn't work, as the top of her head came to my chin. She folded her arms and tried to adopt a casual stance, but she had to tip her head back to look at me.

"Listen to me," I said. "You've lost your job, your boyfriend, and"—I looked around the room—"your self-respect. If I have anything to do with it, you're going to lose your freedom too, because I think you killed Brian."

I expected to get protests, raging denials, or anger. Instead, she looked me straight in the eyes, her shoulders back. "I didn't have anything to do with it. I found out he was dead the same time you did."

She was convincing. Her gaze was steady, her voice calm. The surety of her answer bothered me, and I turned to leave, less certain than when I'd arrived that she was the killer.

Chapter 12

I left Nicole trying to reconstruct her remote. As much as I disliked her, she had managed to leave an impression. She'd certainly shown no signs of guilt or anxiety when I'd asked about Brian's death. Of course, the night he died, Nicole had been heavily self-medicated. She'd claimed she couldn't remember the hour before Brian's death. Was it possible she'd killed Brian and didn't remember it?

The route back to town brought me near the shore and Cliff Point, the place Eric said he was filming bats the night of the murder. On impulse, when I reached the entrance, I pulled in.

There were few cars in the lot, nothing like the crowd this stretch of shore attracts in the summer. In spite of the chilly air, there were walkers down on the beach and surfers in full wetsuits bobbing in the frigid water.

Since I was there, I decided to do a quick walk along the shore. I snagged the jacket and sneakers I keep in the trunk and hiked down the path. For me, the hardest part of exercise is starting, and once I began walking I was glad to be there. Although the sky was dark and cloudy, the hills were unusually green from all the rain we'd been having, and wildflowers were starting to appear. Poppies, lupine, and mallow were making appearances. I walked the shore heading north, maybe a mile up. Cliff Point was marked by a natural arch surrounded by granite boulders several stories high. They looked as though they'd been carefully stacked by a giant. For now, the tide was low, the water's edge a fair distance from the cliffs, but the jagged surface that faced the ocean was lined with caves, a testament to countless years of battering from an unyielding sea.

I turned into the first cave, one of the largest. I hadn't been here since high school, when it was a game of dare to see who would go furthest into the dark abyss. Inside, the air was as I remembered, heavy and filled with the stench of bat guano. In the dim light, I spotted the remnants of several cigarettes and a camera lens. I took a closer look. The cigarettes were rolled in brown paper. Eric had been here at some point. I lasted about ten seconds before leaving. If Eric spent a lot of time in these conditions, he deserved whatever accolades he was getting.

I arrived back in the parking lot certain I'd walked at least five miles roundtrip. Hungry for lunch, I drove the short distance to Sterling and took a seat by the window. Moments later, Ross plopped down in the chair opposite me.

"I don't see you for ages, miss all the excitement, and now you're here two days in a row? What's up?"

"I just walked six or seven miles, and I'm exhausted. Plus, you know, I stress eat."

"The special today is stroganoff."

"I don't know why I'm not here every day. I'll have a glass of wine with that."

As Ross stood, there was a rap on the window. I turned. Connor was there, and I signaled for him to join me.

"Now if I were you, I'd pay close attention to that one," Ross said. "The wine growers association had their meeting here last night."

"I heard."

Ross leaned in. "Chantal was all over Connor." He grimaced. "Connor handled it well, practically ignored her, but honestly, she couldn't have made it any clearer what she wanted." He shuddered. "She had on so much perfume it overpowered the entire restaurant. I finally managed to get rid of the smell this morning."

"I had the same problem myself. Connor came back last night reeking." My cheeks warmed. "I think I suggested he must have been getting pretty friendly with Chantal to smell so much like her."

"Trust me, you didn't have to get that close to pick up the scent. Not that she didn't want him close." He gestured to the chair he'd just vacated as Connor walked up. "Here, take this seat. We were just talking about you."

"Not really." My cheeks warmed.

"True," Ross said. "More about Chantal."

"No! Not about Chantal either." I rubbed my eyes with my thumb and finger.

"I'm confused." Ross actually looked perplexed.

"And you wonder why I keep things from you."

"What? What are you keeping from me?"

Connor brushed his palm against the two-day beard that I find so attractive. "Do you two want me to step out and come back in?"

"Never mind," Ross said. "If you aren't going to tell me anything, I might as well go back to work."

"Everything okay?" I asked after Ross left.

Connor nodded. "Even though it's chilly, as long as it isn't raining the fields are finally drying out. So, what brings you into town?" The abrupt change of conversation caught me off guard, which was likely intended. The giveaway was the twinkle in his eyes and the way he leaned in.

"Nothing. Nope, nothing in particular."

"I saw you leave, bright and early. Seems like you must have left for something."

Sigh. "All right. I wanted to see Annie. She's back at the clinic, and I stopped in to make sure she was all right."

Connor nodded. "She's fine. At least that's what she told me when I called."

"Oh, you talked to Annie?"

Connor smiled. "Yes, as a matter of fact."

"I did go and see her." I bit my lip, wondering how much he knew. I didn't have to wait long.

"I know you brought Nicole her last check. You shouldn't have gone to see her alone. She hates you and Annie and might possibly be a murderer."

"Okay, you're right," I offered, too late. "I did bring Nicole her check."

Connor shook his head. "Did you ever feel like you were in danger?"

"Only from catching something. She isn't much of a housekeeper. And she ate a cake."

His eyebrows gathered. "What do you mean, she ate a cake? Nicole doesn't eat, not much anyway, not looking like that. She's the type that stays away from cake. Any cake, much less an entire one."

I shook my index finger back and forth. "Ah, that's where you're wrong. Now that she doesn't have access to appetite suppressants, she's making up for lost time."

"So, what happened?"

"Well, I asked her about her movements the day Brian died."

Connor started to say something, but I forged ahead. "After she was kicked out of Jason's hotel, she had time to drive to the clinic and kill Brian before I got there with Annie. She denies it, of course. Says she can't remember where she was."

Connor tilted his head like Nanook waiting for a treat.

"Where did I lose you?"

He shook his head. "At the beginning."

I pinched between my eyes. "Let's get your lunch ordered. This is going to take a while."

"So," Connor said, sometime later. "It could still be any one of them." He'd finished his salad and was waiting for me.

"That salad was enough for you?" I asked.

"I had a slice of bread too," he said. "Everything in balance."

"Sure, everything in balance." My idea of balance is to

pace my wine with my food, and once again, I'd succeeded. I pushed away the plate.

"Yes, it could be any one of them," I said.

"So, we've been through this before. How do you propose shrinking the pool of suspects this time?"

"The usual. Look for motives and check alibis, all while staying out of trouble."

He smiled. "Because that's how it always works for you."

"I'm not saying it always goes smoothly, but the process is the same. Ask questions, be nosy, press where it hurts."

"*You* might get hurt if you press the wrong person," he said.

"If I don't do something, then Annie's the one who will get hurt." I stood. "Come on. We aren't going to reach an agreement on this."

"No, we won't," he said. "Not unless you're willing to let the police handle it."

I rolled my eyes.

"Well I guess that's my answer."

I puffed. "Honestly, did you expect me to respond any other way?"

"Not really. You aren't easy, you know that?"

"Of course I am," I said. "I'm easy. So easy. Easy as can be." I chatted away until I realized several tables had stopped to listen. "No, not *easy* easy. Not that easy. No! I mean not *that* easy." My cheeks blazed, and we didn't speak again until we were out on the sidewalk. "Well, my daily humiliation is out of the way, so I've got that going for me."

"I've never noticed you're limited to once a day. Sometimes when you're on a roll..."

"You aren't helping." I sighed. "Let's go for a walk and do a little window shopping."

"Window shopping? That doesn't sound like you."

"I need to stretch. I did just polish off an entire plate of stroganoff."

With its cottages and gardens, and the beach just a short walk from town, Cypress Cove never failed to renew my spirits. Those who live here choose a slower pace. Residents have learned to get by without street lights, take gleeful pride in informing tourists their cell reception will be spotty, and are fine with stores being closed on Sunday mornings.

We walked at a pace too slow to qualify as exercise, and I caught my reflection in the glass of Calla Lilly Flowers. Connor saw my quick self-appraisal and was gracious enough to look away, but apparently I wasn't limited to one humiliation per day.

"I've put on a few pounds."

Connor scoffed. "What are you, a size eight?"

"Ah, sure."

"You're fine." Connor smiled, and my heart skipped around the inside of my chest. "How about this." He opened the shop door. "Why don't I buy you flowers, just because?"

A gorgeous man wanted to buy me flowers. Just because. My day was looking up.

I stepped into the sweetly scented air and a short time later came out with a large bunch of tiger lilies.

"Where to now?" he asked.

"Maybe a few more blocks and we can turn around." We walked in companionable silence, dodging tourists and locals alike. We'd just crossed the street when I spotted a familiar braid enter a store ahead of us.

"I think that was Dot." I looked at the sign. "She went into Martin and Martin Jewelers." I paused behind a tree and got a better look. "It's Dot all right."

In Cypress Cove, the price of all this charm is, well, the price. Of everything. The jewelry stores in town, especially along touristy Ocean Boulevard, were no exception. They were certainly beyond my means, and well beyond the means of a former bookkeeper at a veterinary clinic. I moved to the corner of the building and lifted the bouquet so my face was hidden from view.

"What are you doing?" Connor said from behind me. He was standing in the middle of the sidewalk, his arms folded.

"Dot can't afford to shop there, not unless she was stealing from the clinic after all."

Connor hadn't moved. "Didn't she say her memory was going?"

"Yes, but this morning she rattled off a patient's ten-digit number without even looking it up. I'm not sure I believe her story." Connor was still pinned to the center of the sidewalk. "Get behind me before she sees you!"

"I refuse to hide behind a bouquet."

"Fine, but don't just stand there." I gestured toward the neighboring store. "Look, one of those upscale shave places. Go browse." I loved how he kept that slightly unshaven look, but under the circumstances, sacrifices needed to be made. I pointed. "Go!"

He shook his head. "I can't stop you, but I'm not going

143

to participate. See you at home."

He strode past me without looking into the jewelers. Perfect. I'd managed to alienate him once again. I steeled myself with images of Annie going to jail and moved along the wall to the next tree. I curled around the trunk to get a better look. Penny Lively, master of disguises.

"What on earth do you think you're doing?" Antonia had come up behind me. "Lovely flowers, but you've got tree bark stuck to the side of your face."

"What are you doing here?" I wiped my cheek with the back of my hand.

Antonia sniffed. "I'm here to see one of my tenants, if it's of any relevance." Antonia's family had been one of the first to settle in Cypress Cove, and she still owned several buildings along Ocean Boulevard. "Why are you here"—she gestured with a wave—"pressed up against a tree?"

She had on a large emerald ring. I grabbed her hand, but she pulled it away with determination. "What in heaven's name is wrong with you?"

"Go into Martin Jewelers and tell them the emerald in your ring feels loose."

"Why would I do that?"

"Because then you can see what Dot is doing in there."

"Dot? Annie's bookkeeper with the faulty memory and the lost money bags?"

"That's her. Ex-bookkeeper, and I'm beginning to doubt her memory is all that bad."

"You doubt her story. That explains it," she said.

"What?"

"Why you're wrapped around a tree and Connor stormed off."

"Connor didn't storm off." I pushed thoughts of Connor aside. "Can you just go in and see what she's doing?"

Antonia sighed. "Very well. I don't like it, but I'll do it for Annie. I'll be right back."

I moved down the street to wait. Dot stepped through the glass doors a moment later, and I pushed open the entrance to Mayan Chocolates.

"Chocolate praline sample?" The girl behind the counter held out a tray.

"I really shouldn't," I said.

"We cut them in half, so they really aren't that large."

"Well, in that case." I took one and peered out the door. Dot was nowhere in sight, and Antonia stood in front of the jewelers. I grabbed the second half of my praline and joined her.

"She bought something all right," Antonia said. "It was all wrapped up before I could see what it was. She'd finished paying too, so I haven't any idea how much she spent."

"It doesn't matter, really. If she has money to spend at the most expensive jewelry store in town, something isn't right."

"So, what are you going to do now?"

I buried my nose in the lilies. "Take these home and get them in water."

"Connor buy them for you?" I nodded. "You might want to talk to him," Antonia said. "Get him on your side. Explain Annie might be accused of a murder we all know she didn't commit."

"He knows, and he doesn't care."

"Now you know that isn't true."

"I mean, he cares more about someone coming after me."

Antonia nodded. "Sensible. You should be concerned with the same thing."

Chapter 13

I didn't go home, though. I wasn't ready to see Connor. I was confused and needed to clear my head. I understood his concern for my safety, especially when it had been justified in the past, but he must have known I wasn't going to quit. He knew how I was. Who I was. I hated when we disagreed but couldn't seem to avoid it. He was kind and funny, but utterly too sensible, which led to these moments of impasse. A lump formed in my throat, but I knew I'd make the same decision again if necessary. Annie was counting on me. With her on my mind, I found myself passing the clinic a few moments later. I pulled in, glad for the distraction.

The better part of the afternoon was gone, the shadows long, as I parked up front. Only a couple of cars were left, and the reception area was down to one pug when I pushed through the glass doors.

The pretty brunette I'd seen on occasion smiled from behind the reception desk. "So, Dot isn't working this afternoon?" I asked.

She shook her head. "She worked this morning but had

the afternoon off. We're a little overstaffed right now because Dot was the bookkeeper until…" Her voice trailed off. "Until recently. She's working a short schedule until we have a full-time opening."

So, Dot was only working part time, yet she had money for jewelry?

"Is Annie, I mean Dr. Moore, available?"

"Let me check." She spoke into the phone, then turned to me. "Dr. Moore is finishing up with a patient. It will be a few more minutes."

"No problem. I'll wait outside." As I walked out onto the porch, Eric rounded the corner from his offices. He stopped when he saw me. "Hi, Penny. What are you doing out here?"

"Just waiting for Annie to finish with a patient." He had on another Tommy Bahama shirt and looked like he had stepped off the beach.

"How do you stay so tan?" I asked. "It's been raining here for weeks. The little sun we've had the last couple of days wouldn't have been enough."

"Heredity helps. My family is from South America, but I admit to being a sun lover. When I can get away from the office, I'm outside as much as possible."

He rested against the porch. Except for that ponytail, I had to admit he wasn't hard to look at, but the effect was marred by the confidence in his eyes. He knew he was attractive. Still, plenty of women in town would be willing to overlook a passé hairstyle and arrogance in a man, especially if he was successful.

"Do you get into San Francisco often?"

"Not really. The research is keeping me pretty busy here."

"Nobody special in your life?"

He flashed that smile. "Nope, nobody special." He got a faraway look in his eyes and tightened his hand against the railing. "No one special. Not in a long time."

Claire. He was thinking about Claire. I needed to know if he was still in love with her. "I hear you and Claire used to date. Back in college, before she married Brian." For a moment, I thought he was going to ignore the comment, but then he slowly turned to me. "It was casual, nothing more than friends, really."

"That's funny," I said. "That wasn't the impression I got from Claire, and it certainly didn't look casual when I saw you and her at the ugly dog contest."

"You saw us talking that day?"

"It was more than talking. You pulled her by the arm, and she had to push at you to get away."

"No, no, you've got it wrong." His voice rose at the end. "It wasn't anything like that."

"Then why did you grab her by the arm?"

"What did she say happened?" He tried to shrug, but his voice broke.

"She hasn't said much yet, but I'm sure the police will want more details, especially in light of what's happened to Brian."

His smile slipped. "You don't think I would do anything to Brian because I was once in love with his wife. That's ridiculous. It was ages ago. We were in college. I was in love with half the girls in my class."

"Police look for motive when someone is murdered," I said. "If they think you're still in love with Claire, I'm sure it's something they'll consider."

He looked a little pale under his tan. "All right, here's the truth. I don't have time to be in a serious relationship, but if Claire was up for having a little fun, I would find the time. Okay? That's all there is to it. Nothing more, and certainly no reason to kill her husband. But she made it clear she wasn't interested." His face relaxed a bit. "Hey, you can't blame a guy for trying."

I'd seen his reaction when I'd first mentioned Claire's name, and I wasn't buying this casual business, but I let it go for the time being.

"How are your tests coming?" I asked. "Will you be working on them much longer?"

He took a breath and, with effort, relaxed his shoulders. "You like to ask questions, don't you?" I think he meant to lighten the conversation, but he sounded stiff and awkward. "I'll be here for a couple more weeks, then it's back to field work for me." He looked at his watch. "And now, if you don't mind, I need to be going." He turned toward his offices.

I wasn't going to let him dismiss me, and so I scrambled for another question. "What will Denise do when you go back into the field?" I knew I'd hit a nerve when his shoulders tensed. He turned to face me.

"You'll have to ask her."

"Isn't she your associate?" I asked.

"Only on this project. Most of the preliminary work, the

data gathering, is finished. That's all I really needed her for."

"Huh. I got the impression when I spoke to her that she views your research as a team effort."

His jawline hardened. "I have no idea what you're talking about. The vaccine is entirely mine." He resumed walking along the cement path without a backward glance.

So, Eric viewed Denise as expendable, which was unfortunate for her, but I didn't see any connection to Brian's murder. Denise didn't have a motive, and if I believed Eric's assertion that he was only interested in Claire casually, then there wasn't any reason for him to kill Brian. I mentally worked over the pieces, trying to make them fit, until Annie came out a short time later. Her hair was tousled from being under a cap, she had mascara streaks under her eyes, and her hands were bright red.

"What happened to your hands?"

"Do you have any idea how many times I wash my hands every day? A hundred times. Easy."

I put my arm around her shoulders. "Let me take you to dinner."

"No, honestly, I couldn't. I'm exhausted. Between all of Brian's patients and my own, not to mention people wanting to see how I am and where it happened, I couldn't eat a bite."

"How about a glass of wine?"

She didn't say anything, so I took that as approval. "Somewhere we don't normally go. You look like hell."

She grabbed my arm. "I'd resent that but I know it's true." She massaged her temples with her fingertips. "Can we just go to your house? I don't want to run into anybody.

People either want to ask questions or tell me they're certain I'm not a killer. It doesn't occur to them that when they feel the need to give me their assurance it's completely terrifying for me. And they know details, certainly more than I want to relive. How does everybody know everything right away?"

"You know that's life in a small town."

"Isn't it the truth?" She stopped. "I'll follow you. I need to come back here later to check on a patient."

"You're exhausted. Can't someone else do it?"

Her face crumpled. "Who? This is exactly the kind of thing Brian was so good at. How will I ever replace him?"

I opened the car door. "Get in. I'll drop you off later."

"You don't need to do that."

"It isn't far, and I don't want you here at night alone. At least not for a while." What I meant was, not until the killer was caught, and we both knew it.

She nodded. "Thanks, I know I'll appreciate the offer later."

As we pulled out of the parking lot, I contemplated exactly what we'd be having for dinner. I wasn't the cook in my house; Hayley did most of the kitchen stuff, and I was glad my niece enjoyed it. I called home, and she answered on the first ring.

"What did you and Connor fight about?"

"Why, what did he say?"

"He didn't have to say anything," she said. "He's been stomping all over the place, muttering how stubborn you are."

I rolled my neck to relieve the tension. "We had a bit of a disagreement. I'll tell you about it later. Annie's coming home with me for a glass of wine, and maybe a bite."

"Better than going out and having people stare at her, or worse, asking her a bunch of questions."

"Exactly right." A thought occurred to me. "You aren't seeing Lucas tonight, are you?" Annie tensed next to me. "Not that it matters if you are..."

Hayley finished the thought. "Just not here while Annie's over. I get it. I don't think seeing the officer running Brian's murder investigation would have the calming effect you want."

"Something like that."

"Not to worry," Hayley said. "He's working."

On what, I wondered. "So, it will just be us. Perfect. Do we have anything to eat?"

"Nope. We've been busy all afternoon in the tasting room. I can pick up Fiore's if you want."

"Sure. We'll see you soon."

I glanced at Annie. She rested her head on the seat back, her eyes closed. "When you're ready, I can tell you about my visit with Nicole."

Annie opened her eyes. "Don't keep me in suspense. How was it?"

"She's a mess and her house is a mess."

"Was she alone?"

"Yes, just her and a chocolate cake."

"Wait." Annie raised her head. "She was eating chocolate cake?"

"It was pretty much completely gone."

"An entire cake? Nicole? How did she seem?"

"Full. Lethargic."

Annie shook her head. "If she isn't the killer, maybe spending a couple of nights in jail and being forced to clean up will be a turning point for her."

I had my doubts. She hadn't seen Nicole. Annie was once again resting her head with her eyes closed. "You going to make it through dinner?"

"In spite of my appearance, I will rally."

"Of course you will." I pulled into the winery and parked in front of the house. "One more family trait we share."

There were several cars in the parking lot. Tastings are by appointment, but it isn't unusual for several couples to book at the same time. I was glad Connor would be busy with them and I could delay any talk he might want to have.

We headed outside to the wooden deck, and I opened a bottle of pinot gris. Annie sprawled on a lounger, and I sat on the steps leading into the vineyards. I had my camera and was toying with close-ups of the tasting room. Only one car remained. I focused my lens on it. New BMW. Tan.

"I'm going to make it through dinner." Annie rubbed her bloodshot eyes. "But barely. I could fall asleep right here, and I still have to go back to the clinic."

I poured her untouched glass of wine into mine, and she shot me a look. "What?" I said. "I'm going to make you an espresso."

"You were never one to waste." She yawned.

"One espresso coming up. Look at it this way: your first

day back to work is behind you. Eat a little something, and you'll feel better."

"You're right," Annie said. "The worst is over. It's only going to get better."

I looked over her shoulder at the path leading from the tasting room and tried to keep my voice calm. "It absolutely is going to get better, I promise you, but I'm not sure it's going to get better right *now*."

Chapter 14

She looked behind her. Connor and Jason were walking toward us, and she let out a moan. "You didn't say Jason was going to be here!"

"I didn't know! Don't you think I would have at least told you to comb your hair and get the mascara streaks off your face?"

"I have mascara streaks?" She wiped under her eyes, pinched her cheeks, and ran her hands through her tangled locks before swinging her legs to the floor.

"Don't forget Jason's still a suspect in Brian's murder," I said.

"How likely is it a successful pharmaceutical entrepreneur is also a murderer?"

More likely than Annie knew, but I hadn't had a chance to tell her that Amerigen stock was plummeting, or that Brian had tried to pull out of the deal. That information would need to wait until later, though. Jason and Connor stepped onto the deck.

"Hi, Annie," Jason said. "I hope it wasn't too difficult to

be back at work today." His direct approach was refreshing, and I saw Annie's shoulders relax.

"Good to see you again, Jason," I said. His face clouded as he recalled our last meeting, then he gestured toward Connor.

"We just had a few things to go over for tomorrow's event," Jason said.

"Hum, sure. Tomorrow." I was at a loss, and Connor came to my rescue.

"I haven't had a chance to fill Penny in. Tomorrow Jason is holding a luncheon at Sterling for the press and the medical community to launch Eric's vaccination."

"This is the first of several we're doing across the country," Jason said. "We're expecting a good turnout for this first one. You'd be surprised how many doctors and medical specialists live in Cypress Cove and the Pebble Beach area. Really the entire Monterey Peninsula."

Considering home values, I wasn't at all surprised. If my aunt hadn't bought the winery fifty years ago, I certainly couldn't afford to live here.

"Jason's also asked us to supply the wine for all of these events across the country." Connor raised a brow and the message was clear: group events are easy to ship to, very cost effective, and gave us great exposure to a lot of customers at once. This was good business, and I needed to behave.

"That's fantastic," I said, with as much enthusiasm as I could. We needed the business, but if Jason thought it would be enough to keep me from viewing him as a murder suspect, he was wrong. What if his order was an effort to distract me?

Was he trying to buy my silence?

Hayley arrived with the food, and Jason turned to leave. "I should get going."

"Why don't you stay," Connor said. I tried to wave him off, but he was still thinking of the order Jason had placed. "It looks like there's plenty."

Hayley started opening bags. "I ordered family style. We won't run out, I promise you."

"Well, then." Jason looked at Annie. "Sure, that sounds nice." He grabbed a seat next to Annie, who was now into her second espresso. I'd wanted to talk to him about Amerigen stock and the article I'd seen. Now seemed as good a time as any.

"So, this event at Sterling," I said. "It's for the press and medical community?" At Jason's nod, I continued. "Are investors going to be attending as well, because"—I cocked my head to one side and wore what I hoped was a quizzical look on my face—"I happened to see in the newspaper that a good number of investors are backing out." It got quiet, but I took a deep breath and plunged in the rest of the way. "I believe when I saw you at the hotel you were reading the same article. Sounds like Brian wasn't the only investor having second thoughts."

Jason's fingers tightened on his glass. "I will say that Brian did try and cancel his investment, but I'm afraid, the situation being what it was, that it wasn't in my control."

"You mean because he died, he couldn't cancel his order?"

So much for tact. Jason took his time answering. "There

were some final papers that would have allowed Brian to cancel the order, that no, given his death, he didn't get to sign." With that behind him, Jason continued with more confidence. "In the long run, though, Brian...Claire, now, as his heir, will do very well. Ultimately the investment will pay off handsomely."

"Still, it is curious, why he wanted out," I said. "You told me before it seemed like Brian needed the money."

Jason smiled briefly, but the lines around his mouth were tense. "I didn't ask if he needed it, or what he needed it for. Really, it was none of *my* business..." The implication being that it wasn't any of mine, either.

We ate in awkward silence until Jason asked Connor several questions regarding the winery. I let the conversation move around me. Brian hadn't wanted to invest in Amerigen. Jason got the impression that Brian needed the money, but according to Claire, Brian came from a wealthy family. He was also a successful veterinarian, and his wife was a doctor. He tried to cancel the investment and turns up dead. I studied Jason. It was hard to imagine him as a killer, but killers never looked the part, at least the ones I've met.

Jason left shortly after dinner. His farewell to me was short, but I suppose that was to be expected. We watched him drive away as Connor returned to the winery without looking at me, Hayley following close behind.

"And here I was, worried about how I look." Annie patted my arm. "I'm joking. Sort of."

"I wasn't particularly subtle, was I?"

"Let's just say I doubt he'll want to double date." Annie smiled. "You basically accused him of murder."

"Jason had a motive. Brian dies, and he can't cancel his investment."

"Why don't we go over everything," she said. "Talk it through and maybe find something we haven't thought of yet."

"Sure." I pulled open the glass doors to the house.

She held up her hand. "Connor disappeared pretty quickly." I closed the slider. "I noticed you weren't saying much to each other at dinner. Why don't we ask him to join us?"

"Because he wants me to stay out of Brian's murder. He thinks Lucas has it under control and the police will figure it out without my help."

She smiled. "I'm not sure 'help' is how Lucas would describe your meddling, but I'm grateful for it." She grabbed my arm. "Let's go find Connor. See if we can make this right."

We walked to the tasting room, where Connor was going over orders. He looked up when we came in. "I would imagine after you made it clear he's a murder suspect, Jason is less inclined to give us the order for his company events." He clipped the words off and his face was stern, but he didn't look angry. If anything, he looked concerned.

"Can we sit down and go over the reasons someone might have wanted Brian dead?" I asked. "Annie would like for you to join us." His brow went up. "I wouldn't mind, either."

He stepped behind the bar and pointed at two of the stools. "Can I get you something?"

"Sure, I'll take another espresso," Annie said. "I'm not usually a coffee drinker, but those are pretty tasty."

I plopped down on my stool and waited for her to get settled, then pointed behind the counter. "Grab that wine list and a pen."

Connor handed them to me, then leaned against the back counter.

"Okay." I said. "Suspects and motives." I paused for a moment, then wrote Dot's name.

"Wait a minute," Annie said. "I thought we decided Dot is innocent. She was at the clinic that night because her memory's going and it was taking her longer to get her work finished."

I moved my hand from side to side. "I'm not so sure anymore. I saw her rattle off a patient's file number this afternoon. Ten digits without missing a beat. And later she was downtown at Martin and Martin Jewelers. I don't know what she bought. I was outside. Behind a tree, actually." I snuck a peek at Connor, but his face didn't offer any clues to what he was thinking. "I sent Antonia in to see what Dot was buying, but she was too late. Either way, Dot can't afford anything in there on a receptionist's, or even a bookkeeper's, salary." I wrote *embezzlement* next to Dot's name.

Annie sighed, then nodded. "All right, we leave her on the list. For now." She pressed her hands together. "Let's get to someone much easier to see in the position of murderer."

We each said one word in unison: "Nicole."

"That's an easy one," I said. "She could have arrived before us. Sure, she might have come to collect her last check, but she gets there, she's out of pills, and she realizes she has an opportunity for one last fix."

Annie picked up where I left off. "She knows Dot's in the back but also knows she wears headphones and listens to music when she works. Nicole goes for the drug cabinet, and Brian surprises her. She panics and stabs him."

Connor shook his head, the first sign he'd been listening. "Doesn't work. She didn't have keys for the cabinet. I'm assuming you keep it locked?" Annie nodded, and Connor continued, "Did she have a key, or was the cabinet broken into?"

Annie closed her eyes against the memory. "No, everything was how it normally is, other than Brian."

I touched her arm as she remembered that night. "Maybe she'd just arrived and didn't have time to pry it open before Brian surprised her," I said. I wrote Nicole's name and the word *drugs* next to it.

"Then there's Eric," I said. "I saw him today at the clinic. He's pretty sure of himself, but he doesn't have an alibi for the night of the murder. Said he was filming bats down at Cliff Point when it happened."

Connor shook his head. "At best, he had opportunity because his offices are at the clinic, but I can't see a motive."

"Eric's been in love with Claire for years," Annie said. "Nobody really talks about it, but we all knew. It bothered Brian on occasion, even though he didn't have anything to worry about. Claire thinks Eric's a pompous ass. She always has."

"I asked him about grabbing Claire's arm during the ugly dog contest."

"What was his excuse?" Connor asked.

"He said he was propositioning her, that he didn't have time for a relationship, but if she wanted to have a little fun, he was her guy."

"Ugh," Annie said. "Obviously she said no."

"True, but he wasn't embarrassed about trying." I tapped the pen against the counter. "Still, if Eric thought he might have a shot with Claire, and if Brian was out of the way, there's your motive." I wrote *in love with Claire* next to Eric's name. "Who's next?"

Connor raised a brow. "I'm assuming by the way you were questioning him earlier, Jason is going on that list of yours."

I tipped my head. "As a matter of fact, he is." I wrote Jason's name with a flourish. "It's obvious what his motive is. If Jason wouldn't give Brian his investment back, maybe they fought and it got ugly. I timed the trip from Jason's hotel to the clinic. It was just a few minutes, easy to do at night." I shook the pen at Connor. "And we can't be bought off with an order. How much wine are we talking about him buying, anyway?"

"About 300 cases."

I winced. "That much? Huh." I gave a little shake. "Who's next?"

"Really, the only other person I can think of is Claire,"

Annie said. "And I can't honestly believe she had anything to do with it." She popped up from her stool and paced behind me. Any sign of her earlier fatigue had vanished in direct proportion to her caffeine intake, and now she ran her hands through her hair until it was standing straight up. "Of course, I can't see *anyone* I know being capable of murder."

"That's because you're too trusting," I said. "Believe me, this kind of thing happens all the time, and it's often the spouse." I wrote Claire's name. "She has a gambling addiction, and it's bad. Bad enough for Brian to take her off all of their joint accounts."

Annie shook her head. "When you asked her about it, she swore she was staying away from the casino."

"She also said she was glad Brian canceled all their joint accounts," I said. "What else was she going to tell me?"

Annie shook her head. "I just can't believe it."

"Here's the deal," I said. "It was either someone who had a key or someone Brian knew and let in, because the lock wasn't forced. It was either someone on this list, or it was you." She stopped shaking her head and stared at me. I hated to scare her, but she needed to know someone close to her was a killer. "Was it you, Annie?"

"No." Her voice was soft.

"I know it wasn't, which means"—I picked up the list—"that it *was* one of these people here. Like it or not, someone you know, someone we both know, is a killer."

Annie took a deep breath and pursed her lips, letting the air slowly escape. "Okay, what do we do now?"

"We build on the newest information we've found out."

"You'll be quizzing Dot on her shopping excursion at Martin and Martin Jewelers," Connor chimed in.

"I wasn't sure you were still listening," I said.

He crossed his arms. "If you can't beat them, or talk them out of meddling…well, you know the rest." There was the faintest hint of humor in his voice, and I smiled.

"I do want to hear what Dot has to say, but first I'm interested in talking to Claire again," I said. "Brian wanted to pull out of the Amerigen investment, even though as a veterinarian he must have realized what a good opportunity it was. For some reason, he needed a large amount of money. His wife has a gambling addiction. I'm willing to bet there's a connection." I stifled a yawn. "Come on, Annie, I'll bring you back to the clinic."

Connor straightened. "Why are you going back there tonight?"

Annie shrugged. "I have a diagnosis coming in that I want to check. I won't be there five minutes."

"And I'll be waiting for her," I said.

"Sure, that makes me feel much better," Connor said. "I think I should follow you, or better yet, why don't you let me take her?"

"Stop, we'll be fine," I said. "You heard Annie. Five minutes."

The short drive back to the clinic was punctuated by Annie rattling nonstop. I think it was about the suspects, but I wasn't listening, a fact that finally came to Annie's attention.

"You aren't paying attention to me."

"Well, first of all, you've had way too much caffeine, and I'm too tired to keep up."

She thought for a moment. "First of all? Is there a second reason why you weren't listening?"

I nodded. "I think we're being followed."

Chapter 15

Annie shot around, the car's lights illuminating her face. "How long have they been there?"

"Since we left the house, and they're getting closer." I pulled at her arm. "Stop looking, they'll see you!"

"If they get any closer, they'll be seeing me from the back seat," Annie said.

I stomped on the gas but quickly realized it wasn't making a difference. They were shutting down the distance between us. I felt a rush of fear, quickly followed by a shot of anger, and once again I sped up, pushing the car around a curve. I knew there was a shoulder ahead. When we reached it, I slammed on the brakes and pulled to the far right.

"What are you doing?" Annie said. "They'll catch us!"

"We can't outrun them, and there's nowhere to hide," I said. The car came around the corner. "Either they pass us, or we've shown them we're on to them."

"Oh, sure, we'll show them."

In an instant, the driver saw what we'd done, slammed on the brakes, and pulled in behind us.

"Now what?"

I clicked open my door. "When I say go…" The car was filled with a blue glow, and then the glare of a spotlight.

"Stay in the vehicle," a voice called.

"I don't believe it," I said. "It's the police."

We sat there and waited for what felt like ages. Finally, the door opened and an officer stepped from the car and walked toward us. Moments later, he leaned against my door, his face level with mine. I rolled down the window.

"You must be Penny."

I thought I knew everyone on the force, but this one, a kid really, was new to me. He was a little on the chunky side, and his breath was quick and shallow, like this was a big deal for him. His hand rested on his gun, and the last thing I wanted to do was make him nervous. He kept darting quick glances at Annie.

"What can I do for you, Officer?" I asked.

"Where are you off to tonight?" he asked. I wasn't sure it was really any of his concern but decided to keep that to myself.

"I'm just dropping my friend off at her clinic."

"Right. The vet clinic. Her car's there."

"That's right," Annie said, leaning over me.

He shifted his head to get a look at Annie. "Evening, Dr. Moore."

Annie frowned. "I don't believe we've met, but yes, I'm Annie Moore."

"Wait a minute," I said. "If you've never met, but you know who she is, *and* that her car is at the clinic, you've been keeping an eye on us. In fact, you must have been following us since we left her clinic." I felt my voice rising. "Did Lucas tell you to keep an eye on Annie?"

My casual mention of the police chief's name gave the young officer pause, and I pressed, "I bet he did. In fact, I bet he also said to be discreet and not let us know you were keeping an eye on her."

He frowned. "I could give you a ticket. You took that curve just now at a high rate of speed. I've got you on radar if you care to see it."

"I was only speeding because you were following us!"

"That's right, and getting pretty close too, if you ask me," Annie said. "You haven't had much experience tailing anyone, have you?"

I turned to her. "Quit helping, okay?"

I collected my thoughts and turned back to the window. "We have nothing to hide. I picked her up and drove because she was exhausted from her first day back at work—"

"She doesn't seem tired." He leaned once again on the side of my car, his jacket zipper scratching my door. "She seems like a bundle of nerves."

She did. Her nails were tapping on the center console and one tiny foot was shaking like crazy. I dismissed her with a wave of my hand. "She's had three espressos. She's fine."

He sighed, tapping his ticket pad against my door. Finally, he slapped it against his palm and straightened.

"Okay, I'm telling the chief you just went back to the clinic to pick up her car and then you're both going home. Is that it?"

"I have one test to check on while I'm there," Annie said.

"But you aren't doing anything else tonight, right?"

"No. We covered this," I said. "You act like I'm hiding something."

"The chief said…"

"What?" I felt my face flush. "What did Lucas say?"

"Only that you were prone to getting into…" He paused. "Situations."

"Well." My chin rose a notch. "I'm not sure that's true, but I won't argue the point. Are we through here?"

He tipped his head, leaning over to include Annie in his gaze. "You two have a good night."

We sat there until he returned to his car. Moments later, he drove past us, giving us a final once-over as he continued up the road.

"I can't believe the police are watching me," Annie said.

"They're just looking for some break in the case, although I don't know what they expect to find by following us." I didn't say it, but it wasn't a good sign that Lucas was spending manpower watching Annie.

Lost in our own thoughts, we finished the drive in silence. When we reached the clinic, I parked near the front and Annie jumped out. "It will take me two minutes to grab the test results. You can go."

"Not a chance." We had been in this exact situation— me waiting for her in the car—the night she'd found Brian. "Want me to come with you?"

She knew what I'd been thinking. "Thanks, but I can't be frightened away from my own business. I won't be."

I nodded. "Go on, then. I'll be here."

Annie crossed the porch and disappeared inside while I turned off the engine. Expecting silence, the echo of someone running immediately caught my attention. I stuck my head out the open window and listened. The footsteps were fading, pulling away from me and back out the parking entrance. Moments later a car started and pulled away, the sound vanishing into the stillness. Odd. I stepped out of the car. It was dark, but nothing looked out of place. Nothing, that is, but Nicole's car. When I'd gone through it, I'd left it as I found it, the windows down, the doors unlocked. Now, I wondered if someone was trying to steal it. Cypress Cove is a safe town, but an expensive car, left for several days with the windows open, would eventually attract attention.

The front door to the clinic slammed, and Annie joined me in the lot.

"I just heard someone running. They had a car somewhere." I paused. "I think they came from Nicole's car." I took a few steps forward.

"This does *not* feel like a good idea," Annie said.

"Just a quick look." I pulled her forward by the arm. "They must have been parked out on the street. I didn't see anyone when we pulled in."

Annie shook her head. "I didn't either."

"Come on."

Annie groaned and tucked in behind me. The walk across the lot seemed to take forever, mostly because Annie had a grip on my arm like a vice and was dragging her feet.

"Do you have a flashlight?" I asked.

"Of course not. I have the app on my phone, but it isn't charged."

The moon was blocked by trees, leaving barely enough light to show the soft outline of the car. I got a few feet away from it and stopped. Something was different.

"Hold on," I whispered over my shoulder. "Something's wrong."

"Of course something's wrong. We shouldn't be here."

"No, that's not it."

"I'm pretty sure it is."

I moved around the car. "The passenger door's open. There *was* someone here."

"Just as long as they aren't here now."

I reached in and blindly ran my hand over the seat. It was empty.

"What?"

"I left all of Nicole's junk here, on the front seat. Why move it all back to the rear seat?"

"Are you sure it's there at all? I can't see anything."

"Hang on." I got in the car. "Let me turn on the light." I poked around above my head and found the switch. "Here we go."

"Okay, we know someone was here because the door was left open and Nicole's things were moved. Can we go now?"

I didn't answer her. My mouth was dry and my heart was somewhere up in my throat.

"Did you hear me?" Annie shifted from foot to foot.

"We need to call Lucas." It came out as a whisper, and Annie leaned into the car. When her face drained of color, I knew I hadn't imagined it. I forced myself to turn and look again at the driver's seat. Her head rested against the door, and she was dressed in a skintight teal dress. Nicole might have been sleeping, if it weren't for the dark bruising around her wrist and the needle in her arm.

"Five minutes. You were here for five minutes and you find a body." Lucas shook his head. "That must be a record, even for you."

"If I'd known what was coming, I'd have let your deputy tag along. Then *he* could have found her." I kept the words short and crisp, breathing in through my nose and out my mouth. It's supposed to be calming. It wasn't working. I felt cold and clammy, and my hands wouldn't stop trembling. "Come to think of it, if you hadn't had him following Annie tonight, wasting his time, he might have prevented this from happening." That wasn't necessarily accurate, and Lucas gave me a sharp look.

"Are you planning on telling me how to assign my deputies? Because I'd rethink it if you are." He moved closer. "Might I also point out that Annie is off the hook for this murder, if it is a murder, precisely because she was with you, an alibi that can be corroborated by my deputy. If she didn't kill Nicole, she's much less likely to have killed Brian."

At that, I did manage a swift sigh of relief. Annie sat in a squad car a short distance away, watched by the same deputy who had stopped us earlier. "Does she know yet?"

Lucas held up his hand. "I'm not saying she's completely in the clear, but this helps get her there."

Across the lot, the coroner loaded Nicole's body into the van. I swallowed and looked away.

"When was the last time you saw Nicole alive?" Lucas asked.

"Well," I stalled. "It was this morning, actually."

Lucas made notes. "And where was this?"

"Um, at her house."

He looked up. "You were at Nicole's house. This morning."

"Well, yeah," I said. "She hadn't picked up her last check, and I knew she couldn't drive here to get it…" I gestured to her car. "So I offered to deliver it."

"Just to be helpful, I'm sure." Lucas raised a brow. "How did she seem when you saw her last?"

"She was vague and eating a chocolate cake, an entire one from what I could make out." I closed my eyes, picturing Nicole as she was now. "Her hair was done since this morning, and she had on different clothes. She cleaned herself up."

"I wonder how she got here."

"She might have been driven. Someone else was here."

"How do you know?"

"I heard someone running out of the lot right after we got here, and a car started somewhere up the road."

"Were you planning on telling me this?" Lucas raised a brow.

"I would have. There's a lot going on."

Lucas ignored my comment. "Is there anything else you want to share with me?"

Right. "Well, there is one more thing. It's her car."

Lucas narrowed his gaze and lowered his voice. "What about her car?"

I pinched between my eyes, trying to decide how to proceed. The silence stretched. Finally, I just blurted it out. "The thing is, I went through it yesterday. Her car, I mean."

Lucas dragged his hand across his chin, weighing out his response. "You disturbed the scene of a crime. Again."

"Technically her car wasn't a crime scene until I found the body."

"You know what I mean."

"The car was just sitting there. Unlocked. I wanted to see if I could find anything, and I knew Nicole was still in jail."

"Well? Did you find anything?"

"Just a mess. A bunch of her stuff on the back seat. Personal items. Nothing incriminating."

He wrote a few more notes, then slapped his pad shut. "Okay, one last thing before you go. Let's go take a look at the car. See if you notice anything different from the last time you saw it."

The coroner was pulling out of the lot, and the car now sat empty with both doors open. Bright lights illuminated the entire area, and the items from Nicole's back seat were being pulled out one at a time.

"Give her some room," Lucas said. The officers moved away while I crouched over and scanned the back of the car.

"The other day, I moved all of this to the front seat to go through it. Someone put it back here again."

"Nicole moved everything to the back so someone could sit in the car with her," Lucas said.

"That's what I think, yes." I studied the car's interior. Both front seats were pushed forward. The back seat was covered with the same collection of shoes, makeup, and clothes. Mentally, I pushed it all aside. It took me a minute to register what was new. And there, wedged in the bottom of the driver's seat, was a shiny gold key.

Chapter 16

"That wasn't there before." I pointed to the key.

Lucas signaled one of his men and had the key brought over. It was small, as though belonging to a padlock.

"Under the front seat like that, it could have fallen out of Nicole's back pocket at some point."

I shook my head. "I can see why you'd think that. It's the conclusion someone wanted you to reach, but it wasn't there before Nicole was killed." Nicole's face flashed before my eyes, and my head started to spin.

"You look a little pale. Let's go sit in your car," Lucas said.

When I'd taken a seat and could focus, I nodded to Lucas. "Go ahead, I can answer your questions."

"So, the key wasn't there yesterday morning. You're positive."

"Lucas, I spent years as a photojournalist. All I did was look for the details. That key wasn't there when I went through that car."

Lucas shook his head. "I still can't believe you did that."

"Hey, it's a good thing I did. Otherwise you wouldn't have known the key was planted."

Lucas flipped on my overhead light and examined the key. "We'll figure out what type of lock this goes to. In the meantime, did you notice anything else?"

"She cleared the seat next to her so someone could sit down. Someone she knew and was expecting." I felt cold and hugged my arms. "She let someone in, and they killed her."

"We don't know for certain until we get a final cause of death," Lucas said. "We do know she had a drug problem. It might have been suicide."

"No way," I said.

"Why so adamant?"

"Nicole wasn't the type. She had plans." I shuddered, remembering Nicole's body. "Plus, she had marks on her wrist." I swallowed hard. "Bruises, just a few inches from where the needle was. Someone held her arm down."

Lucas considered my words. "I happen to agree with you. I don't think it was suicide, but I do think someone was going to stage it to appear that way. Looks like you interrupted them." Lucas opened my car door. "Are you okay to drive home?"

I nodded.

"Then that's what I suggest you do." Lucas stepped out of the car. "I'll make sure Annie gets home safely." He shut the door.

I started the car and lowered my window. "You do realize if it wasn't for me you'd still consider Annie the main suspect. Also, you wouldn't have known the key was planted or that Nicole had anyone else in the car with her."

Lucas stopped and turned back to me. "You were fortunate. If what you'd found out wasn't of value, I'd be taking a harder look at your meddling, trespassing, and interference. Go home."

It was quiet when I reached the house, and I made a cup of tea and curled up on the couch. Nanook pressed against my legs while Syrah settled on the pillow near my head. They always know when I'm upset. Nanook rested his big malamute head on my feet while Syrah kneaded my shoulder with her tiny cat paws. The phone rang, and all three of us jumped at the sound.

"It's me." Annie's voice sounded faint.

"Where are you?"

"At home."

"Not exactly the night we expected," I said.

"It rarely is with you. What was the plan? Just a little wine, maybe some dinner, and then I go home. Easy, right?"

"Something good came from all of this. You couldn't have killed Nicole. Lucas admitted as much. This means they'll start looking harder at other suspects."

Annie sighed, a long, full sigh. "That makes it worth it."

She hadn't gotten the close-up of Nicole that I had. I pushed down the memory and agreed.

"This should also help narrow the list of suspects in Brian's killing," she said.

"Unless there are two killers, but that's unlikely. The trick is to find out where everyone was this evening."

"So that lets Jason off," Annie said. "He was at dinner

with us, remember? You were busy accusing him of killing Brian."

"It was still early when he left. He had plenty of time to meet Nicole."

"Maybe, but I have my doubts. At least I'm not the main suspect anymore." She sighed in relief. "Now that I'm in the clear, are you going to do what Lucas and Connor want and stay away from the investigation?"

"Not likely," I said.

"I was hoping you'd say that. Whoever did this to Brian, and even Nicole, needs to pay."

"Exactly." Nicole as I'd last seen her flashed through my thoughts. As much as I disliked her behavior, she deserved better than this.

At some point, I fell asleep right there on the couch. When I woke up, I was covered with a quilt, Syrah was curled up behind my knees, and Nanook was sleeping pressed against the sofa. I struggled to move under Syrah, finally getting my feet to the floor. The sun was well into the sky, and I glanced at my watch. It was after nine. I pushed myself up off the couch and staggered to the kitchen. Hayley walked through the sliding doors as I poured a much needed cup of coffee. Black.

"Looks like you slept soundly," Hayley said.

"First time in four nights. Thanks for covering me up."

"It wasn't me. Must have been Connor."

My heart skipped a beat. The thought of Connor tucking me in got my heart beating better than coffee ever would.

Hayley took the pot from me, poured herself a cup, and leaned against the counter. She kept her eyes on her cup. "I talked to Lucas this morning."

I groaned as the memory flooded back. "He told you about Nicole."

"Oh yeah. He had a few things to say about you finding another body. Apparently, you hold the record for Monterey County, and that's including the professionals."

"He's joking, of course."

"I don't think so," Hayley said. "Regardless, you found her, and because Annie was with you when Nicole was killed, it sounds like she's off the hook for both murders."

I nodded. "Lucas told me the same thing."

She took a sip of coffee. "He's hoping that since Annie isn't really a suspect anymore, you'll leave it to him and the police to solve."

"I'm sure he is. The problem is that Annie *is* still involved. Her clinic's the site where both murders occurred, and we still don't know who's responsible or why people are dying."

"So, do you want to talk about finding Nicole?"

"In time. Just not now." I pushed at the memory. "How does today look?"

"Just the event at Sterling."

"Right, Jason's kick-off for the vaccine. Even though I grilled him about his company and his relationship with Brian, I guess he's still letting us supply the wine?"

"At least for today. The rest of the events are still up in the air." Hayley took another sip of coffee. She started to say something and then stopped.

"What?"

She paced, fingers tapping against the cup. Finally, she put the cup in the sink and turned to face me, hands on hips. "So, here's the deal. Dating a cop can be a tricky thing. You learn to tune out things you weren't supposed to hear. On the other hand, there are things that just come up during a conversation."

I caught where this was headed. "I'm sure if there is something you're about to share with me, it came up in the course of conversation, the same type of conversation you and I are having right now."

"Exactly." Hayley smiled. "For example, Lucas might be stopping into the event at Sterling today, even if it's just to say hi to me. Although"—she paused and caught my eye— "I wouldn't be surprised if there was more to his visit than that."

"Jason, Denise, and Eric will all be there."

Hayley nodded. "Claire too. She's on the acceptance list."

"How did you get that?"

"From Jason, for a head count on the wine. I would guess Claire's trying to get her life back to some sort of normal, as normal as it can be without Brian."

I was planning on seeing Claire today. This gave me an excuse. "You might need extra help pouring."

"Sure, let's go with that." Hayley grinned. "But do me a favor. If you're planning on interrogating anyone, just don't do it in front of Lucas or Connor."

"Interrogation's such a strong word." I cleared my throat.

"So, does Connor know I found Nicole last night?"

"Yes. Sorry, but when Lucas called, Connor was right there. Come to think of it, he left right after that and walked up here to the house. That must be when he covered you with the blanket."

Connor's disapproval was easier to handle than his concern, and I felt a wave of guilt. Hayley seemed to read my thoughts. "He's only worried about you."

"I know. Believe me, the last thing I expected was to find Nicole dead behind the wheel of her car." I thought back to those vacant eyes and felt my stomach flip. "Even though the police aren't looking at her as a likely suspect, Annie's still involved since both murders happened at her clinic. I just want her to be safe."

Hayley nodded. "I know that, and so does Connor. Just remember to keep yourself safe in the process."

Chapter 17

I helped Connor and Hayley carry cases of wine to the truck, keeping one eye on Connor. He didn't have a lot to say, but several times I caught him watching me. Tension framed his eyes, and his face was tight and anxious. I tried to think of a way to reassure him, but everything I came up with required some version of not looking for the killer, which was something I wasn't prepared to promise.

After they left, I showered and tugged on a simple wrap dress in sage green. I piled my curls on top of my head, pulled out black pumps from the back of my closet, and swiped on a little makeup. I'm pretty low maintenance, and twenty minutes later I walked out the door.

The spring day was exactly what we needed to kick off the growing season. Soft, warm air, deep blue skies, and no rain predicted. Within minutes, I pulled into town, taking Ocean Boulevard to Sterling Restaurant. I pulled into the drive, parked next to Connor's truck, and made my way to the front entrance. Ross had opened the restaurant doors, allowing attendees to spill out onto the front patio. I weaved through the crowd but didn't see anyone I knew, eventually reaching the bar where Ross had his hands full with tourists. He waved and squeezed past his bartender, coming out to give me a hug. As tall as I am, he still towers over me, his flamboyant pink dress shirt somehow working with a pale green tie.

"I heard about Nicole," he said. "Although I can't believe I had to hear it from someone else. Why didn't you call me?"

"It was just last night," I mumbled into his shoulder. "Who else knows?"

"In this town?" He raised his brows. "Who doesn't?" He studied my face. "Pretty grim?"

My mouth went dry. "I don't want to talk about it."

"I have just the thing."

He cleared a path to the bar, pulling out the one empty stool. "Sit here. I'll be right back." Moments later, he was by my side, holding a cupcake. Vanilla. My favorite.

"If this doesn't make you feel better, nothing will."

Something about this simple gesture crumbled my resolve. I sat there surrounded by tourists, eating cupcake and feeling sorry for myself, until I felt a hand on my shoulder.

"What are you doing?" Connor had a soft look in his eyes, and he kept his hand on me.

I held out the empty plate. "Cupcake."

"Feel better?"

I nodded. I did, actually. "How did you know I was in here?"

Connor cast a side glance at Ross, who was back behind

the counter washing glasses and studiously avoiding looking at me. "I see. In case the cupcake didn't work, you needed a backup plan?"

"I can't have you bringing down my customers."

I slid off the stool. "Come on. Let's go serve some wine." I pushed at Connor, but he didn't move. His chest felt really nice under my palm, and I let it linger there. "Seriously, I know you're busy. I'll be fine."

He took my hand from his chest and held it in his, rolling his thumb across my palm. I shivered down to my toes. Our eyes met and held as I waited for his next words. "You don't need to go through this all alone. I'm here. Just let me know when you need me."

I need you, I need you, I need you. The words rumbled through my brain, but I just stood there nodding. Like a genius.

"In the meantime, try and stay out of trouble." He said it in a whisper, and with that soft smile, but his eyes held concern, and for once I couldn't take offense.

I followed him through the bar and into the large room that Ross reserved for special events. A video screen was set up, with "Amerigen" splashed across it. Eric stood in front of the screen on a low platform stage, talking to a crowd that knew what immunoglobulin and neurotransmitters actually meant. I listened for a moment, then slowly glazed over. I scanned the crowd and spotted Denise in the back. In a floor-length navy satin dress, complete with a crystal necklace and matching earrings, she seemed overdressed for the occasion. Although she was leaning against the wall, she hardly looked relaxed. Arms crossed, she drummed her fingers against sturdy biceps, her foot tapping away. She looked like a woman with a gripe, and I was more than ready to listen. I slipped through the crowd.

"Hi, Denise. You look lovely. Are you getting ready to join Eric on stage?"

The drumming stopped. "Why would you think that?"

"Well, your dress. It just makes sense you would be presenting as well." I decided to push a bit. "Didn't you tell me it's a joint project?"

Her face crumpled, and her shoulders dropped. "I thought if I kept saying it, somehow it would happen. I've been kidding myself."

She stopped, pulling off an earring. "Go on," I prompted, when the silence lengthened.

"What else is there to say? The terrible pay, long hours, impossible working conditions." She ran her hands through short, no-nonsense hair. "I put up with it because he said we'd share equally in the credit. Even today, I expected a place in the spotlight. What a fool I've been." She watched Eric, her face tightening. "I thought we were going somewhere, you know?" She wanted a response, and I gave a small nod. "Together. None of it was true. Now I just want to grab him by that stupid ponytail and…"

I held my breath waiting for Denise to continue, but she stopped at the sound of applause. Eric stepped from the stage as the audience continued to clap and offer congratulations. While I hadn't understood anything he'd said, it appeared most of the room did, and the applause was heartfelt.

"I'm not staying to watch this. He can have the spotlight, and he can have it alone." Denise pushed up from the wall. "He won't get away with it, though."

"What do you mean?"

"Amerigen might be buying the vaccine from Eric, but I have my research notes, and my memory, which is excellent."

"You're looking to sell information."

Denise shrugged. "Anything's possible."

"Wait a minute," I said. "The night Brian was killed, you said you were in San Francisco. You acted strange when you said it. Were you meeting with a rival drug company?"

Denise gave a flick of her head. "Perhaps. I didn't sign a non-disclosure. I need a job, and I need to worry about my future. I'll do what I have to."

"And that might be taking a job in San Francisco?"

"Or elsewhere. I'm not locked into this town. I'll leave as soon as the right opportunity comes along."

So she wasn't going to be around for long. "I just have one last question. How well did you know Nicole?"

Denise frowned. "Hardly at all. I would see her on occasion at the clinic." She shook her head. "I know about her murder, and if you're wondering where I was last night, I was back in San Francisco. If they want, the police can check my phone records."

As I processed this, Denise turned and, without a backward glance, strode from the room. Eric watched her departure, but his face remained neutral. When the door closed behind her, he gave a slight shrug and walked over to

Jason. If I was going to talk to them, now was the time. I darted across the room before anyone could join them, although I didn't receive the warmest welcome. When Jason spotted me, his jawline hardened. Although he was still the same good-looking man, his eyes were red and it looked like he'd forgotten to shave.

"Hello, Penny," he said, without any warmth. I guess I couldn't blame him. The last time we'd spoken I had basically accused him of murder. It was clear he remembered our last encounter. "Just let me know if you're going to accuse me of killing Nicole as well as Brian. I'll need another drink for that."

"I know you and Nicole were…close, for a time," I said. "I'm sorry."

He took a ragged breath. "She was her own worst enemy."

She'd had a bigger enemy. I'd seen the aftermath, but I kept those thoughts to myself. "The police will be asking everyone who knew Nicole where they were last night."

Jason gave a long exhale. "The police, or you?" When I didn't answer, he shrugged. "After I left your place, I took the long way up the coast and then returned to my hotel." I stiffened. The route took him right past the clinic.

Jason nodded, as though reading my thoughts. "That's right. I was alone, without an alibi, and likely nobody saw me until I reached the hotel."

Eric gave a short laugh. "Well, if you're looking for alibis, you can add me to the list of those who don't have one." He reached for his top shirt pocket that held a pack of cigarettes, then his

189

hand dropped. "That's the problem with most alibis, though. If you're innocent, you never think to have a good one."

"The police will decide what to make of everyone's alibis."

"Well, I was in San Francisco, although I can't prove it."

"Wait a minute," I said. "You were in the city last night?"

"Yes, but I don't have any witnesses."

My guess was that he'd followed Denise. Did he also know she was trying to sell the vaccine?

"So, you went to the city and didn't stop or see anyone. Is that what you're saying?"

He shrugged. "Hey, I wanted to go for a drive. It isn't a crime."

No, but it was unusual, and I'm sure Lucas would want to know about it. The silence lengthened, and Eric turned a shoulder to me. I was dismissed. Most folks would have cut it short at that point. On the other hand, how much more uncomfortable could it get?

I circled around so I was facing him. "At least you had a good turnout today." Eric gave a brief nod, tugging on that ponytail of his. He wasn't going to make this easy. "I spoke with Denise for a few minutes. Before she left." A waiter passed with a tray of champagne, and Eric grabbed a glass. "She seemed disappointed not to be with you for the presentation." At that, he focused on me over his glass.

"As I've mentioned to you before, I never viewed Denise as anything but a research assistant. If she felt differently, that has nothing to do with me." He finished his glass. "Nothing."

I turned to Jason. "So, this is the first of these presentations?"

Jason nodded. "I'm leaving next week for a ten-city tour."

"I assume you're going too, Eric? I bet you're excited to introduce your vaccine to the world."

Eric shook his head. "No, that's not my job. I'm leaving that to Jason."

That surprised me. He denied Denise the chance to shine, and Claire had said that Eric was "full of himself." I continued. "It seems like the launch parties would be something you'd enjoy, Eric."

"I'm much too busy." He stuck out his chest a bit. "My work will continue to come first. As a matter of fact, I'm also leaving next week."

"Where are you off to?"

"I'm back to South America," he said. "Most of the best field work on rabies is done there."

I nodded, but was having a brain freeze. Denise, Eric, and Jason would be leaving town soon, making it harder for the police to solve the murders.

My thoughts were interrupted by a voice right next to me. "What's that? You're heading to South America?"

Claire was standing there. Her shiny, dark bob was perfect, and, although she was pale, her makeup was flawless, the bright pink lipstick framing a smile only slightly forced. She didn't look like a woman who had just lost her husband, and I wasn't the only one surprised to see her.

"Great to see you, Claire," Jason said. "I wasn't sure you'd make it."

"Brian would have wanted me to come. Besides, we Brits have stiff upper lips." She tried a small laugh. "But as I was saying, you're both traveling?"

Eric had been staring at Claire and now gave himself a small shake. "That's right. Jason is traveling for the drug launch, and I'm heading to South America."

As they discussed Eric's work, I studied Claire. This was a different side of her, hardly the grieving widow I'd last seen. Her bob flipped about as she spoke, and I caught the last of the conversation. "...so you should get current vaccines, and you"—she turned to Jason—"you owe me lunch and a synopsis of this company of yours that I now find myself owning stock in."

Jason gave the smallest of nods. "Absolutely, Claire. In the meantime, we have a roomful of investors who wish to offer their congratulations. Coming, Eric?" Eric nodded, his eyes still on Claire, and they walked away.

"Claire, can we talk for a few minutes? Outside?" I asked.

"Of course."

We worked our way through the restaurant and onto the front patio, where I came right to the point.

"Claire, did you know that Brian tried to cancel his Amerigen stock investment?"

She caught her breath. "Yes. How do you know about that?"

"Jason told me. Brian wanted to cancel his order, but Jason said it was too late. That's the only reason you own the stock at all."

"I thought it was something like that. That's why I'm

here. I heard Brian talking to Jason on the phone."

"When was this?"

"The morning Brian was killed. When he hung up, he was upset but wouldn't tell me why." Her eyes teared up, and she swiped at them with a tissue from her bag. "I knew Brian was looking for money."

I touched her arm, and she didn't pull away. I'm not sure she even noticed. "Why did Brian want to cancel his investment?" She didn't answer. "Claire, did Brian need the cash?"

Tears rolled down her cheeks, unnoticed. She heaved a sob, and I pulled her around the corner. "This is more private," I said, digging through my own cluttered purse. Of course I didn't find tissues, but I found mints. "Want one?" She shook her head and wiped away tears with the back of her hand. I waited until I thought she was able to speak.

"The money, Claire."

Claire avoided looking at me, keeping her eyes down. She wrung the tissue between her hands, and I leaned in to hear her whispered response.

"What I told you before was true. I started gambling and couldn't stop." Her head rose. "I haven't been back, though, and I'll never gamble again." Her voice was strong.

"Then why did he need the money?"

She paused, then shook her head as though reaching a decision. "I wasn't honest about how much I lost. The casino found out I was a doctor here in town and gave me a hundred-thousand-dollar limit." She laughed bitterly. "Just like that. They made it so easy. Did you know casinos will take on debt, just like a bank? It's so civilized when you're first borrowing. So pretty in the casino. All bright lights and nice music. And when I didn't know how to play craps, they were more than happy to teach me." Her voice dropped. "The money was gone in two days." She balled her hands into fists and buried her eyes behind them. "They aren't so civilized when you need to pay the money back."

I struggled to imagine it. "You gambled away a hundred thousand dollars?"

"It isn't hard when the nice, quiet blackjack tables in the back room are a minimum of two thousand dollars a hand."

"You couldn't pay the casino back."

"Not by that time. I'd gone through most of the cash we had in the bank, and the rest is tied up in investments with Brian's family." Her hands trembled, and she pressed them together. "He didn't want them to know what I'd done. The casino was hinting that they would be happy to make my debt public knowledge if I didn't work out payments. They said it wouldn't help my career at the hospital, and they're right."

I was tempted to believe her, but in reality she'd just strengthened her motive for killing Brian. Lack of cash wouldn't be a worry for Claire now that Brian's life insurance was coming.

"I assume you haven't paid them back yet."

She shook her head. "No. I've agreed to make payments, and they're more than happy to charge me interest."

She wiped at the last of her tears as I considered my next move. Everything she'd said might be true, but it just felt too tidy and convenient. Brian died just as Claire was in desperate need of money. If she proved innocent, I'd apologize later. For now, I forced myself to continue. "You told me the night Brian died that he'd provided well for you. Now you won't have any trouble paying off the debt."

Claire flinched as though I'd hit her. "I can't believe you'd say such a thing, Penny."

"Surely it's occurred to you. I'm sure it will occur to the police too."

"Perhaps, but I've always considered you a friend. Now, during this"—she raised both hands in the air—"the worst time in my life, you've made me wonder whose side you're on."

"I'm on the side of finding out the truth," I said. "Perhaps I haven't been polite, but until this killer is caught I'm not really worried about hurt feelings."

The tension left her face, and she sighed. "I understand, and actually I should be glad you're so determined to see this through." She dabbed once again at her eyes and wiped away her lipstick. "Brian was a good man. He was everything I ever wanted in a husband, in a friend." She managed a small smile. "You're quite right, you know. Politeness be dammed. Is there anything else you want to ask me?"

"Well, yes. I was wondering where you were last night."

"Ah, right. Nicole's murder." She raised her hands, palms up. "I was home, alone. How did she die?"

The question made me pause. It was an obvious question to ask if you didn't already know the answer, and a smart one to ask if you did. "She was given an overdose."

Claire shook her head. "It was obvious from her behavior as of late she was abusing something. How do you know she didn't accidentally overdo it?"

"I found her. It wasn't an accident." I didn't elaborate.

"I see," she said, after a pause. "Well, I must tell you, I don't have any alibi to speak of. I wish I did." She gave herself a little shake. "And now I think I'll go home." She was pale, her eyes red. "I shouldn't have come."

Chapter 18

Claire turned and walked to her car. Her gait was stiff and plodding, with none of her usual grace. When she'd gone, I stood there a moment, considering my options. There wasn't any need to go back inside. I'd learned all I could. The police station was right down the street, and on impulse I headed that way. The day was perfect, mild with a touch of the summer ahead. Shopkeepers stood outside talking with their neighbors or adding flowers to already overflowing window boxes. Small tables in side gardens held couples sharing wine, while visitors snapped photos of the downtown buildings, many of which looked like they had come straight from *The Wind in the Willows*.

I was nearly at the station when I had second thoughts. I wasn't sure Lucas would appreciate my updates. I was even less sure he'd share anything with me. As I reached the door, still considering my options, I looked to my left. The window to his office was right next to the front door, and of course he was at his desk, watching me. I toughened up and pushed through the entrance.

The desk sergeant behind the half wall started to get up, but I waved him back down and gestured to Lucas's office door. "He knows I'm here." I pulled on the latch as I heard Lucas through the closed door.

"Come on in, Penny."

I walked through the half door at the front counter and paused at the coffee station. I knew it was horrid tasting, but the caffeine sounded pretty good. It also gave me a chance to collect myself. By making Lucas wait, even momentarily, I managed to regain some of my dignity. We were on equal footing. I opened his office door.

"You know I should arrest you." So much for equal footing. "The techs found your fingerprints all over the inside of Nicole's car. I just got done explaining that one to the higher-ups."

"I had no idea when I was going through Nicole's car it would turn into a crime scene. Obviously, I would have worn gloves if I had."

"Do you even *hear* yourself sometimes?" He rubbed the palms of his hands against his cheeks. He obviously wanted to say more but instead settled on a curt inquiry.

"So, what can I do for you?"

I decided to ignore his lack of enthusiasm.

"I thought I might see you at Sterling Restaurant. Amerigen is hosting a launch for the new vaccine. Jason, Eric, and Denise were all there. Claire was there too."

"I was going over in a few minutes." He lowered his head, eyes narrowed. "What were you doing there?"

I sniffed. "I had a perfectly good excuse. Hayley may have

told you that we supplied the wine for the event."

"You were helping Hayley and Connor?"

"Well, no." I knew he'd ask Hayley if I'd actually worked. "Turns out they had everything under control. But I was there in case they needed another pair of hands."

"That means you were free to roam the room asking things you probably shouldn't be asking."

"You know, I came here because I thought you might be interested in what I've learned." I took a step back. "If you genuinely feel I'm hindering your efforts..."

"What, you'll stay out of it and let me do my job?"

"Of course not. I was just going to offer to leave."

He pressed a thumb and forefinger against his eyes. "Have a seat. Tell me what you learned."

I always sit in the same place in his office: on the sofa under the open window. I refuse to sit in front of his desk. Too much like high school. He sighed, moved to the front of his desk, and sat in the chair I'd rejected.

"Well," I said, "I spoke with all four of them—Denise, Jason, Eric, and Claire."

"What did you learn?"

I went over the conversations as Lucas sat back and listened. When I'd finished, he didn't say anything. "What?"

He shook his head. "I don't know how you manage to get people to share what they do, but it looks like some of our suspects have fairly strong motives."

"It gets worse. Three of them said they're leaving town soon."

"When, and which ones?"

"Denise as soon as possible. Eric and Jason next week. You can keep them here, right? Tell them they can't leave?"

Lucas shook his head. "It doesn't work that way, despite what you've seen on television. I can't order them to stay. All I can do is ask for their cooperation and contact information if they leave. Or I make an arrest."

"We don't have a lot of time." Lucas's brow shot up. "I meant *you* don't have a lot of time." He rested his chin on a cupped hand and let me squirm. "It stands to reason you probably want to solve the murders before anyone leaves town, and naturally *you'll* be the one solving them."

I took a breath as Lucas rocked back in his chair and laced his fingers across his lap. "Look, it's helpful to know they're leaving, right?" I said. "And what about Claire owing the casino so much money? That's quite a motive there."

Lucas straightened up. "A hundred grand. Hard to believe, but then again, I'm not much of a gambler."

"It doesn't sound like Claire is either. She appears to be full of remorse."

"Appears?"

I shrugged. "As I said, that's quite a motive. She doesn't have any money worries now, and the casino hinted it wouldn't help Claire's reputation if her gambling problem became widely known."

"They're right," Lucas said. "This is a small town with a long memory. She doesn't need press like that." He started to stand. "Anything else?"

"Well, yes." He sat back down. "We need to talk about Dot."

He turned in the chair, grabbing a file from his desk. "Go on."

I took a deep breath and slowly let it out. "Until recently, Dot was the bookkeeper for the clinic, as you know. What you don't know is that there was an issue with some money."

"What kind of issue?"

"The books weren't adding up. Dot said she's been having trouble with her memory. That's why Annie moved her to the reception desk."

"Does Annie suspect Dot of theft?"

"No. Annie knows something was wrong, but she just doesn't want to believe Dot would steal from her. Dot might have a touch of dementia…"

"But you think there's more to it than that."

I shifted. "I don't want to, but there've been a couple of things that make me wonder." I told Lucas of my suspicions. Lucas opened the file and made notes as I spoke. "Between the purchase she made at Martin and Martin Jewelers, and the way she rattled off that patient's ten-digit number, I just don't know what to think."

I waited silently as he continued to write before finally looking up at me.

"Anything else?"

"What about you?" Probably not the best choice of words. "I mean, anything you care to fill me in on?"

Lucas stared at a spot over my head, lost in thought. Finally, he nodded as though he'd come to some conclusion.

"How well do you know Dot?"

I reflected. "Well, I know she's very active in several

rescues. She's always fostering dogs, which says a lot about a person. She's worked for Annie for years." I fidgeted a bit. "Sorry, I'm just not sure what you want."

Lucas flipped through the file, reading a page toward the bottom of the stack. "Dot grew up in San Francisco. Original hippie."

I nodded. Dot's hair and colorful dresses were her signature. "She's sort of a free spirit. Not someone who keeps up on fashion or possessions. Putting aside her recent visit to Martin and Martin Jewelers, what does this have to do with the murders?"

He flipped through the file. "I don't suppose it ever came up."

"What? What didn't come up?"

Lucas looked up. "Her record."

I let out a long exhale. "Dot has a record. For what?"

"Theft. Breaking and entering."

"It can't be."

"We have it all right here. Naturally we do a background search when someone is a murder suspect. She was right there in the next room when Brian was killed. Doesn't it strike you as odd that she didn't hear anything?"

"She wears headphones and listens to music."

"You know"—he shifted in his chair, as though he hadn't heard me—"Brian might have caught her in the act. A sophisticated thief can systematically empty the accounts of a business before they're caught. If I were Annie, I'd have an audit done."

"Look, I know it doesn't sound good. The jewelers, the

police record—I can see why Dot's a suspect, but it's a big leap to believe she's capable of murder. She lives a very simple life, and most of her spare time goes to animal causes." Lucas grinned, and I stuck out my chin. "I don't care if you don't get my logic. Anyone who fosters shelter dogs just isn't a killer."

Lucas rose. "Well, if it's all the same to you, we will continue to take a good, hard look at Dot."

For the second time today, I was dismissed. This time, I didn't fight it. "Sure, no problem." As I walked back to my car, I called Annie.

"Is Dot working today?"

"No," Annie said. "It's her day off."

"Do you know where she is?"

I was short, and Annie caught it. "What's going on?"

I took a breath. "I'll explain later. Right now, I just need to talk to her."

"Try her at the shelter. She goes there most days she's free."

"I should have guessed," I said.

The shelter wasn't far from the center of town and served both Cypress Cove and Monterey. A well-designed, newer building financed mostly on donations, it was a prime example of a community pulling together for a good cause. I pulled into the lot and spotted what I was sure Dot drove: a VW bus with a Grateful Dead sticker. I parked and followed the chorus of barking through the open double doors. One wall of the reception area was glass and allowed visitors to see the play yard. Two families were sitting with dogs, considering their options.

"Please take them, please take them."

I didn't need to turn around to identify the voice. Dot walked up behind me. "They both seem like such nice families." She bit her lip. "Here, I've got someone I want you to meet."

"I just wanted to ask you a couple of quick questions." I followed her down the hall.

"Fine, fine, ask me anything, but you have time to meet Hollie."

"Let me guess," I said as we stopped at a door. "Hollie isn't your coworker."

"Do you remember the song 'Bus Stop?' A boy meets a girl at a bus stop, and he offers to share his umbrella?" She pushed open the door. I followed.

"I think it rings a bell," I said. "Wasn't that a hit ages ago?"

Dot tossed the braid over her shoulder. "The sixties. Best decade for music the world has ever seen. Anyway," she went on, bending to open the door of a bottom cage, "this is Hollie." She turned and handed me a scrap of a dog, dingy white with big brown eyes. "The Hollies were the band that recorded that song."

"Why did you name her after the band?" I asked.

Dot relocked the cage. "Because that's where we found her. At a bus stop."

"I don't understand some people." I hugged the little dog to me. "You know, I really just started thinking about getting another dog." Hollie settled into my arms.

"No time like the present. I'll leave you two alone for a

minute." Dot left, and I stood rocking Hollie. Her heartbeat slowed, those brown eyes willing me to keep her safe, and she finally relaxed. Still holding her, I retraced my steps until I found Dot in the lobby. Dot smiled. "Well?"

"She's a love." Dot waited, holding her breath. "We'll give it a try, but I think Hollie might have found her new home."

Dot smiled. "I was hoping you'd say something like that."

"We need to see how she gets along with Nanook and Syrah."

Dot nodded. "They're both rescues as well. Animals seem to know. They'll get along fine." She rubbed her palms together. "Now what did you want to ask me?"

"Is there somewhere we can sit down?" I heard the tension in my voice. Dot did too.

"Here," she said, taking Hollie from my arms and handing her to a passing volunteer. "Prep Hollie for check-out. She's going home."

Hollie looked over her shoulder at me, and that did it. "I'll be five minutes, sweetie."

Dot led me to a back office. Four desks occupied the room, but we were alone. Dot gestured to the nearest desk. "Let's sit here." She took a seat and fingered a beaded earring. "What's up?"

I took my time, wondering where to start. It was easier to press people for information when they didn't expect it. This was more of a formal interview, and I acquired a new respect for how well the police manage it. The silence stretched as I settled into the chair in front of the desk. Finally, I gave up working on my approach and just dove right in.

"So, you heard Nicole was murdered last night."

She nodded. "It's all over town. Poor lost soul." Her compassionate answer gave me pause as she continued. "I know she struggled with drugs. Are the police even certain it was murder?"

I remembered the bruises on Nicole. "There isn't any doubt."

"Oh, dear Lord." Dot covered her face in her palms. "What a terrible way to die."

"The police are talking with everyone connected to the clinic. They're going to want to know where you were last night."

"Well, I'll be happy to tell them I was here until late. Left about ten."

"Was anyone else with you?"

Dot thought for a minute, then shrugged. "I was on my own after seven."

"Are there security cameras?"

"Nope."

"Any other way to prove you were here?"

"Not really. We do have a security code that lets us in, but it's never been changed and doesn't record when people come and go." She gave me a smile. "I could easily leave and come back without anyone knowing."

I twisted in my seat. She wasn't understanding the trouble she could be in. "Look, Dot," I said, pulling in the chair, "the police will be talking to you. They looked up your record. Breaking and entering. Theft."

"Well of course I have a record." Dot airily waved her hand in the air. "You couldn't claim legitimacy to the cause if you weren't arrested at least once in the sixties."

"What cause?"

"Whatever one you believed in. Take your pick."

"But these are serious charges."

"The Vietnam War was dragging on. We managed to shut down a draft office for a couple weeks. It was a badge of honor at the time. Still is with a few of my crowd, the ones left."

"I'm not sure the police are going to look at it that way." Still, it did sound a little better after her explanation. I wasn't finished, though. "Dot, do you recall our conversation when you told me your memory isn't what it used to be?"

She stiffened, and her chin jutted forward. "Of course I do. I'm slowing down, but I'm not senile."

Right. "Well, I saw you yesterday morning, when I came into the clinic."

She crossed her arms. "Believe it or not, I remember that too."

This wasn't going well. "You told me that your memory was going, but I saw you when that patient came in. You rattled off his ten-digit patient number from memory. Out of hundreds of patients."

Dot stared at me, then started laughing. "Are you kidding? That's Clyde."

"Who's Clyde?"

"A decent enough terrier mix. Little grumpy. His ears are magnets for foxtails." She leaned over the desk, still smiling. "However, his daddy is a lot more than decent. Now, he's about as attractive as a man can be. You bet I've got his number memorized. I make sure I'm front and center every time he comes in."

That made perfect sense. I've done similar things. What woman hasn't? Dot started to rise and I stopped her by raising my palm. "There's just one other thing."

Dot sighed and dropped back into the chair. "You know, I'm trying not to take this personally, Penny."

"I appreciate that, but there isn't much that's more personal than murder."

That got her attention, and she nodded. "Go ahead. Ask away."

"Yesterday afternoon I saw you downtown."

"That's twice the same day you managed to spot me. If I had anything to worry about, I'd think you were following me."

"So you were in town?"

She nodded. "I had a few errands to run."

I took a breath. "One of those errands was to make a stop at Martin and Martin Jewelers. I saw you there. Now, I'm sorry, but it just doesn't make sense that you're making expensive purchases right now. I know you're only working part time at the clinic, and now that you're a receptionist you're probably making less than you did as a bookkeeper." I paused, but she didn't answer. "I can check with Annie on your salary. How can you afford to be spending money on jewelry right now?"

"The tiger lilies!"

"What?"

"You were out in front of the store, hiding behind the bouquet of tiger lilies. I thought that was you." She shook her head. "You still think I might have been stealing from the clinic, and that maybe I killed Brian to hide embezzlement."

"It's something the police are looking at, and your record doesn't help. For what it's worth, I told them I don't believe you're capable of murder."

"I suppose that's something to be thankful for, but you would have saved yourself some trouble if you'd come into the jewelers and said hello. If you had, you would know I was just getting my watch repaired." She held up her wrist. "If the police want to check with Martin Jewelers, they can." She fingered the watch. "That's all it was. Cost me forty dollars, if you're interested."

I felt like crawling under the desk. "I had to ask, Dot. My focus is clearing Annie and finding out what happened to Brian, and now Nicole. It's probably not going to make me any friends."

She nodded and gave me a smile. Not as wide as it had been, but a smile all the same. "You aren't losing me as a friend, and since I have nothing to hide"—her smile widened—"there's no harm."

"The police will be asking you about your arrest all those years ago," I said.

She gave a small laugh. "Let them. It'll be fun to talk about the old days."

Chapter 19

I finished the paperwork and collected Hollie, holding the little dog close to me. She didn't move as I carried her to the car and sat her in the passenger seat. "You don't know it yet, but today is your lucky day."

Big brown eyes studied my face, then she curled into a ball and slept the entire way home. After a quick bath that she didn't seem to mind, I took her out onto the patio to dry. Holding her, I let Nanook and Syrah meet the newest member of the family. Nanook nudged her with his big wet nose, then waited. He seemed to realize the small dog had been through a lot and was gentle, lying beside Hollie and letting her take the lead. Syrah did what any self-respecting cat would do and ignored her.

Hayley came out a short time later and took Hollie and Nanook for a walk through the vineyard. The little dog followed Nanook down the back steps like she'd lived there for ages, passing Connor as he came onto the patio. He stopped and watched the trio disappear into the closest row of grapes.

"Who's that?" he asked, dropping next to me on the back steps.

"Hollie. I found her in the shelter."

"Cute." He stretched, reaching over his head with both arms. His blue shirt, with the sleeves rolled up to just below the elbows, showed the outline of his shoulders. I tried not to stare but wasn't very successful. Connor tipped his head toward me. "What?"

How do some women do this so easily? Chantal flirted without even being aware of it, and I didn't have a clue how to tell Conner I was interested. I studied his blue eyes, waiting for an answer, and scrambled for something to say. "Nothing, um, nothing, it's just that you look good. I mean, you got some sun today." Very smooth.

"Yes, finally some good weather." He studied me. "You look a little tired yourself."

Not what I was looking for. He leaned closer.

"You're as beautiful as ever, but you're pale. When was the last time you ate?"

He said I was beautiful. It took me a minute to answer. "That cupcake at Sterling. It doesn't surprise me that I look tired. I haven't been sleeping very well."

"It doesn't matter. You're still beautiful." He dropped one step closer to me and turned my way. A soft breeze lifted the hair off the nape of his neck. He was waiting for me. All I needed to do was meet him halfway. I inched closer. The silence stretched. I inched a little closer. Finally, his lips touched mine, soft and demanding in equal measures.

It wasn't the amount of time that had passed since my

last kiss, or my imagination—Connor knew how to kiss. Winery? What winery. Every thought flew from my head. I was completely gone. Minutes or hours passed, and it took a little heavy breathing in my ear to bring me back. Not by Connor, unfortunately. I reluctantly pulled away. Hollie was on the steps next to me, and Hayley stood at the bottom of the stairs.

"She wanted to come back. I don't think she wants to be away from you. It will take a while." Hayley surveyed the scene. Connor settled back onto the step and raised his face to the sky, the sun now low on the horizon. Hayley raised a brow. "Looks like maybe I'm interrupting something?"

"No, nothing at all," I said.

"Sure, nothing at all." Hayley walked up the steps and into the house, giving me a thumbs up behind Connor's back.

"So." Connor turned to me, resting on one elbow. "More on that when we have a little more privacy?"

"Can't wait." Great answer, but he smiled.

"In the meantime, we haven't had much of a chance to talk lately."

"I know."

"I haven't pressed you, but I'm here if you need me."

I thought for a minute. My emotions were running all over the place, a mixture of excitement, confusion, and fear, all in equal measures. "You know what I really need? Someone just willing to listen." I held up a hand. "Not to fix it, not to try to talk me out of anything. Just to listen."

"No fixing. Just listening. Got it."

"So, where do I begin?"

He smiled softly. "What happened at the clinic?"

I flashed back on Nicole, her tiny body slumped in the driver's seat. My stomach did a flip, and I rubbed my damp palms together.

Connor's voice floated toward me. "Are you all right? I thought you were pale before. Now you're nearly translucent." He moved closer, placing his arm around my shoulders. "It's okay. It's going to be okay."

His calm reassurance only seemed to make me feel worse. I wasn't sure anything would ever be okay again. I pressed my fingers to my eyes, but it didn't help, and moments later the tears came. Connor just held me, letting me cry into his shoulder. I cried for ages and still he held me, letting me finally push away when I was ready.

"I guess I needed that. Thanks."

"Sure. Happy to help." He leaned in. "I will always be there to help. You just need to let me."

I smiled. "Fair enough." The sun disappeared in the distance, slipping behind a cloud layer tucked in over the Pacific. I gave a shiver as Connor stood.

"Why don't you take a hot bath and then try and eat something? I'll go help Hayley in the kitchen, and between us we can figure out something."

I stood. "No argument on the hot bath." I left him and went in through the glass doors, stopping to poke my head into the kitchen. Both dogs were in Nanook's bed, Hollie's chin resting on Nanook's side, while Syrah looked on in disgust.

"Hollie's making herself at home," Hayley said.

I nodded. "See you in a bit." I made it to the bedroom, kicking off my boots before I decided to rest for a minute. My head hit the pillow, and that's the last thing I remember.

Chapter 20

The morning kicked off with a small, wet nose working its way under the covers. I tried to straighten out but couldn't, and I opened my eyes. Syrah guarded her place on the pillow next to mine, pointedly ignoring the new intruder. Hollie ignored her right back, squirming to get closer, while Nanook stretched out along the entire foot of the bed. I looked at the clock. It was nine. I'd been asleep for twelve hours.

I pushed everyone out of the way and stood, then took a quick shower and dressed in jeans, boots, and a burgundy knit top. Piling my curly damp hair on my head in what I hoped resembled a stylish yet avant-garde bun, I headed to the kitchen to find a full pot of coffee and a note from Connor. I opened it, my heart kicking around a little in my chest.

Now that you've slept, hope you are feeling better. I had to run into town to hand-deliver a couple of cases to Sterling. They went through all the wine we brought yesterday, and most of the restaurant's. By the way, you have the cutest snore.

Hmm. I was not a snorer. I was, however, famished. I grabbed the phone and dialed Ross's number. He picked up on the second ring.

"Yesterday's party was a huge success," he said. "We're almost out of your wines and won't have enough for the dinner rush."

"I've heard. Connor's making a special delivery."

"He's here now."

"What's your breakfast special?" I don't know why I asked, since anything he made was better than what I could prepare, which was, well, nothing.

"Quiche."

"What kind?"

"Does it matter?"

"Hmm, no, not really."

"I'll be sending Connor home with some. You're welcome."

I grabbed an apple while I waited and took a few pictures of Hollie getting used to her new home. Nanook willingly shared his bed and Syrah grumbled from afar as Hollie walked every bit of the house, finally settling down on the outside deck. I joined her at the patio table with the sales book and recorded the orders for the week. Wineries are bonded cellars and don't pay taxes until the wine is removed and sold, so it was something I needed to keep up on. Thankfully it wasn't difficult, and I could manage it with a bit of simple math.

Connor arrived as I was finishing up and handed me a Sterling-To-Go bag. "Here. Ross called it a pity quiche."

"He sent me an entire quiche?"

"He said to share."

I peered in the bag. "Desserts too?"

"I know you aren't good at sharing."

I pulled out the container. "Oh man, why did you have to pick the Napoleon? You know I can't resist a cream-filled flaky crust." I grabbed a fork and dug in. "Besides, I didn't have dinner last night, and I plan on going for a hike this afternoon."

After polishing off half the dessert and a large piece of quiche, in that order, I grabbed some hiking boots and spent the next hour roaming through the vineyard. These rows of vines, with the mountains to the east and the rocky shore to the west, marked the borders of my youth. My parents were both academics who traveled a lot when I was young. It might have been a lonely childhood, but Aunt Monique had made a home for me here. Walking the vineyards now, they felt to me as they always had—a comfort and a reminder that I was lucky to have the chance to live in such a beautiful spot. The dogs plodded behind me, Hollie tripping over her feet as she followed Nanook, looking for gophers or other pests. I didn't see any signs of unwanted insects or rot, not that Connor wouldn't also spend the day looking. I stopped at the highest point in the vineyard. For now, the skies were clear and the weather warm.

It took me longer to get back than I had anticipated, partially because the dogs were calling me left and right to show me their findings, but mostly because I'm out of shape and easily winded. It was early afternoon when I kicked off my dirty boots and threw myself on the patio chaise.

The phone rang, and I reached for it.

"I think it will do us both good to have a night out." Annie picked up the conversation without preamble.

"Oh, sure, because our last night together was such a roaring success."

"That's why we need to get back out there. Erase the memory."

Nothing was going to erase the memory of Nicole, but I let that pass. "What did you have in mind?"

"The charity auction is tonight."

Held at the Marquis Hotel, the auction is an annual event that supports local organizations. Joyeux Winery had donated two cases of wine.

"I wasn't planning on going." The sun was warm on my limbs. "Frankly, I could just eat quiche and watch old movies tonight."

"Don't even think about it. This year it's for the shelter."

"I don't have anything to wear."

"Find something. You *have* to go," she wailed. "I have to go, and I need you there."

"I make regular donations, and did I mention I adopted from the shelter just yesterday?"

"Dot told me. Hollie. I can't wait to meet her, but tonight you are coming to the auction."

"Fine." I knew I'd end up going. A nice meal in a spectacular setting, with top shelf martinis. It could be worse.

"I'm going to shut my eyes for a few minutes. See you

later." I hung up, rolled over, and promptly fell asleep in the setting sun. I would have slept for hours if Hollie hadn't nudged me awake for the second time that day. I moaned, spun to the side of the chaise, and sat up just as Hayley crossed the deck. She wore a long silver dress that showed off her lithe figure.

"You look great," I said.

"Thanks. We're presenting the wine we donated at the auction."

"We?"

She nodded. "Connor is going too." Her eyes grew wide. "Speaking of Connor, what's going on there?"

"I have no idea what you're talking about." I knew exactly what she was talking about, but it was too new, and I wanted to hold it close to me for a while longer. "He was just checking in with me."

"Okay, sure, let's call it that. Anyway, Connor is going to be there tonight with me."

"As it happens, so am I. Annie talked me into it."

She eyed my outfit. "It's dressy."

"I promise I won't embarrass you."

I managed to be ready in under thirty minutes. A quick shower, a pile of curls, an extra swipe of mascara, and I was pretty much done. I even had the perfect dress, a fuchsia number I'd bought in Las Vegas and never worn. Its floaty, loose style hid ten extra pounds, easy.

I came around the corner of the kitchen and stopped dead in my tracks. Connor in a tux is something worth pausing for. Tall and broad-shouldered, his skin bronzed by a day in the sun, he stood at the desk reading the order book I'd updated earlier. It gave me a moment to gather my composure, and I forced myself to breathe.

He closed the book and turned, taking in the dress. "You look pretty."

"Thanks." I managed a little spin without hitting the desk. "You too. I mean, you look really good."

Connor raised a brow, and my cheeks got hot.

"I'm glad you're going," he said.

Suddenly I was too. "Where is Hayley?"

"She went on ahead. I'll drive." He walked to the door and held it open for me. "I brought my car."

The sleek German model was parked out front. He reached the car first and once again opened the door for me. Slipping into the seat, I felt like a princess...until the lingering scent of Chantal's perfume reached me. When he joined me in the car, I wrinkled my nose. "That fragrance of hers really permeates hard surfaces, doesn't it?"

He grimaced. "I can't get rid of it. She was in here days ago. I've been driving around with the windows down ever since."

It was nice to be with him, feeling pretty and having a little laugh at Chantal's expense. I felt my shoulders relax, the tension easing in my chest for the first time in days.

We rode in comfortable silence, pulling into the hotel's circular drive a short time later. Connor left the keys in the ignition as the valet opened the door for me. I floated up the steps to the lobby. "I should get dressed up more often." I twirled, nearly taking out a Bellhop. "This is fun."

The hotel lobby was softly lit, the same musician once again playing the piano. Classical music drifted through air scented by oversized vases of gladiolas placed on gleaming mahogany tables. A buzz of activity rose from the terrace across the lobby, and I spotted Dot seated at the entrance.

"Looks like we're in the right place," Connor said when we walked up. Dot had her usual braid, but she'd wrapped it into a bun on the top of her head. She wore a purple jersey dress that hugged her ample curves. Silver rings adorned most of her fingers, and lots of bangles on both wrists completed her look.

"You are indeed in the right place." Dot handed us cards. "Here are the items we're auctioning off tonight, and thank you again for your donation. I'm sure your wine will bring in a good price. Don't forget we want you to be there when your item is up." I looked at the card. Several wineries had donated items for the auction. Joyeux was listed right after Martinelli Winery.

"Is Antonia here?"

Dot nodded. "She arrived a while ago with Chantal."

"Oh goody, Chantal's here." I let my eyes sweep the room, spotting Antonia along with several faces I recognized. I rescanned the room, but this time I focused on a special group, the ones who might be guilty of murder. "They're here. They're all here."

Connor knew who I was talking about. "This is a big event in town. Not showing up would be a mistake, especially if you have something to hide."

Connor gently guided me out onto the patio. Beyond the

tables, the sun was setting over Monterey Bay. Below us, otters played without concern in the protected waters. The air, tangy with salt, felt clean and crisp on my skin. We watched in comfortable silence as the sun slipped below the horizon.

"Well, look at the two of you. Penny, you look different. Feminine."

Now *that* was the kind of back-handed compliment I've learned to expect from Chantal. I knew it was her, though, even without the comment. Her perfume easily cut through the ocean breeze.

"Hello, Chantal." I turned and took in the brunette at my side. She was poured into a strapless, sequined dress that fell to the floor, with a long slit up one leg. She reminded me of Jessica Rabbit. The dress matched the red soles of her Louboutin shoes, which added at least four inches to her height. She studied me over a martini glass, long red nails tapping against the rim.

"Yes, that's it. You look feminine." Classic Chantal. Certainly not a compliment, but not insulting enough for me to make a scene. At least, not this early in the evening. I spotted Annie at the bar. "I'm going to mingle," I said to Connor, ignoring Chantal. "See you in a bit."

I almost felt sorry for him as I moved away. Chantal grabbed his arm and leaned against it, leaving him little choice but to stay with her. I pulled up a bar stool next to Annie. "What are you drinking?"

"A Chrystalini, I think it's called. Raspberry vodka, Chambord, champagne, and fresh raspberries."

I signaled the bartender to bring me one of the same and studied Annie's face. There was a faint blue tinge under her red eyes. "How are you feeling, because you look done in."

Annie rubbed her temples. "Afraid. Afraid and tired. First Brian, then Nicole. And as for the rest,"—Annie looked into the mirror behind the bar—"they're all here, every one of them." She kept her eyes on the mirror. "Eric's at the appetizer table, and Claire came in a few minutes ago. Dot's working the check-in table, Denise is around here somewhere, and Jason came down from his room a couple of minutes ago." Annie perked up, her cheeks turning a pretty shade of pink.

"You're blushing."

"I know he might be a murderer," Annie said. "But, from a purely esthetic point of view, well…"

"You're saying he looks pretty fantastic in a tux."

Annie turned an even brighter shade of pink. "He does. He really does."

The bartender returned with my drink, and I took a sip. "This is fantastic." I licked the edge of the glass. "What is this?"

"Sugar," Annie said.

"No wonder I like it so much." I took another swig. "So, we have this group of people together, and one of them is our killer. At least here we're safe."

"That reminds me." Annie dug through her bag. "Look what I found." She handed me a bullet-shaped device. "It's a flashlight, with a strobe and a siren. We never seem to be prepared for those times when, you know."

"We find a body?"

"Exactly. Let me show you how it works." Annie twisted the top and immediately a blinding light spun around the room. That wasn't the worst part. The ear-shattering squeal wasn't on long before Annie turned it off, but it still brought a halt to all conversation in the room.

"Oops. I thought I had it on low."

"Not sure that would have made a difference." I took another swill of my drink. "I wonder why I'm not more embarrassed right now?"

"Because we have too much experience at embarrassment, and you're tucking into that Chrystalini pretty well?"

I nodded. "That sounds about right." I gave myself a little shake. "Back to the suspects. Do you have something to write with?" Annie nodded and handed me a pen from her bag. I grabbed a cocktail napkin. "Let's go over them one more time. Maybe we missed something." I wrote Jason's name down, tapping it with the pen.

Annie sighed. "A town with few to no eligible bachelors, and when I do find one, he might be a killer."

"Yes, that does tend to put a damper on a relationship." Annie didn't answer. "He had motive, Annie. Brian tried to back out of investing in Jason's company. He also had a relationship with Nicole. Maybe Jason was just sick of Nicole embarrassing him."

"That's a stretch," Annie said. "You don't kill someone for embarrassing you."

"You might if a multi-million-dollar investment was on the line." I wrote Claire's name next. "Claire has a gambling problem. Maybe her husband wasn't as supportive as she claims he was. Brian was wealthy, and now she inherits everything. She probably has the best motive of all."

Annie shrugged. "Why would she kill Nicole?"

"Maybe Nicole was there early the night Brian died, like we originally thought, only instead of killing Brian, Nicole saw the murder. She could have been blackmailing Claire, or any of them, for that matter."

"I'm still having a hard time believing Claire is an out-of-control gambler," Annie said.

"I know. I'm not sure what a gambler should look like, but it usually isn't the town's favorite doctor. She racked up a hundred thousand dollars of gambling debt, though, so it's clear she has a problem."

"It boggles the mind when you think about it," Annie said. "And it *is* a little strange that she's showing up at social events so soon after losing Brian." Annie pointed toward the mirror and I followed her line of vision, finally spotting Claire in a stunning cream-colored gown, leaning up against the piano. "She doesn't seem like the recently heartbroken widow."

"As a matter of fact, she doesn't. Maybe she just wants to be out. Maybe she's lonely."

"Maybe." Annie shook herself. "Okay, who's next?"

"Eric." I added his name to the list. "He's still in love with Claire. I don't care how much he denies it." I found him in the mirror. "There he is now." Eric was leaning against the railing looking out over the bay.

Annie nodded. "You may be on to something, but

225

getting rid of someone's husband doesn't mean you'll have a chance with the wife, even if you do think you love her."

"That kind of logic might escape someone if he's obsessed," I said.

"True. What about Denise?"

"I don't think it's likely, but for now we'll keep her on the list. She claims to have been in San Francisco the night Brian died, and I don't see her as the killer. There isn't any motive."

I wrote one last name on the napkin. "Finally, Dot. All we really have is her word that her memory's going."

"You know I can't believe she's guilty."

I pushed back. "We've discussed this. Don't forget, there's still money unaccounted for, isn't there?"

Annie nodded.

"So, where did it go? And don't forget, she's the only one with a police record."

"She was young and broke into a draft office a long time ago."

"Perhaps. It's possible she's innocent." I spun the napkin with my fingers until the names blurred. Eric, Jason, Dot, Denise, and Claire. "The only thing I'm certain of is that one of these people is guilty. Guilty of two murders, Annie." I handed her the napkin. "Put this away, and let's figure out how to make sure it isn't three."

Chapter 21

Lost in these thoughts, I jumped when Dot came up to us moments later, hands clenched, bracelets jangling all over the place. "Oh, this is dreadful, simply dreadful."

"What is?" I asked.

"Our auctioneer was in a car accident. He won't be here, and may have a broken arm." She twisted the rings on one hand. "I don't know what to do. We may have to postpone the auction."

"Nonsense." Antonia had walked up behind Dot. As always, she wore black, this time a floor-length beaded dress, her silver hair swept up and held in place with an intricate silver and onyx comb. "We'll have someone fill in for the auctioneer."

"It isn't as easy as it sounds," I said.

"Well, it certainly can't be that hard, and it's better than canceling."

"No, we shouldn't cancel," Annie said. There was a moment of silence while we contemplated our options, then I focused on Antonia.

"I think you should do it. Think about it. You know the Martinelli name has clout. Half the people in the room are politicians who want to do favors for you, and the other half you can just browbeat."

"I can't do it," Antonia said. "For some reason, people tend to find me—"

"Scary. You can be scary," Annie said. "At least, you've always scared the hell out of me."

The corner of Antonia's mouth twitched. "I was going to say intimidating."

Annie nodded. "Sure, that too."

"Don't we need to get clearance from the shelter to make a change?" I asked.

"I can do it," Annie said. "Approve the change, I mean. I'm on the board, and frankly, who's going to stop us?"

Antonia was lost in thought. "No, no, I'm not the right person, but I think I know who might be." Her gaze was focused across the room. I followed her line of sight to where Chantal held court, surrounded by no less than three tuxedoed guests.

"No way," I said. "You can't be serious? Chantal?"

"What is an auctioneer? Someone who can keep the attention of a room full of people and convince them to spend more than they intended." Antonia shrugged. "Nobody is better than my daughter at parting men from their money."

Annie cocked her head. "That makes sense, in a strange kind of way. Let's give it a try. I mean, what choice do we have?"

"Right on," Dot said. "We're going to crush this thing."

Dot walked away, bracelets clanking, as Antonia shook her head. "Why can't I ever understand what that woman is saying?"

"She said she thinks it will work," I said. The terrace was packed, and guests spilled into the lobby and around the piano player. "This is quite a crowd. Do you think Chantal will be nervous?"

"Of course not. There isn't anything my daughter likes better than an audience."

Chantal was now basically resting on top of the railing, the ocean a mere ten feet below. Her dress was putting up a valiant fight to stay in place but was losing the battle. "If she isn't careful, she's going to topple out…" Antonia turned to me. "I mean *off,* topple *off* the railing."

"Yes, well, let me go tell her."

"You need to tell her? You'd think she'd feel a draft."

Antonia stopped. "I'm not talking about her dress. I need to tell her about filling in for the auctioneer."

"Sure, I knew that." I studied Chantal. "I just don't see this working out well."

"There are things about my daughter you've overlooked, Penelope." Penelope. Antonia only used my full name when I was in trouble. "Her behavior is questionable at times, and often her choices aren't the best. But Chantal isn't stupid, and she can laugh at herself. Sometimes, she can be downright charming."

Half an hour later, Chantal was proving Antonia correct.

"Now, are you going to let that gentleman back there

outbid you?" Chantal ran a finger across the shoulder of a man in the front row. "I think your wife deserves that diamond bracelet, and remember, it's for a good cause."

I couldn't believe it. The wife was nodding her head enthusiastically as her husband basked in the glow otherwise known as Chantal. After he nodded, Chantal bounced back to center stage. "Do I hear three thousand from the back?" *Bounce.* "I'm certain we can do better." *Bounce bounce.* "Someone?" She pointed to the rear. "Three thousand from the back!" She held up a hand, shielding the spotlight, and peered toward the back of the room. "My, aren't you a handsome one."

Chantal turned back to the man in the front row. "So, what do you do for a living?"

"I'm a lawyer," he said.

"And Mr. Handsome in the back. What do you do?"

"I work for the government. Internal Revenue."

Chantal smiled at the audience. "So, I have a question for the rest of you. If these gentlemen go over the side and we can only rescue one, do we open a bottle of red or a bottle of white?"

Laughter rang out as Chantal banged the gavel. "Sold! Sold to the man in the back of the room, who makes his money by taking all of yours!"

Antonia came to join us at the bar. "Well, what do you think?"

"I'll admit it, she's doing a good job," I said. "Even the wives are loving her."

"That's because several of them will be going home with diamonds, thanks to Chantal."

Annie listened to us as she studied Chantal. "She reminds me of someone, especially in that red sequined dress."

"Jessica Rabbit," I said.

"YES," Annie said. "It was driving me crazy. Except for the brunette hair she's a dead ringer."

I picked up the list to see the remaining auction items. We had donated estate- bottled cabernet sauvignon, but I stopped when I saw Antonia's contribution: a rare bottle of Chateau Lafite Rothschild.

"Antonia, this is a really expensive bottle. Are you sure?"

"Of course I'm sure. Have you ever seen me do anything I was unsure of?"

"Well, no, actually, although this is certainly generous of you."

Antonia shrugged. "It's for a good cause, and I do have a deep cellar."

Before I could respond, Chantal cooed into the microphone, "You know, it would be easier if I had someone to present the items to the lucky recipients. I think I need an assistant."

The hand of every unaccompanied male within hearing distance shot up. Even the waiters. Chantal shook her head. "I couldn't ask any of you lovely gentlemen." Chantal pointed to the bar. "Penny! Penny, come and be my assistant."

Antonia turned to me. I held up a hand. "Absolutely not."

"Penelope, go up there." Antonia gave me a small push.

"Penny, come help me. Penny!"

This was embarrassing. The longer I resisted, the worse it was going to get.

Annie shrugged. "Listen to Antonia. You know Chantal isn't going to stop. I'd say the best course of action is to go up there and shut her up."

"Fine. I'll go, but it's under duress."

Antonia smiled. "It's also for a very good cause."

For the next half hour, I shuttled items across the room. We were nearing the end, which was a good thing. Chantal was enjoying the evening a little too much. *"Penny! This is for the gentleman at the bar!"* Bounce. *"Here, for the two women in the back!"* Bounce. *"Let's time her! Do I hear one hundred dollars if Penny can make it across the room in ten seconds? Somebody time her!"* I shot her a look, but the audience thought it was great fun. *"Come on, Penny, it's for charity!"*

Perhaps, but I was feeling less charitable as time went on. Chantal pounded the gavel as I collected a hundred-dollar bill from the man in the front row. He smiled. "It is for a good cause."

"Right." I gave the bill to Chantal. She flashed a smile and handed me the Chateau Lafite Rothschild.

"Penny, hold it up for everyone to see." I raised the bottle. It was a good opportunity to scan the crowd, and I sought out certain faces. Jason sat a few feet in front of me, while Eric lounged against the railing. Claire sat at the bar talking with Annie. Dot stood at the rear of the room, next to Denise. It could be any of them. It could be any of them…

"Penny!"

Startled, I twisted around. "What!"

It was the twist that did it. My foot slipped out from under me, and I knew I was in trouble. One minute I was standing there, and the next I was sprawled on the floor. To make matters worse, I heard glass shatter. The room froze in stunned silence.

"Oh, you've done it now." Chantal backed away.

"It was an accident!" The front row dabbed at very expensive wine stains. "An accident!" Guests shuffled awkwardly, then Antonia spoke from the rear of the room. She's never had any problem raising her voice, even at her age, and especially at me.

"Never mind. No harm done, unless, of course, you factor in Penny's embarrassment." She walked toward the stage. "The bottle was insured, and I will be happy to donate the replacement value to the shelter directly."

Applause broke out as she leaned over me. "I assume you're okay?"

"Just mortified." I stood and wiped the wine from the front of my dress. "I'm sure glad you had it insured."

"The insurance company will hardly believe this story, but the shelter is financially much better off with the insured amount."

"You had a lot of insurance?" I asked.

"Of course. I believe in being well prepared."

"Sure, so do I." I mean, if I had anything worth insuring, other than the winery, which was barely profitable. I left the stage to go clean up, passing Jason on my way.

"Don't worry," he said. "Could have happened to anyone." Gracious of him, considering he had wine splatters all over his pristine white shirt.

Annie handed me a bar towel when I took a seat next to her. "It wasn't that bad," she said. "And the shelter did benefit."

"I landed in a heap, in front of a room full of people. Not one of my better moments." I dropped the towel onto the counter. "I'm covered in wine and managed to completely embarrass myself. My work here is complete."

She didn't answer. "Annie?"

Annie dug in her purse, then scanned the bar. Slowly she swiveled on the bar stool.

"What's wrong with you?" I said. "You're as white as a sheet."

"It's gone." Her hands shook as she pressed them against her cheeks. "The list of suspects. It's gone."

My stomach lurched. "You didn't put it away?"

"I thought I did. I know I meant to, but then the auctioneer canceled, and Dot…" Her voice trailed off. "It's gone." She gripped my arm. "Everyone on that list was near me at some point."

Fighting down panic, I took a deep breath. "You don't know one of them took it. It was a napkin. Maybe the bartender just threw it away."

"Do you think that's what happened?"

No, I didn't, but I needed to keep Annie calm so I could think. "It's possible." I placed my hand on her shoulder. "Let me walk you to your car."

We managed to get out of the hotel without speaking to anyone. "I self-parked," Annie said. "There's my car, under the light."

I was glad the area was well-lit as we moved across the lot. "Go straight home and call me." I turned to go as she opened the door.

"Penny, wait." She pointed to her windshield. "There it is."

I knew what she was talking about. I turned and looked where Annie pointed. The napkin was wedged under the wiper. I moved past Annie and pinched the corner, pulling it clear. "It's our list, all right."

Annie stared at the back. "There's been a modification." Her voice was tinny and hollow. I turned the list in the air and read, *"You should leave it alone, while you still can."*

Chapter 22

"I don't *know* who might have taken it," I said to Connor for the tenth time. "We made that list before the auction."

"It's my fault," Annie's voice faltered. "I was facing the other way watching the auction. Everyone on that list was at the bar and near me at least once or twice."

We were driving Annie home. She didn't want to go alone, and I didn't blame her. We pulled into her driveway.

"Neither of you are mentioning the obvious," Connor said. "Someone is keeping an eye on both of you. While you were writing that list, someone *on* that list was watching."

Annie nodded. "I wonder what they felt when they saw their name?"

"Angry," I said. "Angry and worried enough to try and warn us away."

When we arrived at Annie's, Connor walked her to the door, making sure that everything was as it should be. Annie stood at the living room window and watched us drive away, worry evident on her face even from a distance.

I drummed my fingers on my purse, the napkin tucked

into a side pocket. "I'll bring it to the police station for Lucas tomorrow," I said. "He should know."

"He should know? He *should* know?" A flood of emotion Connor had apparently been holding back now burst forth. "If the killer suspected you were sticking your nose where it didn't belong, you've just confirmed it." He shook his head. "You *listed* the pool of suspects and left it on the bar for anyone in the room to see."

"Annie was supposed to get rid of it."

"That isn't the strongest defense."

"It's the only one I have. If I hadn't been pulled into the auction..." The excuse sounded weak, and I tried again. "Yes, that list should have been torn up and thrown away. Someone now knows we suspect them and also knows who else we think might be involved." My voice broke at the end. "It shouldn't have happened."

Connor turned to glance at me in the soft car lights. "You don't usually admit when you're wrong. You certainly don't admit it that quickly. Or quietly. What's going on?"

I closed my eyes. "I can't afford to make mistakes like this. I'm missing something. It's like I have pieces to the puzzle but no idea how it's all connected, or how to solve it."

Connor pulled into my drive and turned off the car. "Unfortunately, it's too late to tell you to let the police handle it. Someone has you in their sights now."

I nodded. "And they're feeling desperate, if they took a chance like that to threaten me." My mouth went dry, and I tried out the words again. "They threatened me." Stronger this time. "They threatened Annie." There was a spark of anger in my voice. My head cleared, and I took a deep breath.

"I know, but you're going to be okay," he said.

"I know I am. They're hoping to scare me away. If I stop because I'm frightened, they win. And I have no intention of letting them win."

Connor opened the door, and in the light I could see his smile. "You had me worried there for a minute. I can handle you angry and indignant. I can work with you fighting to clear Annie's name and getting into trouble for it. A few moments ago, though, when you were quiet…" His voice was soft. "That scared me. You being afraid, well, that isn't you."

I shook my head. "I have been afraid. Afraid that someone was going to get away with it." Strength flowed through my shoulders, and I sat up straighter. "That's it. I've been worried I wasn't going to get them, but tonight someone let it slip. They're worried. Good. They should be. I'm going to figure out who is doing this. I'm not stopping until I do."

Connor nodded but didn't respond.

"What?"

He drummed his fingers on the steering wheel. "Do you want me to stay the night?"

My cheeks grew hot, and I didn't answer. I couldn't trust my voice. Was he asking because he wanted to be *with* me, or out of concern for my safety, which suddenly didn't seem so pressing. Of course I wanted him to stay the night, and it had nothing to do with feeling safe. Safe was the last thing I was feeling.

"I think that sounds wonderful." I winced. I sounded like I was in high school. "I mean, that would be fantastic." Oh, sure, that was better.

He studied my face. "Right now, I'm worried about you being alone. Someone sent you a clear warning tonight, but there will come a time when I'll be asking to stay for a different reason."

How embarrassing. "Of course. I knew what you meant. Are you ready to go in?" I was glad he couldn't see me blush in the dark, but it didn't matter, because he wasn't looking at me. He was peering through the window. "Connor?"

"There's a car up the road."

"What's it doing?"

"Sitting there, pulled over," Connor said. "They just turned off their lights."

"That's odd." I shivered. "Do you think someone followed us from Annie's house, or even from the hotel?"

Connor shook his head. "I was watching. We weren't followed. This car just pulled up."

"I wonder if they're waiting for you to leave," I said.

"Then they're going to be disappointed." He turned to face me. "I'm staying. If I don't, I'll just be awake all night worried about you." He peered through the darkness. "They haven't moved. Go inside."

We stepped from the car. "What are you going to do?"

"See if I can find out who's in that car."

"I'm not letting you go alone," I said. "You might need help."

"If you're my backup, I definitely need help."

We entered the first row of grapes. The canes were leafless and offered little cover.

"Stay low," Connor said over his shoulder. "And be quiet."

"I know how to be quiet," I said. "Just don't forget I'm tall."

"What does that have to do with anything?"

"It's a leverage thing. It's proportionately harder for me to crouch." My thighs were already burning.

He stopped. "I'm taller than you, and I don't have any problem crouching."

"That's because you're also proportionately stronger than I am."

He groaned. "Please, just stay here."

"Fine, I'll wait." Anything to avoid crouching. He started to walk away. "Hang on!" He turned back to me as I dug in my purse. "Here, take this. It's a flashlight, strobe, and alarm, built into one."

"I know. I saw you set it off at the auction. Everyone did."

"Just take it."

"I can see. There's enough moonlight."

"Take it!"

"If I take it, will you go away?"

"Yes!" I slapped it into Connor's palm with enough force to flip the switch. I knew this right away, because an earsplitting screech pierced the night.

"Turn it off!"

Connor twisted both ends, and the wail was now synchronized with a laser beam bright enough to be seen from space. He managed to turn it off, but the damage was done. As we listened, a car engine fired and roared away.

"Touchy little thing, isn't it?" I took the alarm from Connor. "Well, that was bad luck." Connor mumbled something under his breath. "What was that?"

"I said it was hardly luck, bad or otherwise." He shook his head. "If you had just listened to me and let me go by myself, I might have seen who it was, or at least seen the car."

"I was only trying to help." We walked to the house.

"That's what gets you into these messes." Connor climbed the front steps, and I followed. "How many bodies have you managed to find since you returned to Cypress Cove? And that isn't even the worst of it."

"It is if you're the one finding them." I unlocked the door. "Trust me on this."

Connor continued, "No, the worst of it is that you keep putting yourself in danger. Haven't you learned you need to let the police handle these things?"

"If someone asks for my help, what am I supposed to do, ignore them? Ignore Annie?" I pushed open the door and stomped past him. "I can take care of myself. If you want to stay the night, you know where the couch is."

He followed me into the house. "I'm just asking how you manage it."

"Manage what?"

"Manage to always be involved when there's a murder in town."

I stopped to give both Hollie and Nanook neck hugs as I considered my response. It was a fair question. Connor had been on hand more times than I cared to admit when I'd needed him. He deserved a deep, well-thought-out answer.

"I blame it on curiosity."

He rolled his eyes. "Really? That's the best you can do?"

I shrugged. "It's the truth. I can't stand not knowing something, even if it's none of my business. I'm curious. I always have been, and it increases the odds that I'll be there when something happens. Like murder."

"So, that's it. Curiosity."

"Pretty much." I pushed past Nanook and turned on several lights. "That, and determination. I just keep looking."

Connor pointed at me. "There it is. You keep looking, and that looking gets you in trouble."

I squirmed. He had a point. If I hadn't insisted on checking out Nicole's car, for example, I wouldn't have been the one to find her.

"That may be." I spoke quickly, defensively. "But then we're back to how this all started. Annie was suspected of murder." I handed him the quilt from the couch. "If I had to, I'd do the same thing all over again."

Chapter 23

Knowing that Connor was on the couch helped me sleep better than I had expected. The animals also had a good night, which of course dictated how well I slept. Hollie was getting to know the routine, allowing Syrah to settle first, as was a cat's prerogative.

When I finally managed to get out of bed, I wrapped a robe over my sweats-turned-pajamas and peeked into the living room. Connor was gone. After feeding Syrah and letting the dogs out the back, I reached for the coffee. When I had a cup, I pulled the warning note from my bag. In the morning sun, I studied the writing. The print was in block letters, and I doubted Lucas would be able to determine anything from it, but I would let him decide. I held the note up, looking from an angle. The author had torn through the napkin while writing, and the letters were deep. Someone was angry. Someone was scared. Good. The phone rang as I was pouring a second cup of coffee. It was Ross.

"Come see me. I'll make you breakfast and I *have gossip.*"

"I'll be there in half an hour." I pulled myself together,

gave cookies to the dogs, and headed out the door.

It was another warm day. The air was balmy and scented with newly mown grass. I would have enjoyed a drive up the coast if I didn't have breakfast and gossip waiting at the restaurant, so I took the Ocean Boulevard off-ramp and pulled into Sterling's parking lot.

I recognized Chantal's car right away. She only drove red sports cars, this one a Porsche. I walked past it and pushed my way through the rear entrance to the kitchen. Ross stood over a pot stirring something.

"What is that?" I peered into the pot. "It smells amazing."

"Hungarian goulash." He covered the pot. "Now I leave it alone for the next six hours." He guided me from the kitchen. "Let me check with the servers and get you something to eat." He leaned in. "And I need to tell you something before I burst. Someone's here having breakfast."

"Let me guess. Chantal?"

His face fell. "How did you know?"

"I saw her car."

"Oh." His face brightened. "Then you don't know who she's having breakfast *with*."

"Don't tell me, let me see for myself." I stepped into the dining room and froze. Chantal was at a corner table with Jason and wearing the same dress from last night's auction. Before I could move, Jason turned his head to yawn. When he spotted me, his cheeks brightened to the same shade of Chantal's dress. She caught his look and turned as well, a slow smile playing across her face as she reached out to grab Jason's hand, which he had the decency to slowly remove from the table top.

I grimaced and turned away, nearly running into Ross.

"That's what I was trying to tell you," he said. "They've been sitting there for an hour, and let me tell you, if the conversation I've managed to hear is any indication, they had quite a party last night."

"Ugh. I think they only met last night at the auction." I indicated Chantal with a slow tip of my head. "She was wearing that same dress. He told me he was really interested in Annie, and now here he is having breakfast with Chantal after obviously spending the night with her?"

Ross waved his hand. "Oh please, you should have asked me. I could have told you he's a player. Annie can do much better than him."

"She just doesn't need this right now." My stomach grumbled. "I can't eat in there, not with the two of them all cozied up."

"Come sit at the bar." Ross led me across the room. "I'll bring you some eggs Florentine."

I took a seat while he disappeared into the kitchen. Chantal and Jason? I sat, trying to figure that one out. Then I smelled the perfume.

"Chantal." I turned and pasted on a smile. "You're out early, and in the same dress you had on last night." She didn't seem the least embarrassed. Of course, she's been down the walk of shame so many times she needs her own star. Jason hovered by the back door. Looking at his watch. The ground. Anywhere but at me.

"Well, I was just starving, and we thought we'd eat here because there was a wait for breakfast at Jason's hotel."

Maybe. More likely she brought him here hoping to be seen with him.

Chantal continued, "Wasn't last night fun? The auction was a complete success. Of course, it would have been better if you hadn't managed to break the most expensive bottle of wine there."

"It was an *accident*."

"Sure, an accident," Chantal said. "They do seem to follow you wherever you go." She did a hair flip. "And at least mother had the bottle insured, so the shelter still gets the money."

"Yes, the proceeds go to a good cause. And speaking of going…"

Chantal ignored my hint. "There are so many dogs that need homes," she said. "I may have to get one."

That got my attention. "It's a commitment. They aren't fashion accessories, and I don't see you walking a dog or cleaning up after it. Besides"—I struck the death blow—"they like to chew. On shoes. The more expensive the better."

"Oh!" She glanced down at her Louboutin-clad feet. "Maybe I'll think about it a little."

As if she could think any *other* way. She gave me her standard little finger wave and strolled to the door. Jason held it open for her and whispered something as she walked out. She shrugged and left as he came up to me.

"I know what you're thinking," he said.

"Oh, you couldn't possibly imagine what I'm thinking of you right now."

"Look, Chantal had too much to drink last night. I offered her my couch."

I waved my hands in the get-to-the-point gesture. "Where she stayed all night, right?"

"It didn't go as far as you're thinking, but it didn't end there, either." He shook his head. "Chantal isn't even my type."

"Oh, come on, Nicole and now Chantal? I'm definitely seeing your type, and it's clear you aren't going for MENSA members."

"Look, can you just tell Annie…" He paused. "Just tell her I wish her well, and I'm sorry I didn't get a chance to know her better."

"Sure, I'll give her the message."

He nodded and headed for the back door. "Wait a minute," I said. He turned, eyes wide, a hopeful look on his face. "Speaking of messages, you didn't leave one for Annie and me last night, did you?"

"A message?" He drew his brows together. "No. After the auction, I…" He had the decency to turn red. "We went upstairs to my room. I wanted to change shirts. Mine had wine on it, if you recall."

"Yes, I know. You didn't come back down?"

"No, not until this morning." I drew up my eyebrows, and he tapped his chest with his fingertips. "Why would I leave a message for Annie or go anywhere near her? At that point, I knew I might not be alone for the evening. Look, it wasn't my finest hour, but at least I wanted to be discreet."

I shook my head in disbelief. "So, you want credit for

discretion? Showing up here with Chantal in the same dress she had on last night is hardly inconspicuous. This is a small town."

"I see that now," he said. "But either way, I didn't leave you a note last night."

"I didn't say a note, I said a message."

He shrugged. "Note, message. Same thing."

Perhaps, or perhaps it had been a slip, but I couldn't do anything about it for now. He raised his hand in a goodbye gesture and stepped out the back door. Moments later, Chantal's Porsche pulled out into traffic, Chantal laughing at the wheel. I couldn't see Jason in the passenger seat, but it didn't matter. He blew it. He might not realize it now, but he would in time. Ross came up behind me.

"Have Annie come in. Tell her I'll make her something special."

"Your cures are always so calorie-laden." I nudged him in the ribs. "And very effective. I'll tell her."

I left the car at the restaurant and walked to the police station. When I arrived, I stopped at the window of Lucas's office. He was at his desk on the phone, but he saw me and waved me in. By the time I got to the counter, he was standing in his office doorway.

"So, I heard about the auction last night," he said. "I particularly liked the part of the story where you showered half the audience with a five-thousand-dollar bottle of wine. Quite the accident."

I handed him the note. "Someone leaving this on Annie's

car windshield was no accident." He walked to the window to study both sides of the napkin.

"Just so I understand what I'm looking at, on this side there's a list of potential suspects for the murders. I'm assuming that's your writing?"

"Yes."

"And you wrote this last night, at the auction?"

I nodded. "I was at the bar. With Annie."

"Of course. When I find one of you, I usually find the other."

I sniffed. "There's no need to be sarcastic."

"Just pointing out the obvious." He turned the napkin over. "Lot of force was used to write this warning. They mean it."

"I *know* they mean it. That's why I brought it to you. And last night when I got home, a car was stopped up my street. Looks like they were watching the house. My house."

"Could you see what kind of car?"

I shook my head. "I didn't see it at all. Connor did."

"Did he recognize it?"

"No, they left before he got a good look." No need to go into the alarm incident.

"Well, I'll keep this," he said. "See if we can get anything from it in the lab. I don't suppose I can convince you to keep a low profile until this is all over?"

"Now that Annie is off your list of suspects...she is off your list, right?" Lucas nodded. "I know you want me to stop poking around. I've been in this position before, though—"

"I know that better than anyone," Lucas said.

"My point is that even if I was willing to leave it alone, would the killer be willing to leave *me* alone?"

Lucas gestured to the napkin. "Unlikely, given that you and Annie are leaving lists of potential suspects to be found by, gee, I don't know, one of the suspects."

"Exactly," I said.

"Don't you know sarcasm when you hear it?" Lucas rubbed the back of his neck. "Do me a favor and try to stay out of trouble. We're making progress on Nicole's murder, tracking her movements between when Brian was killed and her own death. In the meantime, don't give this person any reason to consider you a threat." He held up the napkin. "I mean, any more reason."

"Here's the problem," I said. "We both know I'm genetically incapable of doing nothing. Sitting home until you solve it isn't in the cards. Not that you can't solve it. I know you will. In the meantime, though, I think it's in everyone's best interests if you let me help you."

I thought I sounded rather convincing, and for a brief moment it appeared Lucas did too. He leaned against his desk, silent, which I took to be a positive sign. Then he walked to his office door, opened it, and pointed. "Go, and don't let me hear you've been back to my crime scene."

"Come on, Lucas, give me something."

He idly twisted the door knob with one hand, considering. Finally, he gave a short nod and walked back to his desk, opening the top drawer.

"This is a copy of the key we found in Nicole's car." He handed it to me. It was a small key. Gold. The number 61 was stamped on one side. I turned it over in my hand.

"Maybe a safe deposit box?"

Lucas turned his palms to the ceiling. "That's what we thought but no luck. It isn't for a safe deposit or mail box."

"The drug cabinet at the clinic."

"That's the first thing we tried, considering Nicole's addictions."

"Maybe something in Nicole's home?"

"Like a safe? We didn't find anything."

I reached to give the key back to Lucas, but he held up his hand. "Keep it and think about what it might open."

"Thanks."

"Don't give me too much credit. I'm just trying to keep you out of my way."

"Just for that, I'm going to find what it opens."

He smiled. "I sincerely hope you do. I expect you to call me if you come up with anything." His smile stayed in place, but he was watching me with laser focus.

"Of course. You'll be my first call." With as much dignity as I could muster, I left his office, pushing through the counter-high gate. Lucas watched from the window as I stepped outside. When I got around the corner, I called Annie.

"Did you bring the note to the police?" Annie asked.

"Just left Lucas in his office. He wasn't happy we left a list of suspects lying around."

"Did you tell him we aren't thrilled it happened either?"

"I'm pretty sure he knows it. What are you doing?"

"With the clinic closed again, I'm free. Going a little stir-crazy, so if you have anything in mind, I'm available."

"I wish we could place everyone's location during the auction. Dot was near you all night, and I saw Claire, Ted, and Eric get drinks at least once."

"Don't forget about Jason," Annie said. "I mean, not that I consider him a likely suspect."

Here we go. "Actually, I got a chance to talk to him already. At Sterling. He was having breakfast." I turned the corner into Sterling's parking lot.

Annie's voice got a little higher, and she spoke in a rush. "You saw Jason today? How was he?"

I stopped, frozen at the sight of my car, and tried to breathe. "He was fine when I saw him. Better than I am right now."

"Penny, what's wrong?"

"Someone slashed my tires." I walked around the car. "All four of them."

Chapter 24

"Let me call you later." I walked back into the restaurant and found Ross.

"Come sit down. You're shaking. What happened to you?"

"Someone slashed my tires." My voice sounded muffled, and I had to repeat myself before Ross heard me. I sat at the bar while he got Lucas on the phone.

"Someone slashed Penny's tires. All four of them." I heard a lot of commotion on the other end. Ross held the phone away from his ear. "Strangely enough, he isn't all that surprised."

Ross waited until there was a lull and then brought the phone back against his head. "What do you want us to do?" I heard another round of short sentences all ending with exclamation points. Ross kept nodding his head, until finally, it was silent. "Sure, we can all agree Penny should go home and stay out of it." He shrugged. "Have you ever actually *met* Penny?" Ross nodded a few more times. "Right. We'll be waiting at her car." He hung up the phone. "He wants to meet us at your car."

"Yes, I heard."

Ross shook his head. "Trust me, you didn't hear all of it."

We walked into the lot, and Ross gasped when he saw the damage. "I can't believe this happened. Right here, in my parking lot! First thing tomorrow I'm having cameras mounted." He took me by the shoulders. "Look at me." I raised my head back to meet his gaze. "Lucas is right. What you're doing needs to stop, or you're going to get hurt." I didn't say anything, and he gave me a gentle shake. "This time it was your tires. Next time, who knows?"

We stood in silence until Lucas joined us. He walked around the car shaking his head. "Someone took a big risk. Broad daylight. People going in and out of the restaurant."

"I thought the same thing." My ears were ringing, and I felt lightheaded. Only a few cars remained in the lot, stragglers from the breakfast rush. "The restaurant itself blocks the lot from the street, but I agree someone took a chance."

"They wanted to make sure you got the message," Lucas said. "If you weren't ready to listen to me before, is this clear enough for you?"

A breeze had come up, and I shivered. "Yeah, I got the message." The gashes were deep and angry. "Whoever did this was strong."

Lucas shook his head. "The tires for a car this old don't have steel inserts. Someone good with a knife would be able to manage this." He sighed and took out his pad. "Did you see anyone here this morning who's involved with the case?"

"Jason was here earlier, with Chantal."

"Jason, the guy from the pharmaceutical company?"

"Yes, and he had a history with both victims. Brian tried to cancel his investment in Jason's company, but Jason wouldn't let him. As for Nicole, Jason just broke up with her. She didn't take it well."

Lucas took notes. "You say he was here with Chantal?"

"Having breakfast."

"Did they leave together?"

"Yes. Well, wait. Let me think. They left together, but they didn't walk out together. I spoke to both of them, separately." I knelt next to my rear left tire and ran a finger along the gouge. The gash was deep and raw. My mouth went dry, and I held onto the car to get back to my feet. Lucas took a good look at me.

"You don't look so great. Ross, can you call for a tow and see that she gets home?"

After Ross nodded, Lucas turned to me. "I'm going to let you tell Hayley and Connor about this. I bet they'll both have a few things to say, like maybe you take a vacation until this is over."

In the end, I had Annie come and get me. I'd thought it was a good choice, until she saw my tires.

"What have I gotten you into?" Her voice was a whisper.

"You didn't get me into anything. I was involved right from the start, when I drove you back to the clinic and you found...*we* found Brian. Even if I hadn't been there that night, do you think I'd let you go through this alone?"

255

Annie took a deep breath and squeezed my hand. "No, I don't. Just…thanks, okay?"

We waited in silence until my car was towed, then, with unspoken agreement, walked to the center of town, stopping at one of our favorite boutiques. Annie tried on a turquoise scarf while I reached for a pair of copper-colored boots with a slim fit that ended right under my knee.

"How many pairs of boots does one woman need?"

"Apparently at least one more pair than I will ever own." I nodded to the sales woman. "I'll take these, and that scarf she's wearing." I turned to Annie. "My treat. No arguing."

"Who's arguing? It looks great on me." She gave me a small smile.

We left the store a few minutes later. "Here's the reality," I said, getting back to the subject on both our minds, "someone is trying to scare us. The trick is to not let them."

"But look what they did to your car."

"Tires. Just tires. Easily replaced." I spoke with more conviction than I felt, and I jumped when the phone rang.

"How are you?"

"Hello, Antonia. I'm fine, how are you?"

There was a sharp exhale. "Better than you are. This tire slashing is nothing to take lightly."

I didn't even bother to ask how she'd heard, although I suspected Ross was to blame, a suspicion confirmed with her next words.

"Ross said that Chantal was at the restaurant when it happened."

"Yes, she was."

"I understand she was having breakfast with Jason."

"We can talk about that later. I'm here with Annie now."

"Yes, yes, I understand." There was a sigh. "My daughter will live her life as she sees fit. I'm just sorry because I know Annie was interested in him."

Antonia always managed to surprise me with her insight. "Well, she was, but she'll be fine."

"Of course she will. Now, what do you have planned for the remainder of the day?"

"We were just trying to decide."

"How about bingo?"

"Um. Okay…" Nothing about Antonia said bingo. "You mean, like, the game?"

"What else would I mean? Honestly, Penny…"

I sputtered, "It just doesn't seem like you would fit in with the bingo crowd."

"You'll see. All sorts of people play."

"But still."

"The reason you don't see me playing bingo is exactly the reason I like it. There, I'm not a winery owner, or the landlord, or anyone, really. I'm just another player. Toni, the bingo player."

"*Toni?* You go by Toni?"

She sniffed. "Only at bingo, and never by you."

"What church is it at?"

"Church?"

"Of course," I said. "Bingo's played at church, by, um, mature people, and there's a song. Something about a farmer's dog."

Antonia sighed. "I play at the casino, with other adults of all ages, and millions are spent each week on bingo games in this country alone."

I paused. "The casino, huh?" I'd have a chance to see where Claire's troubles began.

"Yes. Now, would you care to come along or not?"

I turned to Annie. "Antonia wants to know if we want to go to the casino and play bingo."

"Bingo?" She shrugged. "Why not?"

"Okay," I said. "We're in."

"Excellent. I will pick you up at Sterling in half an hour."

We waited, sipping espressos until Antonia arrived. She was driving one of the old pickups used on her winery, and she pulled into the lot and parked next to Annie. She rolled down her window, her mouth a thin line.

"Where's your car?"

"They towed it already," I said.

"Someone means business," she said, then studied the two of us. "Neither of you should be going anywhere alone until this is cleared up."

"Not to worry," I said.

We piled into the front next to her. She had on a scoop neck, black knit top edged in lace and black slacks. She caught my look. "What?"

"Nothing," I said. Antonia expertly shifted gears. "Why are you driving the truck? Is it part of your bingo image?"

Antonia sniffed. "I have no idea what you're talking about. I like driving this occasionally, and yes, usually when

I come to the casino, this is what I drive."

I continued to study her. "Now what?" she asked.

"Nothing. You look nice. Different, but nice." She looked younger today. Her eyes sparkled, and her cheeks were flushed pink. "So, bingo."

"I'll have you know bingo has a proud and illustrious history," Antonia said. "It's Italian, you know." She gave a small toss of her head as though this explained everything, and perhaps for someone with a name like Martinelli, it did. "It can be traced all the way back to 1530, to an Italian lottery called Lo Giuoco del Lotto d'Italia. It's still played every Saturday in Italy."

We didn't answer, and Antonia glanced over. "Okay, you aren't impressed with my bingo lore, and you're both distracted. The tire slashing is worrisome, no doubt. Is that what has you troubled? Or are you still bothered by last night." Antonia waved her hand. "The auction was a wonderful success, even with you drenching half the audience with wine."

"If only that was the worst thing that happened last night."

"Why, what else happened?"

"Let me tell it," Annie said. "Before the auction began, we were sitting at the bar listing suspects. I lost track of the list. I thought I put it away, but it wasn't in my bag and I must have left it on the counter. I don't know how it happened, it just did. It turned up later on my windshield, with a warning for us to back off."

"Who was on the list?"

I counted off on my fingers. "Claire, Eric, Denise, Jason,

259

and Dot. They were all there last night. It could be any one of them."

"So, someone knows you're on to them," Antonia said. "Someone on the list is guilty, otherwise they wouldn't have bothered to warn you off. Then, this morning they slashed your tires."

I nodded. "That's about it."

We drove in silence while Antonia processed this turn of events. The pickup was an old Chevy with worn shocks and a big bench seat. The windows were down, and we passed through the countryside, the air fragrant with wild mustard. A touch of coolness lay underneath the warmth. A perfect spring day, the kind that is usually my favorite…when I can enjoy it, that is, and don't have someone threatening to kill me.

We turned the last corner. The size of the casino struck me first. In a part of the country where most buildings are a couple of floors, this building was at least twenty stories high.

"I can't believe how tall it is," I said.

"That's the hotel tower. Because it's on Indian land, they have different codes and requirements. Building height wasn't a concern." Antonia turned into the drive. "It's very nice. They hold a lot of conventions here, and there's a beautiful spa and athletic club."

We passed a large fountain and waterfall that divided the drive and pulled into the parking structure. The attendant tipped his cap.

"You come here often enough to be recognized, I see."

"Don't be impertinent." She worked her way through the parking structure and finally pulled into a space in the far corner.

"Lucky spot, huh?" I'd been joking, but Antonia nodded. "When it's working, you don't mess with it."

A few moments later, we stepped through the front doors. The inside looked like any other casino. The slots were whizzing, and there were craps tables and the usual card games going. The surprise came when we rounded the corner to the bingo room. It was packed. A table just inside the entrance was topped with piles of bingo cards, big fat pens, and other items I couldn't identify. A hefty lady sat behind the table wearing a name tag: Gladys. She had an unlit cigarette dangling from her mouth and a mass of hair bleached beyond any redemption. She wore cowboy boots, jeans, and a red plaid shirt. She leaned over to Antonia. "Brought a couple of first-timers with you, huh, Toni?"

I jumped. Her voice was raspy enough to strip paint.

"How do you know we're first-timers?" I said.

"'Cause you're gawking with your mouth hangin' open." She gestured to the cards. "Let me get you the basics. You need a dauber?"

"A what?"

"The pens are called daubers. Some people have different colors for different games." She shook her head. "Where'd you get these two, Toni?"

"Yes, well. Let's get them what they need."

As Gladys outfitted us, Annie circled the room. She came

back moments later, her eyes wide. "Have you heard that guy?"

"What guy?" I said.

"The guy up front calling out the numbers. At least I think that's what he's doing. I'm only understanding every fifth word."

Gladys nodded. "That's Stan. He normally speeds up when he's had a few."

"It's not even noon yet."

Gladys nodded. "That's what I mean. An hour from now, you'll really need to pay attention."

Antonia turned from the table. She was holding several things I didn't recognize, along with a box of daubers. The side of the box said, "Be the envy of the bingo hall with Dazzle Glitter Bingo Daubers."

"I've got your admission packs and cards," she said. "Pick out a dauber you like."

I studied the daubers, finally selecting a hot pink one. "How much are the jackpots?"

"Five hundred dollars," Gladys said.

"You're kidding."

"No, she isn't," Antonia said. "Let's go."

We followed the sound, a non-stop little ditty performed by a diminutive, bespectacled fellow. He could barely see over the podium. We listened for a moment. "I agree with Annie," I said. "It doesn't sound like he's calling out numbers. It sounds like he's singing in some weird language. Maybe Dolphin. I can't understand a word he's saying." The caller peered over his glasses, snapping his fingers to the beat.

Antonia shrugged. "They work the numbers into a fun song. You get used to it."

We worked our way through the crowd and finally found three seats together up front. Across from us were two women. The one in front of me was thin and wiry, the table in front of her covered in bingo cards. I smiled, but she didn't make eye contact. She studied her cards, a line of daubers in different colors uncapped and ready to go.

The woman next to her was plump and pretty, at least what I could see of her. She was also focused on her cards. She was a two-fisted dauber, a pen in each hand, and was swaying back and forth over her cards in time to the caller's chant.

"We're late. Quick, take a look at the numbers on the board and see if you have anything," Antonia said.

"If I do that, I can't listen to the new numbers he's calling," Annie said.

The whippet-thin player across from me took a slug of coffee. "Quiet!"

I studied my cards. "I have three in a row so far."

Antonia shook her head. "This game is airplane. You need to get the numbers in the shape of an airplane."

"You mean we're making *designs*?"

Antonia nodded. "Sure. Turtle, picnic table, champagne glass, tree, all kinds of things."

I studied my cards and tried to keep up with the numbers being called out. I was busy searching for something yelled three numbers back when the frazzled lady across from me yelled "BINGO!" at the top of her lungs.

The players cursed and groaned under their breath, the losers tossing their cards into the trash bins.

"Fun, isn't it?" Antonia asked.

"Oh, sure," I said. "Loads."

Annie lasted one more game before she threw up her hands. "Too stressful for me." She handed me her cards. "I'm going to take a stroll."

"I can't take these," I said. "I can't even keep up with what I have in front of me."

That got everyone's attention. Suddenly I had all kinds of eye contact as people vied to receive the extra cards. I slid them down the center of the table. Before they came to a complete stop, they were gone.

"What's next?" I asked. Antonia quickly went over the shapes and how to keep track of what was being called, but it wasn't any use. Right before the next game began, the caller said something else I couldn't understand. Immediately everyone in the room tensed and hunched further over their cards.

I nudged Antonia. "What's going on?"

"Now you really need to pay attention. This next game's a blowout."

"It's a who-what?"

"A blowout. It's the same as a quickie."

I put down my dauber. "Are we still talking about bingo?"

"It's when the caller reads the numbers as fast as he can."

"Hasn't he been doing that already?"

"Shhh!"

"I agree with Annie," I whispered to Antonia. "Too

stressful for me." I waited for a pause in the action, standing when someone across the room yelled "BINGO!" and the cursing began anew. "I'm going to check out the rest of the casino. See you later."

Antonia nodded without looking up. I threaded my way through the packed room and spotted Annie sitting in the coffee shop. She was reading a casino brochure.

"You can do all sorts of things here," she said. "They have clinics for the games. There's one on bingo if you ever want to try again."

I shook my head. "Those people were a little high-strung for me." I took a seat. "What else is here?"

"The spa, the gym, the sports courts."

"What's a sports court?"

"You know. Tennis, basketball, racquetball."

I turned. "Racquetball? Brian played racquetball here. Claire said so."

Annie nodded. "He played a couple times a week, but I didn't know it was here. Never occurred to me to ask."

I dug into my purse and held out the small gold key. "I bet they have lockers."

Chapter 25

I called Lucas. "Of course we thought of the gym lockers at the casino," he said. "It's on Indian land, and we've started the requests. We don't have jurisdiction, though, and it's always a little tense when they perceive us as stepping over boundaries." He paused. "Where are you now?"

"At the casino," I said. "I wouldn't have thought of the lockers otherwise. Annie and I are having coffee. Bingo was too scary."

"You played bingo?"

"With Antonia," I said. "She's really into it."

"Never would have guessed. So, let's cut to it. I'm assuming you're going to try and see if that key fits a locker."

"Are you going to tell me not to?"

Lucas grunted. "I should, but I know it wouldn't do any good. Would you actually listen to me?"

"Probably not."

"That's what I thought. The correct approach is through the Indian Council. I've made the request, like I said, but I don't know when I'll hear back."

"I can ask to tour the facility," I said. "The women's section will be easy. I'm not sure I can get into the men's locker room—"

"And I'm not asking you to," Lucas interrupted.

"Right."

He lowered his voice. "I mean it. I can't bail you out. I have no authority at the casino. Be careful."

"Got it. I'm on my own. I'll call you later."

It was easy to get into the women's gym. I talked Annie into taking the tour with me, and the club manager was happy to show us around. The gym stocked the usual torture devices I've been avoiding all my life, and the manager confirmed members could rent out lockers on a monthly basis. While Annie walked ahead with the manager, I tried locker 61 without success. Touring the men's section would be more difficult, and I didn't see an opportunity until we reached the pool. It was co-ed, with doors that connected to both the men's and women's changing rooms. If you weren't paying attention you could easily select the wrong door, which is exactly what I was going to say if anyone noticed me. I signaled Annie and she caught my meaning, leading the manager away from the pool and back into the women's gym.

A rolling cart, stacked with towels and fresh robes, sat near the pool. A baseball cap dangled from one corner. I grabbed the cap and tugged it low over my face, pulled on a robe, and, before I could change my mind, pushed through the men's entrance. The showers and changing rooms were empty, and my luck held as I made my way down the center aisle. I cut across two more aisles, trying to get my bearings. Halfway down the third row, though, my luck ran out. Three men blocked my path, and I swerved down a side aisle, breathing hard as they passed. When their voices receded, I started around the corner, then stopped. I was in the right section. Counting lockers, I found number 61. The moment I inserted the key, I knew it was the right locker. The key slid in easily. I held my breath, turned the key to the right, and opened the door. There was only one thing in the locker, a notebook, and there wasn't any doubt who it belonged to. I flipped through the first few pages and recognized the same shorthand I'd seen at Claire's house. It was definitely Brian's.

I shoved it into the folds of my robe and headed for the exit, dodging men in various stages of dress. I missed the main row and somehow ended up near the Jacuzzi and saunas. The need for towels was greater in this area. I pulled the cap lower and tried to avert my eyes, with limited success. After a series of wrong turns, I finally managed to retrace my steps to the pool. I ditched the cap and robe and darted into the women's gym, hurrying past the equipment. I'd nearly reached the exit when I heard my name. I stopped and turned. Denise stood at a machine that looked like something used to draw and quarter people. Lean and strong-looking, she dropped a pulley and several weights clanked back into place. Grabbing a water bottle from a nearby bench, she took a drink and walked up to me, using the small towel around her neck to wipe her face.

"So, you've decided to start working out?" she asked, without a trace of sarcasm. "Anytime you want to walk through the machines, let me know."

"You bet. Absolutely," I said, hopefully also without a trace of sarcasm.

Denise shifted her head and her eyes narrowed. She was focused on the notebook. Warning bells went off in my head, and I held it tightly at my side. "Isn't that Brian's notebook?"

"Why do you ask?"

"I just recognize it." She dragged her eyes away from the book. "He always had it with him. I wonder if it can clear up what happened that night. Maybe things can get back to normal."

"Two people were murdered. Nothing's ever going to be the same again."

"No, of course not." She made a sweeping gesture. "Well, it has nothing to do with me." She kept her voice low, but her breath was quick and I saw the rapid pulse along her neckline. "Have you opened it?"

"I just discovered it. I'm going to give it directly to the police to examine." Primarily because I couldn't read Brian's shorthand, but Denise didn't need to know that.

"Of course, of course. That's exactly what you should do." Her words were at odds with her expression, which said she wanted to rip the book from my hands. I tightened my grip.

"Well, I'll let you get back to your workout."

"I'm finished here." Denise hesitated, seeming reluctant

to let me leave. Finally, she shrugged. "I need to change and get to the clinic."

"You and Eric have a lot going on?"

She nodded. "We're leaving for South America soon."

"I didn't realize you were going with him," I said.

Denise's nostrils flared, and she tossed her head back. "Naturally I'm going."

"What happened?" I asked. "Last time we spoke you were thinking you might be out of a job."

Denise smiled, and her face softened. "Eric and I talked it out. He just didn't realize how I was reading the situation. He said we would talk about my taking on a larger role in the future. Getting the credit I deserve."

"And you believe him? That isn't exactly how Eric described your role. According to him, you're a research assistant."

I knew the jab hit its mark when the pulse quickened once again along her neckline, but she kept her composure. "It doesn't matter what you say. I know what my input has meant to this project. I know how Eric feels." Her voice dropped when she said his name. "Nothing else matters. Nothing." She eyed the notebook once more, then nodded and turned toward the changing rooms.

Annie was pacing at the gym entrance. "I thought I'd lost you."

"Let's walk and talk." I gestured to the book under my arm. Annie's eyes widened.

"That's Brian's notebook. You found it."

I nodded. "It was in his locker."

"Let's look at it."

"We need to get out of here," I said. "Denise was in there, working out. Trust me, she wants to know what's in this book as much as we do."

Annie nodded. "The bingo room is right around the corner. Let's find Antonia."

We filtered through the players as they surged toward the exit, finding Antonia at the cashier's window. She waved a stack of bills. "I won the last game."

"Of course you did. Lunch is on you." I motioned to the notebook under my arm. "And we have reason to celebrate."

Chapter 26

"What do you mean, it's gibberish?" Antonia leaned across the table. We were eating crab salads overlooking the bay at the Marquis Hotel, the same spot where the auction took place the prior evening.

"I mean I can't read it."

"What rot. Here, let me see."

I pushed the book across the table to Antonia, while Annie took one look and sat back.

"It's no good. It's his shorthand," Annie said.

Antonia shook her head. "This isn't shorthand. I took shorthand in school, and I can tell you this isn't like anything I've seen before."

"You took shorthand?" I asked.

"All the girls did, back then. There weren't as many options available to us. Secretary or teacher, that was about it."

"And now you run the largest winery in the region."

Antonia nodded. "You have no idea how much the world has changed." She shook her head. "Now, back to this."

"You can't read it," Annie said. "Claire's the only one who can. Let me call her." She pulled out her phone and punched in the numbers.

I nodded. "She's right. Claire told me herself. It's a shorthand she made up with Brian in college."

Annie shook her head. "No answer."

"Try her house phone." I said. "She isn't using her cell phone right now, not since she learned you can gamble on-line."

While she left a second message for Claire, Antonia and I leafed through the pages. I flipped to the last entry. The only thing I recognized were several exclamation points. With a sigh, I closed the cover. "I suppose we need to turn it over to the police."

Annie nodded. "That's what we should do."

"It's really the only responsible solution," Antonia agreed.

We finished lunch in silence, all of us alone with our thoughts. Finally, I slapped my hand against the table. Both of them jumped at the sound.

"Really, Penelope, was that necessary?" Antonia asked.

"Sorry, but let's be honest. We all want to know what Brian's last entry says."

"That requires Claire, and we don't know where she is."

"So for now, let's go over who might have hidden it in the locker." Antonia grabbed my arm. "What about Nicole? She could have taken it from the clinic the night Brian died. Maybe she was blackmailing someone, and it got her killed."

I shook my head. "No good. How could she threaten anyone with the contents, if she couldn't read it to know what it said?"

"Then maybe Jason or Eric," Annie said.

"But they couldn't read it either, and when would they have gotten it? Also, how would they get the key?" I bit my lower lip. "I wonder if we'll hear from Claire. Maybe it holds something incriminating, and she's the one who hid it."

Annie raised her hand in protest. "But why hide it? Wouldn't she just destroy it?"

"Good point," I said. "Wait a minute. How about Brian himself?"

Antonia shook her head. "Then how did the key get in Nicole's car after Brian was killed?" She dragged her napkin over the notebook. "None of this is helping. We need to know what it says. We need to find Claire. In the meantime, I suggest we keep this to ourselves."

"Who else would we tell?" I said. "For one thing, the police would be furious. I can just hear Lucas now."

"Still, we need to be discreet. Isn't Jason staying at this hotel?"

I did a quick scan of the patio. "Yes, and I've seen him out here before." Hearing Jason's name reminded me of the little breakfast he had with Chantal, and my attention shifted to Annie. Antonia was watching her too.

"What?"

Putting off the conversation wasn't going to make it any easier. "It's Jason. I need to tell you something. He and Chantal were having breakfast together this morning at Sterling."

"That doesn't necessarily mean anything happened between them," Annie said. "Does it?"

"It does, actually. She had on the same dress as last night."

Annie sat back in her chair and let out a long exhale. "Okay. That's that." She gave herself a quick shake. "I'm just glad it didn't go any further. I was willing to put down his dating Nicole as a fluke, but now, if he's interested in Chantal... Antonia, I realize she's your daughter, but anyone interested in Chantal just isn't someone who's going to be a match for me."

Antonia waved off the comment. "I understand completely. My daughter hasn't shown a lot of common sense regarding her love life. Regarding a lot of things. I'm just glad you aren't hurt by this, um, new development."

Annie patted Antonia's hand. "I'm fine. Really. I think I might have avoided a lot of trouble, if you want to know the truth."

My phone beeped, and I glanced at the screen. "My car's ready. Four new tires."

The remark gave all of us pause, and Antonia shook her head. "We need to be careful." She patted the book. "Enough. Let's take this to the police before anyone else knows we have it. Whatever is in here could have cost Brian his life. Nicole's too. Let's make sure we don't join them."

Antonia drove us back to Sterling, stopping at Annie's car. "Do you want a lift to the tire shop?" Antonia asked me.

"I can bring her," Annie said. "It's on my way."

"Very well." Antonia studied my face. "You're going straight to the police, correct?"

"Yes," I said. "I can't read it, so what's the point of keeping it?"

"Very well, then," Antonia said. She gave a slight wave and drove off. We watched the truck turn out of sight.

"Before we give it to the police, you want to try Claire again," Annie said.

"Of course I do." We took a seat in her car, and Annie dialed Claire once more. "Still no answer." Annie left another message, and we reviewed our options.

"We can go get my car and try again later," I said. "Meet at the clinic and go from there?"

"Fine with me." Annie pulled out of Sterling, and a short time later we reached the garage. Annie left while I waited and paid for the tires. I'd just gotten on the freeway heading south when my phone tweeted with a text from Annie. *At the beach near Cliff Point. I found Claire.*

Why the beach? I tried calling her, but she wasn't picking up, and she didn't answer my follow-up text. I took a shortcut through town and moments later pulled into the parking lot overlooking the point. The fog was rolling in as it often did in late afternoon. There were only a couple of cars in the lot, and I parked next to Annie's Mini. It was empty, and I didn't see any other cars I recognized, including Claire's.

I considered my next move. Very few people were down on the beach, and those that were on the sand kept a safe distance from the angry, steel-gray sea. The tide was coming in, pushing further up the shore with each wave. Annie had to be somewhere down on the beach, and with a growing sense of apprehension I reached in the back for a windbreaker. I circled Annie's car. It was unlocked, which didn't ease my concerns. Annie always locks her car.

The fog was coming in thick now, heavy swirls of dampness that clung to my skin. I pushed my hair back, my face wet, and navigated down the steep path. The few people I'd spotted earlier all passed me now, leaving the beach. I turned north and headed to the point, invisible in the thick air. I kept walking and finally spotted Annie through the mist, relief filling me when I recognized her new turquoise scarf. The feeling died when I got closer. Annie wasn't the one wearing it.

"Why do you have Annie's scarf, and where is she?"

Eric pulled the scarf off his shoulders. "Pretty, isn't it?"

"Answer my question."

"You always have so many questions, don't you?"

I needed him to tell me where Annie was, and I fought to keep my voice calm. "I didn't know you were meeting us here."

He shook his head. "Penny. Always in control during a crisis."

I bit the inside of my lip to keep from crying out. I hardly felt in control.

"Come on, admit it." He flashed those white teeth. "You were surprised to see me." He moved closer. "Especially when you were expecting Annie and Claire."

I went numb, fighting to get the words out. "How do you know we're meeting Claire? What have you done?"

Eric tugged at the scarf, snapping it taut between his

hands. "I'd never hurt Claire. I mean, I don't think I would. I found out before she did that you have the notebook. That was a lucky break for her."

My throat was dry and it was hard to speak. "Denise told you we found it. She spotted me in the gym."

Eric laughed. "No, I've been avoiding Denise for days. Won't take her calls. She still thinks she's going back to South America with me."

"If Denise didn't tell you we had the notebook, it must have been Claire. We've been trying to find her."

He nodded. "I know. She wasn't home when you called and conveniently left those messages."

"You were in her house." My heart skipped a beat.

"She's at work. I erased the messages, so it should be hours before anyone misses you." He looked at his watch. "Not that we have that much time. Especially Annie."

My throat went dry. "Where is she?"

"First, I need you to confirm the notebook's in your car." I didn't answer. "Come on now, Penny. You came here to have Claire read it, so where else would it be?" He lowered his head, his eyes locking on mine. "Let's just hope for Annie's sake you haven't done anything stupid, like give it to the police."

I didn't see any point in lying. "No, it's in my car." He visibly relaxed. "So when Annie sent me the text that she was here with Claire…"

He nodded. "It was me. I sent it from Annie's phone. Which reminds me…" He took a step closer. "Time to give me your phone. Your car keys, too."

"Where's Annie?"

"If you want to know that, Penny, then give me your phone."

Reluctantly I handed it over, along with my keys. "Why are you doing this to Annie?"

"I don't have anything against Annie, really I don't. If the two of you had left it alone, and I'd found the notebook first, that might have been the end of it."

"All this for something in Brian's notebook?" I mentally worked through the possible scenarios. "Wait, you don't know what it says. You can't even read it."

Eric shook his head. "I couldn't take the chance. He was writing in that thing all the time. Every little comment. Whatever you said, there he'd be, making notes."

"He found out something and you killed him for it, but you couldn't be sure he hadn't written about it," I said. "I thought you might be jealous, might still want Claire."

Eric wagged his finger. "Not at all. She's always been special, with that cute British accent, but I wouldn't go to all this trouble for a woman."

If it wasn't jealousy, it was money, and the fragments finally pulled into place. "It's your research. What happened? Did Brian find some mistake, and you had to stop him from telling anyone?"

Eric snapped Annie's scarf between his two fists. "I don't make mistakes."

I swallowed and pushed the panic down. "Then what was it? What's in the book?"

He tilted his head, silently trying out different versions of answers, finally selecting one. "The drug has unanticipated side effects."

Unanticipated side effects? "Like what?"

He shrugged. "Nothing we couldn't have figured out with time, but I needed to get the drug to market. The trials were expensive." He twisted the scarf around one hand. "Too expensive. I'm out of money, out of time."

He shifted to avoid the waves, now pushing further up the beach. "I asked Brian about a pattern in the trial results." He shook his head. "Stupid, stupid. I thought he'd agree with my findings. I've known him since we were young. I never dreamed he'd disagree. He knew what this means to me, to my career. We were going to be rich beyond our dreams. Instead, he gave me two days to either reveal the risks or report a delay and take the setback. Two days."

He moved closer, the scarf now wrapped around one fist. I took a step back. "Why did you kill Nicole?"

"She was at the clinic when I spoke with Brian. I wasn't sure she'd put it all together, but you could never tell with Nicole. Really, though, she was just in the way."

Just in the way. I was the one in his way now, but to my surprise he turned and began walking back toward the parking lot.

I raised my voice over the pounding surf, the waves breaking high on the shore. "What are you doing?"

He stopped. "I'm leaving you here. Why not?" He gestured down the beach, now fully eclipsed by fog. "Not a soul in sight. No one to help you. I have your phone and your car. And everything I've said here, well, you don't have any proof, because now I also have the notebook."

"Just tell me where Annie is."

He moved once again to avoid the incoming waves. "It's amazing how fast the tide can change."

The tide. My voice was shaking as I struggled to get the words out. "Where is she?"

He laughed and turned away. "Last time I saw her, she was further up the beach, taking a nap on the sand." His last words hung, bodiless, as he disappeared into the fog. "You better hurry."

I did, running along the shore until I found her. She was lying in the surf, soaking wet and icy cold, but still breathing. I pulled her up the shore onto dry sand. Her lips were bluish but she managed to open her eyes, the panic in them calming when she spotted me.

"It was Eric."

I nodded. "Save your strength. I need to get you warm."

"Walking will help." She shook her head. "At first I thought he was working in the caves. But then he pressed a rag against my face. Chloroform. I knew it right away but couldn't stop him." She shifted, looking at the ocean. "He left me in the water, with the tide…"

"Come on, let's get you moving." I put my arms under Annie's and pulled her to her feet.

We pushed through the fog, Annie finally able to walk on her own. "Where is he?"

I hesitated, hating the words I needed to say, unwilling to believe the truth. "He got away."

Chapter 27

"So, he got away." Her voice low and heavy, Antonia sounded dejected, even over the phone. I didn't blame her. The early morning light warmed the sun room, but I felt chilled. Hollie and Nanook were sprawled on the floor and Syrah was asleep in my lap, but losing Eric had left me cold and depressed.

"By the time I got to the police to tell them what happened, he was gone. Eric had our phones, and it was a slow walk back to the car with Annie."

"No surprise, after what he did to her," Antonia said. "Have you had any updates from Lucas?"

"He called earlier. Airport police found my car parked at the international terminal at San Francisco. Eric's gone."

"Which country?"

I stroked Syrah's warm fur. "Lucas didn't tell me, but he did say it was in South America and, more importantly, doesn't have extradition."

"Well, that's it then."

"That's it." I hesitated.

"What?" Antonia said. "There's something else, I can hear it."

"I don't know," I said. "Maybe it's just that I don't want Eric to get away with it, but I can't help feeling there's something out of place. Something I've overlooked."

The feeling stayed with me, even after a morning spent hiking the vineyards, Nanook and Hollie at my heels. The usual comfort I find taking photos eluded me. I needed to talk to someone, but Connor and Hayley were busy, and Annie was at the clinic. Finally, I jumped in the car, intending to drive once again to the point, but when I got to the exit I turned away from the shore, instead finding the street leading to Claire's home. When I reached her house, I stopped. She didn't appear to be home, but suddenly the door opened. She saw me sitting in the road, and with a slight gesture signaled me to pull into the drive. She waited on the porch as I parked, her robe pulled tightly around her. The robe was bright yellow and scattered with small roses, too cheerful for the pale woman in front of me, pain etched on her face. She pushed open the door as I climbed the front steps.

"I don't want to bother you," I said. "I don't even know what I'm doing here, actually. I can't seem to let it go."

Claire nodded. "Shock. I'm just glad you and Annie were found, and that…" She paused. "That he didn't hurt you as well." She gestured toward the table and a steaming teapot. "Care for some? I just made it." I nodded.

"What happened with his assistant, Denise?" Claire asked.

"The police cleared her. Apparently, Eric kept her away from the test results."

"I understand he managed to catch a flight." Claire's hand trembled slightly as she poured the tea. "Presumably with Brian's notebook, unless he destroyed it."

"That's what the police think," I said.

Claire handed me a cup. "I guess we'll never know if it mentioned Eric, or the vaccine."

"I'm surprised Brian didn't tell you the drug was having adverse side effects," I said.

"He would have, in time, but he wanted to give Eric a chance to make it right. That was Brian's strength, and his weakness. He always saw the good in people, and it cost him his life." She pressed her fingers into her forehead. "Also, we hadn't talked about much more than my gambling lately. Our last week wasn't our best, and I'll have to learn to live with that." She took a sip of her tea. "It's likely, though, Brian made some note of his conversation with Eric. That was just his way."

"What did he usually write about?" I asked.

"Usually it was just random thoughts, things about patients, or notes for clients. Sometimes he was funny." She smiled at a memory. "He thought the ugly dog contest was fabulous. Said Bubbles really earned the title."

"Yes, Bubbles was pretty homely." I thought back. "He must have written that just a few hours before…" I stopped. "Before we found him." I shook my head. "I wonder when he had the chance. You brought him back to the clinic, right?"

Claire set down her cup. "That's right. He was scribbling in the car as I drove."

The doubt worked its way in, peeling away my assumptions. "But then it disappeared. Everyone thought it was taken from the clinic."

Claire didn't move. "Presumably so, yes."

I leaned closer, not wanting to believe what I knew to be true. "It doesn't work, Claire. If you had a chance to read that last entry, the notebook wasn't stolen from the clinic. It never made it back to the clinic in the first place."

Claire took both hands and gripped the sides of her cup. "It's chilly today. I can't seem to get warm."

I didn't answer, just waited. Finally, Claire's shoulders dropped, and she gave a single nod of acceptance. "I'm tired, and it won't change anything if you know. Brian left it in my car that night."

"Why didn't you tell the police?"

"At first I didn't know it was there. I didn't go anywhere after Brian died. I didn't even go out to the car. A couple of days later I found it on the floor of the passenger seat." She leaned back and looked resigned, waiting for the questions she knew were coming.

"You found the notebook and read it. Was there anything about Eric, about the vaccine?"

Claire nodded. "I knew the police would ask me to read it, since I was the only one who could. Before I gave it to them, though, I wanted to read it myself. I was sitting right here"—she patted the chair arm—"reading Brian's notes. His words." Her voice hardened. "Then I came to his entry

285

the day before his death. I read it several times before I realized I'd found Eric's motive." A flash of rage darkened Claire's face. "Eric wanted Brian to lie, as if Brian would ever do such a thing. People could have died, and all Eric thought about was the profits."

"But even then, after you read it, you didn't go to the police and give them the notebook." I worked through the timing. "It was you. *You* left it in Brian's gym locker." My voice rose. "And you put the key in Nicole's car. Why? Why would you do that?"

She picked at her robe belt, tracing the floral design with her finger. "Well, I could say I don't know what you're talking about, and if the police ever ask me, I'll deny anything I've shared here with you." She put a hand to her throat. "I don't mean to be harsh, but you don't understand how I was feeling. At the time I needed to think, and to do that I needed some distance between myself and the notebook. Don't forget, I might have been a victim too. I was the only one capable of reading Brian's shorthand."

I shook my head. "All the more reason to get to the police. They would have been able to arrest Eric that much faster." Anger and frustration tightened my voice. "If you'd told the police earlier, Eric wouldn't have gotten away."

Claire took a long time answering. "What makes you think he got away?"

She was calm, unnaturally so, and I felt a chill run through me. She waited, pouring herself another cup, while I replayed everything she'd told me, looking for some direction. Finally, I found it. "You said you needed distance between yourself and the notebook. You didn't want...what? You needed distance..." I sifted through motives.

"Distance. Not because you were afraid of Eric. You would have gone straight to the police if you were. Instead, you did the opposite. Distance..." I put down my cup. "You didn't want the police to know you had it. Wait." I held up my hand. "You didn't want them to know you *read* it. You knew Eric was the killer, but you didn't want the police to know. At least, not right away. Why?"

She lifted the pot. "Care for some more?" I put my hand over my cup as she poured herself the last of the tea. "That's very good, you know. You really do have a natural talent for this." When I didn't answer, she sighed. "Very well. Yes, I needed to buy time."

"Time for what?" I asked.

"Are you sure you want to know?"

I wasn't sure, actually, but her next words took away any ambivalence I was feeling.

"Don't worry, I'm not going to confess anything." She laughed. "That would be foolish, and I'm no fool." She thought for a moment. "Do you know the symptoms of rabies in a person?"

The change in topic surprised me. "Annie told me just the other day. There aren't any symptoms, until it's too late. Then it's a death sentence."

"That's about the sum of it," Claire said. "Six months after you're exposed, the symptoms finally begin, and then there isn't any treatment. It kills you. From the cases I've seen, I can promise you, dying from rabies is as bad as it gets." Her face hardened. "That's why Eric's vaccine, if he hadn't been lying, held so much promise. So many lives could have been saved." Her eyes snapped with anger. "Starting with my husband's. Brian died so Eric could continue to lie." She paused, lost in thought, and stared into her cup.

"It sounds like a terrible death," I said, "but surely most people know when they've been infected."

"Usually, but not always." She smiled, but it didn't reach her eyes. She tapped a nail against her cup, her gaze locked on mine. The silence lengthened.

"What aren't you telling me, Claire?"

"Well, think about it. He's safe from the law now, but he needs to pay. What better way than from the disease he professed to cure?" Her voice was low but strong.

"Rabies? Are you saying somehow he was infected?"

She just sat and finished the rest of her tea, watching me. The last piece clicked into place, and I knew.

"You saw Eric this week, didn't you?"

"Sure," she said. "Several times."

"No, you saw him as a doctor. You urged him to get his vaccines for his next trip. I heard you." She gave me a passing smile, as though pleased I'd guessed. "That's why you needed time. Did he come in?"

She sat back with exaggerated slowness, stalling, giving herself time to formulate an answer. "Yes. Eric and Jason were both behind in their vaccines."

My pulse started racing. "Jason too?"

She waved her hand. "Jason's fine. I imagine he was as

surprised as anyone at what Eric did." She shrugged. "Eric's shots were, well, let's say Eric's shots were more tailored for him." She leaned forward in her chair, her gaze holding mine. "If you really want to know, I think we've heard the last from him. In fact, I'm quite sure of it."

I didn't respond. I couldn't. Eric was going to pay for what he'd done, with a vengeance I hadn't suspected Claire capable of. I wasn't sure what I felt. Shock, certainly. No matter what he'd done, Claire was now also guilty of murder. I couldn't grasp the terrible grief that had driven her to this. And yet, hidden behind everything I knew to be right, I was relieved Eric hadn't gotten away with it. The tangled emotions raced through my mind and must have showed on my face.

"I can't tell what you're thinking," she said.

"I don't know what to think." I closed my eyes, focusing my thoughts. "That isn't entirely true," I said, after a moment. "Even though I'm trying to understand what you've done, you shouldn't have gone that far. It doesn't bring Brian back, and now you're—"

"I see." Claire stood. "You're wrong. You can't possibly understand what I'm feeling. You've made yourself clear." She crossed her arms, her words short and clipped. "I've nothing, absolutely nothing, to apologize for, and I reiterate, this discussion never happened."

I nodded and also stood. Her word against mine, if it came to that. "What are you going to do now?"

Claire flipped her head, her bob swinging. "It's early days yet, but I think I might return home to England. There's nothing to keep me here."

She was right. There wasn't any way to prove what she'd done. She was free to leave. "It isn't such early days, Claire. I think you should go." This time I dropped my tone, giving each word meaning. "I really think you need to go."

She took her time, pain, anger, and loss shifting across her face in equal measure, until finally she moved to open the door, closing it softly behind me moments later. I made it to my car and sat, shaking for several minutes. Finally, the chill eased and my breathing slowed enough for me to pick up the phone. I punched the top button, the one I knew would lead to the person I wanted most. He answered on the first ring.

"I need you."

Connor responded exactly as I knew he would. "I'll be right there."

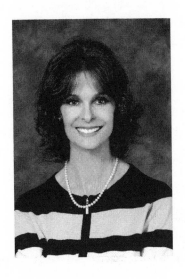

Carlene O'Neil is the author of the Cypress Cove mystery series, set along the central California coast. *Hair of the Dog* is the third book in the series. A former television writer and current wine lover, she is certified by the Wine and Spirits Education Trust. She lives in Southern California, where she is at work on her next Cypress Cove mystery. Visit her online at http://carleneoneil.com or on facebook at facebook.com/CarleneOneilAuthor. Her email is carleneoneilmysteries@gmail.com

Made in the USA
San Bernardino, CA
02 May 2018